A LONG STRETCH OF BAD DAYS

A
LONG
STRETCH
OF
BAD DAYS

MINDY McGINNIS

KATHERINE TEGEN BOOKS
An Imprint of HarperCollins Publishers

Katherine Tegen Books is an imprint of HarperCollins Publishers.

A Long Stretch of Bad Days
Copyright © 2023 by Mindy McGinnis
All rights reserved. Printed in the United States of America.
No part of this book may be used or reproduced in any manner
whatsoever without written permission except in the case of
brief quotations embodied in critical articles and reviews. For
information address HarperCollins Children's Books, a division of
HarperCollins Publishers, 195 Broadway, New York, NY 10007.
www.epicreads.com

Library of Congress Control Number: 2022940766
ISBN 978-0-06-323036-1

Typography by Erin Fitzsimmons
23 24 25 26 27 LBC 5 4 3 2 1
First Edition

For my hometown

ONE

I don't mind living in a small town; I just don't want to die in one.

I also am not interested in serving time in one, either, but that possibility is growing exponentially, as I seriously consider murdering the guidance counselor's secretary. But, of course, I'm not allowed to do that. For one thing, it's illegal. For another, I'm Lydia Chass, and being a Chass in a small town like Henley means something . . . mainly that you're good and kind, earning the respect of everyone around you.

"I'm sorry, what?"

I say it the right way, the nice way. With a smile. But my eyes must be hard, or maybe my smile is showing too many teeth, because Mrs. Pascale can't quite meet my gaze.

"We don't know how it happened, Lydia, truly," she says, her hands fussily rearranging things on her desk. A coffee mug that reads *pencils* but holds only pens. A photo frame that proudly announces *My Grandchildren!* that exhibits only one child. A red Expo marker cap that sits loosely over the tip of a black Sharpie. Nothing makes sense here, and everything is wrong, yet Pascale still somehow manages to seem struck with wonder that a mistake has been made in this office.

A very big one. One that could stop me from graduating.

"Walk me through this again," I say calmly, leaning forward. "I don't have enough history credits to graduate, is that right?"

"Yes," Pascale says, nodding in apparent relief that I have grasped the conversation so far. "And we're very sorry about that."

She adds a quivering smile to this, maybe hoping that that particular silver lining will be relayed to my parents, along with the news that their only child just got screwed—even though I'm still totally a virgin. Which has nothing to do with morality; it's much more a factor of having overloaded myself with courses, college credits, extracurriculars, teams, boards, and advisory committees. I put my sex drive on hold in order to organize blood drives, food drives, dog-adoption drives, and anything else that would look good on a résumé. Because Ivy Leagues aren't impressed when you're the valedictorian of a graduating class of sixty-eight students.

And they're definitely not impressed when you don't even graduate.

"I'm very sorry about that, too, *Gladys*," I say, glancing at the plaque on her desk for her first name before dropping it.

She winces, and I know that particular bomb hit the target, as it should; Gladys is a terrible name.

"But being sorry doesn't put me any closer to what I need," I say, keeping my voice calm. "So, before I go home and tell my parents that the guidance department at Henley High has ruined any chance I have of getting into a first-class journalism school, why don't you tell me how this is going to be fixed?"

There's a rapping of knuckles on the door behind us, which stands open. I know it's Principal Walton without turning around in my chair. He's exactly the kind of person who doesn't have the confidence to walk through an open door without permission.

"We have an idea about that, Lydia," Walton says, coming around to Pascale's side of the desk.

She visibly relaxes, like having a witness means I will back down. The Chass veneer has always kept me on the safe side of social acceptability, but while I might have my dad's eyes, the volatility that lurks beneath them can't always be hidden.

"Which is?" I ask.

"The board and I came to an agreement that this is a very unfortunate incident," he says, leaning back against the wall, like we're buddies having a chat about baseball. Not discussing my future, or the fact that Henley High just went to town on it with a chain saw.

"And we came to the conclusion that no one is really at fault here," he finishes up, giving me a quick shrug like, *Things happen, Lydia. You understand.*

Things happen. They do. They just don't happen to *me*.

"'No one is really at fault here,'" I repeat, narrowing my eyes. "It's an interesting point of view. I guess, if we want to worry about blame—which, I can see why that would be a topic of conversation—we wouldn't want to put it on a particular person, right?"

Principal Walton is nodding along, like he's sure the words I'm saying are in agreement with his own, but for some reason the tone is making him uneasy. It's called *being facetious*, and I might explain that later. But right now I have a point to make, and I'm about to drill down.

"Because if we said a particular person was responsible for this mistake, that would probably be Mr. Benson, the former guidance counselor, right?"

Gladys nods quickly, like I'm doing a good job of identifying school staff. I tilt my head toward the closed door to the right, which has the words *Guidance Counselor* painted in black on the window. Underneath that, the outline of Mr. Benson's name can still be made out; a janitor scraped it away only a few days ago. The room beyond is darkened, the square of the window a black hole that my GPA is about to be sucked into.

"And if Mr. Benson were responsible, that would reflect poorly on the people who hired him, wouldn't it?"

Walton shifts against the wall, recrossing his arms.

"Lydia." Glady's jumps in, eager to deflect. "You know that Mr. Benson has been going through a really tough time."

I do know. Everyone knows. It's Henley. But the fact that his wife left him for another woman doesn't strike any real chords with me. My grandpa died holding my hand, and I still took the SAT the next morning.

And got a 1600, thanks.

"A tough time," I repeat. "And we wouldn't want to make that any worse, right?"

"Oh, no," Gladys says, but Walton is watching me, suddenly aware that there's blood in the water, and it's probably not mine.

"Or tarnish his reputation," I continue. "Maybe we're even worried about his feelings a little bit?"

"Very much," Gladys says, like the self-worth of incompetent guidance counselors are at the top of Maslow's hierarchy of needs. But none of this is a surprise to me. I've lived in Henley my whole life, so I know this game. We're all going to be nice. We're all going to say the right thing and not use words that could hurt. The only salt that gets passed around in this town is at the dinner table in private homes. In public, we might as well be spitting fudge in each other's mouths, we're so damn sweet.

But I'm Lydia Chass, and I'm done with that. Being a Chass means two things—people expect you to be nice and polite, and I expect to get my way. Sometimes those two things are in conflict with each other; this is one of those times.

"So, let's not blame Mr. Benson," I say, getting up from my chair and crossing over to the darkened room. The knob turns in my hand, and I breeze into Benson's office, the motion-sensor lights flickering to life above me.

"Lydia! Wait!" Gladys's rolling chair hits the wall behind her, just as Principal Walton says, "You can't just—"

Of course, someone who knocks on open doors would think that I *can't just*.

But I can, because I choose to, and I will, and because I am Lydia Chass, and they're about to find out that if they're going to screw with me, they're going to need more than muttered apologies and one-shouldered shrugs.

"It's okay!" I tell Gladys as I reach for the bottom left-hand drawer of Benson's desk. "I don't blame him," I reassure her when it slides open. "I blame this."

I set the half-empty bottle of Jim Beam in the center of the former guidance counselor's desk. I rest my hand on the lid, tilting the bottle back and forth as I talk, listening to the slosh of the bourbon inside.

"We can't blame Mr. Benson and hurt his feelings, tarnish his reputation, or get the board and administration in any type of trouble," I say. "So we'll blame this bottle. I'm happy with that for now, as long as your idea about how to fix this is a good one."

"Well, Lydia," Walton says, clearing his throat and eyeing my palm as I roll the bottle under it. "The board and I thought an independent study project could be a substitute for your missing history credit. Assuming, of course, that it's of sufficient scope and depth—"

I tap my ring finger against the neck of the bottle; the circle of metal there—part of a meteorite whose trajectory I calculated in fifth grade—rings against the glass, reminding him that scope and depth are not going to be a problem. NASA representatives have only been pictured in the *Henley Hometown Headlines* once, and they didn't come here to meet *him*.

On the other hand, I don't think I can barge into the offices of the state Department of Education and start opening desk drawers and flashing space junk while demanding that they change graduation requirements because my guidance counselor was a drunk. The truth is that verbally sparring with Walton and Gladys might be a great outlet for my rage, but in the end, I'm going to have to take whatever deal they give me.

And I'll scope and depth the crap out of it.

"All right," I say, and they both visibly relax. I toss the bottle of Jim Beam at Walton, and he snatches it out of midair. There might be an ex-athlete under all those desk Twinkies and gas station sandwiches, but he's buried deep, and he doesn't have the recovery time to stop me when I open the second drawer to unearth a baggie of unmarked pills.

"And if Mr. Beam doesn't want to take the blame," I tell them, "we can always pass it off on Mr. Benzo, am I right?"

TWO

"So what was that all about?" MacKenzie asks in yearbook class.

On my schedule it's listed as a publishing class, but what that really means is that MacKenzie and I are camped out on bean bag chairs in the corner of Mrs. Wilhelm's earth science room. There aren't enough people interested in being on yearbook—or enough students in the high school—to justify having an entire block dedicated to it. So MacKenzie and I just kind of chill and occasionally upload pictures or format things on our laptops.

I'm working on the cross-country pages right now, flipping through the five different action shots we have and deciding if I want to pretend that I care about the sport by making sure everyone gets some exposure, or if I should just feature the sole senior—Brian Phillabrant. Unfortunately, he's extremely sweaty and seems to be in an incredible amount of pain in all the pics, so I decide to go for the group ensembles instead.

"Why do people even run?" I ask MacKenzie, blowing up a shot of Brian's face until his anguish pixelates, turning my screen around for her to get a look.

"It burns calories and builds character," she says, glancing up. "And are you just going to ignore me or what?"

"Probably ignore you," I say, turning my laptop back around. "Why? Did you say something?"

She makes sure Wilhelm isn't looking and then flicks me off. "Why'd you get called to the office?"

Of course this was coming. Lydia Chass was called to the office, and everyone is probably wondering if there was Xanax in my locker or if Harvard said *no thanks*, and a team of purebred emotional-support dogs have been summoned in to console me. While I'll be landing on the senior personalities Most Likely to Succeed category in the yearbook, if there were a Thinks She's Better Than Everyone Else page, it would be my picture, full-frame. I've always aimed high and never made a secret of it.

And while it would feel really good to throw Mr. Benson under the bus and tell my bestie about his utter failure at his job, I can't quite bring myself to do it. He hadn't even blinked when I trotted into his office as a freshman and told him I needed the most rigorous academic schedule possible and that he had four years to cultivate contacts at Columbia, Emerson, Princeton, and maybe NYU if I decided to lower my expectations.

Benson never sat me down and reminded me that I'm from Henley. Benson never said that I should keep in mind that the only truly famous person in our Hall of Fame (located directly across from the bathrooms) is the CEO of a plastics factory who is currently in jail for violating roughly thirty-five different EPA regulations. Benson encouraged me, right up until I detected the alcohol on his breath and the tremors in his hands. He'd lost focus by then, either constantly checking his phone while we met or staring off into the space over my left shoulder, depending on whether he'd popped a bennie yet or not.

The truth is that the game that Walton and Gladys wanted me to play with them back in the guidance office is one I know all the rules to: be nice, smile, and nod. The efficacy of that approach has put families like mine at the top of the Henley food chain over generations, proof that you catch more flies with honey than with vinegar. But I've got a lot of vinegar inside of me, and keeping the stopper in has become harder and harder as I get older.

I've been smiling and nodding my whole life, Lydia Chass, benign bobblehead. A couple of cracks have let the poison slip out once or twice, but I've always mopped away the mess and followed up the faux pas with a teeth-whitening session, so that the smile would flash even brighter the next time. I might've flown my dark flag a little high back in Benson's office, but generations of Chasses gone before have built a foundation strong enough for me to flash my temper now and again and still come out safely on the other side of public opinion. Besides, the mea culpa offering they'd devised hadn't been half-bad.

"I'm missing a history requirement in order to graduate," I confess to Kenzie, whose eyebrows shoot right up to her hairline.

"How?"

I wave off the question as irrelevant, relying on the magic of someone being too polite to push for the truth. It works; Kenzie has also lived here her whole life.

"It's okay," I tell her. "Remember my podcast?"

"The one that you made me follow, like, and review on every single platform?" Kenzie asks. "No, I forget. Tell me again?"

I really didn't need that reminder, since her reviews and follows are among the very few *On the Ground in Flyover Country* actually has. Many of the top-tier journalism programs ask for a highlight reel along with your application, assuming that every applicant attends a high school that has a serious student news channel. One that has things like anchors, desks, blue screens, microphones, and their own budget. Henley High doesn't even have a newspaper, and I don't think Columbia will look too kindly on me just linking to Heather Chapman's Instagram account, which is where we all get our news anyway.

I'd started *On the Ground in Flyover Country* as a way to illustrate some slice-of-life reporting, the kind that runs right before the credits, hoping to leave the audience with a little bit of feel-good after letting them know that their favorite sports team lost and it's not going to rain anytime soon, so all the crops are going to die.

So far, my podcast has bought right into the smile-and-nod mentality. I talked to Jennifer Phillabrant, who runs the food pantry, about the number of families they feed each month. I spoke with Mrs. Levering, my fifth-grade history teacher, about the Prepacked Packs Program, where every kid in the elementary got a new backpack, filled with school supplies. Today's episode was with Mrs. Nathans, the senior-class adviser, and featured the upcoming blood drive along with a reminder of why donating is so important. Other college applicants might have exposés on distracted driving and teen drinking, but I'm going to pretend like everything is fine and we're all going to be okay, right up until the red button gets pushed and everyone becomes ash particles in a great big mushroom cloud in the sky.

I kind of hate myself for the angle I'm taking, but I also know that the review board at Princeton will probably be eyeball-deep in pie charts and infographics, along with emotionally controlled, acne-sprinkled teens who really, really care about global warming. When my enthusiastic coverage of the annual dog costume winner from the Halloween parade hits them, they might just be grateful for the levity. Plus, keeping it positive means keeping Mom and Dad happy, which we need at home right now, even more than the human race needs to chill with the CO_2 emissions.

"Walton suggested that I refocus the podcast," I tell MacKenzie. "I'll toss up a couple of episodes about the history of Henley, and we'll call it even. I get my history credit, they get to pretend—"

I'm about to say, *They get to pretend that they didn't just drop the biggest ball since circles were discovered* when a horrible screech erupts over the PA.

"Give that back!"

Everyone jumps in their chairs, jerked out of the half sleep that Wilhelm's sonorous monologue about igneous rocks had induced.

"You can't— *Hey!*"

It takes a second for me to place Eva St. John's voice. She's the school secretary, and always does both morning and afternoon announcements in a voice so chipper it can't be faked. She actually really does love saying things like "meat loaf sandwich" and "emergency medical forms." But right now, she doesn't sound happy at all. St. John sounds pissed, but she's eclipsed in about two seconds by a voice that is neither chipper, nor professional.

"Can I have everyone's attention, please?" a coarse female voice asks. "I want the whole school to know that I'm about to get fucked, and I don't mean in that free-YouTube-porn kind of way, either."

"What the hell?" MacKenzie whispers to me, but I can only shake my head.

Mrs. Wilhelm is staring up at the ceiling, her mouth working like a fish out of water. The freshmen in her class are glancing at each other, probably wondering where the motherly, happy, high-fiving staff of the middle school has gone to.

There's a scuffle over the intercom, then the sound of a door slamming, and someone pounding on it, demanding it be unlocked.

"No more commercials, I promise," the voice continues. "Just a straight-up PSA from Bristal Jamison."

"Ohhhhhh . . . ," MacKenzie says. And suddenly everything makes sense. Bristal Jamison.

A fellow senior who has been suspended more times than a piano has keys (eighty-eight—I know these things) is mad about something . . . again. The only thing that makes this time different is that she's taken her usual method of communication—screaming obscenities in the hallway—to a different level by hijacking the PA system.

"It looks like I won't be graduating," Bristal continues. "So all you underclassmen bitches can look forward to another year of getting Jamisoned."

My ears perk up as one of the freshmen puts his head down on his desk. Bristal nailed him with a baseball during gym class, claiming to be confused; she thought they were playing dodgeball. She also said it had nothing to do with the fact that he had just dumped her little sister, making Mariana cry in the hallway.

"Not graduating, big surprise," MacKenzie sniffs. "Probably doesn't have the attendance."

"No," Bristal immediately contradicts her via the speaker. "I'll be here next year because—news flash—our guidance counselor is a drunken idiot."

"She buried the lede," I say.

"I don't know." MacKenzie shrugs. "The YouTube porn line was pretty good."

There's a crash and a huff as Bristal pulls the mic right up to her mouth. Her words come out low and fuzzy, her voice dropped deep in a mocking tone. "Tune in next week for my next episode titled, 'Sorry, kids! Nobody's going to college, because somebody has to pump the gas.'"

That gets a snort, and Mrs. Wilhelm covers her mouth, faking a sneeze.

"Get your goddamn hands off me, Walton! You nasty-ass son of a—"

There's a crack and the PA goes out, breaking the spell Bristal Jamison had very forcefully cast over the entire school.

"I really hope that didn't go out to the whole district," Mac-Kenzie says, her thumbs flashing over her phone as she texts her brother in the elementary wing. "I don't want to sit through Mom and Dad explaining what porn is over dinner tonight."

"How old is Jude again?" I ask.

"Nine," she answers, and I wave off her concern.

"He already knows."

THREE

Bristal's car—a battered and rusty Neon, with four miraculously nonmatching doors—is still in the parking lot half an hour after school lets out. I'm running out of ways to make myself look busy as I sit in my own car, but it's not like there's anybody watching. I let the engine idle and the heat run. We're at the end of fall, when the chill is taking the turn from pleasant to bitter, right along with the mood of our football fans, who are starting to realize we're not going to win a single game this season—again.

The dead leaves that skitter across the parking lot serve as a reminder that time is running out. All my applications have been spell-checked, spit-polished, and submitted. I've been hitting refresh on a tracking app since mid-September, but the little gray box next to the logos of all my dream schools continue to simply read *Processing.* Every time I check the stats for *On the Ground in Fly-*

over Country and I've got a listen from any state that holds an Ivy League, I break out into a sweat, wondering if an admissions officer just heard my deep dive into the plucky alumni baton twirler from the class of '68 who broke her ankle during the homecoming halftime show. She finished her routine anyway, smiling through the pain because—as she told me—*twirling ain't for the weak.*

Mom had wanted me to edit the quote graphic and opt for the grammatically correct *isn't.* But I didn't, and had felt a little thrill when I ran the episode with that same title. This woman had splintered a bone to prove that she was still relevant, and to stand as an example to the single baton twirler—freshman Hazel Lawson— that twirling is . . . kind of badass. And badasses don't have to use proper grammar.

But now, sitting in my car with the heat on blast and my hands shaking, I have to question if the review board of any decent university is going to look at that and realize that I'm going for local color and accurately representing my subject . . . or if they're going to think the mistake was mine.

"Shit," I mutter when I spot a listen from Massachusetts. It could be a rando. It could be the dean of admissions from Harvard. It could be a bot. I don't know, and it doesn't matter. That single listen sends my anxiety spiking and a flash of quicksilver through my belly. I might defend seventy-year-old, plucky Henley housewives and their choices, but I sure as hell don't want to be one. *On the Ground in Flyover Country* needs some grit, stat. Something that's going to turn those little gray boxes of *Processing* into green go-lights of *Accepted.*

And I know exactly who can help me out with that.

The police cruiser that had been cozied up next to the entrance doors (apparently fire lanes don't apply to the law) pulls away, and I sit up straighter in my seat.

Bristal walks out a few minutes later, her long dark hair tossing in the wind, her not-quite-warm-enough jacket whipping around her. She's got her shoulders hunched against the chill and her hands jammed in her pockets, but by the look on her face this girl is far from beaten. If you sat me down across from a police officer I would freeze up at the mere implication that I'd done something wrong. Bristal, meanwhile, is walking away from a chat with the cops looking slightly amused, even as her cheeks redden from the cold.

I pull up next to her Neon, and she glances at me through the windshield. I get an up-nod of recognition, but that's it. I've got to roll down my window to really get her attention.

"Hey," I call. "Want to get in?"

She pulls a vape pen out of her pocket and considers me for a second, taking in a long pull before speaking.

"Why?"

She exhales, the vapor pulled from her mouth and torn away by the wind, as she holds my gaze impassively.

"Because it's cold," I tell her. "And because I also got screwed."

She pulls open the door and slides into my passenger seat, bringing with her the smell of wind, river water, and the faintest hint of strawberries, which must be from her vape. She doesn't ask if she can smoke in my car, but she does crack the window before taking another pull. I decide to keep this conversational instead of confrontational and let it go.

"What'd they offer you?" she asks. "Did they just say, *we know you're really smart, so we're going to let this slide*? Or do you have to go directly to jail and not pass go and collect your two hundred dollars?"

"I'm not going to jail, like, ever," I tell her. "Mostly because I don't assault people."

"Assault is just one way in," she says coolly. "And you didn't answer me."

"Independent study project," I tell her, my eyes trailing her exhalation of vape that she doesn't bother blowing toward the cracked window.

"Of the appropriate depth and scope," I add mockingly.

"Sounds like a trigger warning before a porno," she says. "They told me the same thing, but I told them where to stick it."

"Sounds like the script for the same porno," I shoot back, and she turns to face me for the first time.

"Wow, Lydia Chass. I didn't know that was in there." She shifts her gaze back to staring out the windshield, her fingers drumming on the center console. Her nails are stubby and bitten to the quick, and the knuckles on her right hand are scraped, like she's thrown a punch recently. I really hope it wasn't at any of the staff; I could be making some dangerous liaisons here. But the scrapes are scabbed over, and I mentally chalk it up to something I don't want to know more about.

"You think it was just us?" Bristal asks. "We're the only ones who got called in today."

I'd noticed that, too. And it's the reason why I was creeping in the parking lot, waiting for her to come out of the school and hoping it wouldn't be in cuffs.

"Yes, and I have a proposition for you," I say.

"'Kay," she says, disinterested.

I turn in my seat to face her, put on my sale smile, and even pop out the jazz hands from those early days of dancing lessons that came to a screeching halt when I corrected the instructor on the pronunciation of *chassé*.

"How would you like to cohost my podcast?" I ask.

"Why?" Bristal asks, the single word escaping with another lungful of vapor.

"Walton didn't just give me a pass," I tell her. "They want me to do a few episodes that focus on local history, and they'll call it a credit."

"Why?" she asks again, and I'm left with my hands held out to either side, my smile fading as she remains completely unmoved.

"So you can get your credit, too," I say. "It's a win-win."

"No, I get that," she says, tapping the vape pen against my dashboard. It leaves little indentations in the leather that I try to ignore. "I mean, why are you offering? What are you getting out of it?"

"I'm just . . . I'm being nice," I say, somewhat flustered. Dad is the county public defender, and Mom the head of every fundraising group in the area. I'm not accustomed to having to explain the concept of being nice; I've always moved in circles where kindness was the social contract, the assumption that allowed you through the door.

"Nah, this isn't about that," Bristal says. "You said it yourself. Win-win. So, what are you winning by handing a Jamison girl a microphone, other than an FCC violation?"

That sets me back, and I'm not quick enough to cover it.

"Yeah, I'm not stupid, Chass," she says. "I know what the FCC is."

"Perfect," I say, crossing my arms and leaning back into my heated seat. "You know what else? It's been kind of a long day, so instead of me trying to convince you that I'm doing a good deed, why don't you show me exactly how smart you are. *You* tell *me* why I asked you."

"So now I'm auditioning?" she shoots back.

"Call it what you want," I say, my breath coming in heated gasps. The car is too hot, the air filled with stale vape. My head is starting to spin, and I'm wondering what exactly she's got in that pen when she tilts her head and holds my gaze.

"You made sure that Phillabrant mentioned your volunteer hours at the food pantry in that episode. Mrs. Levering got in a great plug about you spearheading the Backpacks for Brats—"

"Prepacked Packs," I correct her, but she sails on.

"And you definitely dropped the fact that you're the organizer of the blood drive into that ep. It's not a podcast about Henley, it's a podcast about Lydia Chass and how wonderful you are. And no, I didn't say how *nice* you are. Because you're not. You're calculating, and I'm willing to bet that the angle you're working right now is a charity piece."

"A charity piece?" I repeat, truly lost.

She puts her hands out to either side, shaking them in a clear mockery of my enthusiasm from earlier. "Valedictorian throws a rope to struggling fellow senior, hauling her along for the ride to graduation."

"That's not—"

"A story that ends well for me," Bristal says. "And I don't need your help."

I'm quiet for a second, weighing my options. When I finally speak, I don't try to push my better qualities, pitch the pros, or argue that she can't come up with anything better on her own. I drop the formalities and ask an honest question.

"How do you know I'm not nice?" I ask her.

"Kindergarten, playground, Lyle Hunter," she says automatically. "Back before any of us did a good job of checking each other's clothing labels and before we decided who we sat with at lunch. A bunch of us were hanging from the monkey bars, seeing who could hold on the longest."

"I remember," I tell her. "You don't have to—"

"Your friend Kenzie dropped fast, then Heather, then me and Jason Franklin. It was you and Lyle Hunter still hanging," she says. "Your fingers were dead white, and your skin was turning blue where your shirt had pulled up. It was the middle of January, and you were a couple minutes shy of frostbite. But you weren't going to let go."

I do remember, and I don't need her to remind me.

Lyle and I had hung face-to-face, little bodies dangling, effort turning our cheeks red as the wind whipped around us. At some point it had turned from a game into a battle of wills, and I was not about to back down. My arms had trembled, and my feet had twitched in midair as I'd battled gravity, begging it to give me a single second longer of reprieve than it did my opponent. And then I'd decided to take matters into my own hands.

Or, rather, my feet.

"You kicked him in the balls," Bristal says. "Solid strike to the sweetmeats."

"And you told on me," I say. "You and Jason ran to the monitor."

"And they didn't believe us," Bristal finishes up. "Because I'm a Jamison and Jason is a Franklin, and you are Lydia Chass. So, no, you're not nice, and I damn well know it. You'll go along to get along until you've got to put your foot down in order to get ahead. And I want to know if that includes stepping on my neck if things don't go the way you want."

"I told you earlier—I don't assault people."

"*Anymore*," Bristal corrects, then narrows her eyes again. "That I know of."

"It's not . . ." I sigh, waving away another cloud of vape when she exhales. "Look, you're right—I'm not nice. And that's exactly the problem, because I'm *supposed* to be."

"Which is why your podcast is all puff pieces and party streamers," she says.

"Uh, you're the one who listens," I stab back.

"Mr. Blanloss gave us extra credit," she says with a sniff.

Oh, great. While I appreciate the hometown support, that means that the little boost I saw midweek wasn't from reaching eager organic listeners. Instead, it's exactly what Bristal is accusing me of—charity work.

"I'm not handing this to you to make me look good," I tell her. "I know that what I've got isn't exactly lighting fires and making waves, and I'm tired of pretending like everything is fine. That recess monitor didn't believe you back in kindergarten because of who you are and who I am, but twelve years later we're both in the same boat, and it's sinking. We need to graduate, and we might not because our guidance counselor is an alcoholic. But nobody wants to say that—except you. You said it loud, and you said it to everyone."

"And you want to cash in on my voice," Bristal says, putting it together. "Add a little edge."

"Which you benefit from," I remind her. "Like I said, win-win. Now, what do you think?"

Bristal shifts in her seat, folding her legs into a pretzel and resting them against the dashboard while she considers my words.

"I think no one from my family has ever graduated from high school," she finally says.

I stare back at her for a moment, weighing my options. Bristal Jamison has a lot of things—a bad reputation, a crappy car, and a dirty mouth. But she's also got gravity. I've felt it before when the crowd parts for her in the hallways, when teachers backed down from her dead-eyed stare, and when a hush fell over the entire school as she used the PA system to vent a personal diatribe.

I could try to sell her again, give her a speech about being an unlikely duo overcoming their dual obstacle and bridging the social divide between them in their shared best interest. I could do that; and I could even make it convincing. But I have a feeling that Bristal Jamison would call me out on my bull, then get out of my car and leave me in her wake of strawberry-scented vape cloud.

"I don't just need a history credit to graduate," I confide to her. "I'm the valedictorian of Henley High School. . . . Do you know what that means?"

"*To say farewell*, in Latin. Don't be too impressed," she says. "I only know that because in seventh grade I thought my dog was possessed and I tried to exorcise him using a homemade speech and Google Translate. Turns out he just had rabies."

I shake my head, trying to recall my point. "It means that I'm the smartest person out of sixty-eight people. That's not a huge pool."

"No, it means you have the *best grades* out of sixty-eight people," she contradicts me. "That doesn't mean you're the smartest."

"Oh yeah?" I bristle. "How many keys are on a piano?"

"Eighty-eight," she says smoothly. "How much does a gallon of milk cost?"

"I . . ."

"Somebody else buys your groceries for you, don't they?" she asks, looking smug.

I feel the blood rising in my cheeks. "I don't care what you think of me, and we don't have to like each other," I tell her, straightening in my seat. "We just have to work together. It'll be good practice for adult life."

"Right, when you're at the White House and I'm in the poor-house," she says.

"Poorhouses don't exist anymore," I snap back.

"Really?" she asks. "When's the last time you drove down Far Cry Road? Lots of poorhouses out there."

"Okay, look," I say, flexing my hands on the steering wheel. "I just want this to happen because—"

"Because you want to rip the polite off like a Band-Aid to take a good look at the wound underneath, but you don't quite know how to do it. You've had a nice, comfy life. I haven't."

"Yes," I confess. "Yes, that is exactly it."

"And," she adds, still eyeing me coyly, "if it goes badly you can always blame it on me."

"Uh . . ." I waver my hand in the air, teetering it somewhere between being honest and getting what I need.

"Whatever," she says. "I'll take it."

A sigh escapes me, and the breath I'd been holding comes out sounding a little more relieved than I care for.

"That's it?" she asks, tucking away her pen.

"Well, no," I say. "We need to put together a timetable, brainstorm, talk about episode topics, who wants to cover what, whether we're each hosting our own episodes, or both of us are recording together. We've got a lot of work to do."

It's one of my favorite phrases in the world. I love having a lot of work to do.

"No, I mean like—that's it? No strings attached? You don't want to bang me, or anything?" Bristal asks.

"What?! No! I—"

"You hesitated," Bristal says.

"I. Did. Not," I say through clenched teeth.

Bristal rolls her eyes. "Listen, if we're going to do this thing, you're going to have to lighten up, or I'm going to poke at you until you explode."

I straighten my spine. "I accept your conditions."

"We're going to have some fun." She smiles at me. "At least, I am. You might just get an aneurysm out of the deal."

"That's doubtful, given the data and my age," I tell her as she cracks the door open, letting in a cold finger of air. "Wait—we should exchange numbers. We need to get on this, right away. Can I text you tonight?"

I think she's going to have another go at me, but Bristal just digs out her phone and taps my number into a new text as I recite it. Seconds later, a new message pops up on my phone. It reads:

An aneurysm can occur at any age. Check your sources.

It's followed by 💀, and as Bristal Jamison gets out of my car, I have the feeling I'm going to need to use that particular emoji quite a bit in the upcoming months.

FOUR

Highlighting the silver lining of having a drunken guidance counselor is not easy; pitching it to your parents—one of whom happens to be on the school board, and the other on the village council—is even harder.

"Excuse me, what?" Mom says, putting down her fork.

It's spaghetti night, and I'm sure Bristal would be shocked to know that the sauce came out of a can, and the pasta out of a box from the local food pantry. Dad inherited the three-story brick mansion on what's known as the "nice street" in Henley. He makes enough money that we get to live the American dream: two-car garage, a stay-at-home mom, and a cat. But we're not as well-off as some people would believe. My car is leased, the deck on the back of the house needs to be replaced, and Mom and Dad have been leaning on me a little more heavily about applying for scholarships—state and national, of course. Not local. That would be embarrassing.

And we actually only own half a cat. We adopted Uneven Steven (who only has his two front legs) from the Humane Society after he got hit by a ditch mower a few summers ago. He came with a Pinterest DIY wheelchair for his back half and a lot of congratulatory Facebook posts about our selflessness. Steven is wheeling his way through the dining room when Mom delivers her follow-up invitation to repeat myself after I dropped my bomb for the evening.

"What's that?" I ask, cupping my ear.

Steven's wheels could use a greasing, but Mom isn't fooled. She knows I heard her.

"I said, the guidance office is incompetent and I don't have enough history credits to graduate."

Mom's eyebrows stay where they had been before—right up next to her hairline. But she did get her Botox refreshed at the beginning of the school year, so I can't really say if she's shocked or still in recovery.

"What? How?" Dad asks. "When did this happen? Why didn't I know about this?"

Since he's covered everything but the *where*, I assume he's done throwing interrogatives at me, and I finish up with the good news.

"It's fine," I say, twisting my spaghetti onto my fork. "They know it's on them, and they offered me what I think is an acceptable substitute. They want me to retool the podcast, cover some local history. And I think it could actually work in my favor. Remember Jeremy Dayforth?"

Mom and Dad exchange glances and nod warily. Jeremy Dayforth had been Henley's most recent golden boy, the minister's son, an all-state scholar athlete, and clean-cut good looks in tandem with teeth that came in straight without the aid of braces. Jeremy could have made a living in front of the camera, but he wanted to be behind it. When Ithaca College turned him down for their film school because it was impossible that Henley High could have prepared him for their rigorous academic programs, it put every liberal arts–bound teen in the county on high alert.

The message was clear—your GPA doesn't matter. Where you are from does. Be better than smart. Be better than special. Be *spectacular* if you want to get out.

"I think this is going to light the fire that I need under me to take *On the Ground in Flyover Country* to a new level, a more honest level."

Mom and Dad are listening, her with the same half smile she reserves for patiently bathing Steven, and him with the resolved I-should've-taken-that-job-offer-in-Cincinnati look that has haunted his face since I was in fourth grade.

"What do you mean by *more honest*?" Mom asks carefully.

"Sort of like . . ." I mentally hit rewind, looking for the phrase that Bristal had used. "Ripping off the Band-Aid of politeness and taking a good look at the wound underneath."

Mom visibly winces at the word *wound*, and Dad's hand tightens on his fork.

"Is that really a great idea?" he asks, his voice inquisitive but controlled, a planned approach no doubt taking form in his lawyer brain.

"I think it is," I say, my riposte already loaded. "I mean, how long have we all known that the guidance counselor was an alcoholic? For a while, right?"

Mom and Dad look at each other again, food forgotten as I talk openly about the things that everyone else wants swept under the collective town rug.

"Lydia . . . ," Mom begins, but I feel the same rush of anger I'd felt in the guidance office. Somebody is going to get fucked, but let's keep everything nice because we all have to see each other at the same grocery store every day.

"No," I say calmly. "Mom, just no. How long has everyone known and nobody said anything? And then your daughter ends up almost not graduating from high school."

"Fair enough," Dad says, leaning back in his chair. "But what specifically are you thinking about covering in your podcast? You can't just go around saying whatever you *think* is true. Remember, most of what you hear is gossip, and the last thing this family needs right now is a libel charge."

He's not wrong, as the sagging deck on the house and food pantry spaghetti can attest to. Everyone assumes that being a lawyer automatically translates to being rich, but much like the oh-so-valuable trait of kindness, the equation doesn't always balance out to equal success. Dad has represented more than a few people in the past who couldn't afford him—at all.

Instead of defending white-collar criminals and making bank, Dad stands up for people who stick up the dollar store, try to casually walk their cart of groceries out the back door of the market, or drive away from the gas pump without taking the step of actually paying. While Dad can defend someone who crossed the legal line when trying to find the money to pay for their kid's surgery, feed their family, or make the drive to a job that doesn't pay them enough to get there, the end result is that our family finances are slowly creeping down to mow-your-own-yard levels.

If we got a libel charge because I ran my mouth on a podcast, Dad might find himself in the unenviable position of not being able to afford his own services. So, I step carefully with the next part.

"First of all, this is going to be historical, so I won't be slandering anyone living. And no, I'm not going to mention the reason for the pivot, either. We don't need to advertise that Benson's personal problems screwed our public education."

"We?" Mom asks. "Our?"

"Bristal Jamison also needs a history credit, and she's going to be joining me on the podcast so that she can be the first person in her family to graduate from high school."

"Oh Lord," Mom says into her wineglass. "A Jamison girl?"

"We had a saying about them back when we were in school," Dad says, sharing a conspiratorial smile with Mom. "There's always a Jamison girl in each wing—elementary, middle, and high school—"

"And it's a good bet that the oldest one is pregnant," Mom finishes.

"Well, that's . . . rude," I say, but Mom only shrugs. "You guys realize that if I become a famous journalist you might have to work on pretending to be less judgmental, right?"

"Honey," Dad says, "all we're saying is that there's a lot of Jamison girls."

"Sure," I agree. "But you're also implying that they breed like rabbits and because of the last name continuing down a female line, they don't marry the fathers of their children."

"Don't marry or can't hang on to them," Mom mutters, and I reach across the table to pull the wineglass from her hand.

"First of all, changing your last name upon marriage is an archaic form of transferring ownership of a woman from father to husband. And secondly, Bristal isn't pregnant."

At least, I don't think she is. If she is she should probably stop vaping and starting fistfights.

"Fine, you've given your evidence against the patriarchy," Dad says, the trappings of lawyer mode still hanging from him even though office hours are over. "And you've rather artfully changed the course of this conversation. What does Jeremy Dayforth have to do with anything?"

"And can't you just start a different podcast, honey?" Mom asks, her worry lines deepening. "*On the Ground in Flyover Country* is so nice!"

I flinch at that word the way she did at *wound*. "Exactly," I tell her. "And so was Jeremy Dayforth. Ithaca didn't accept him, and he rolled over and didn't argue. Now he stocks the paper products aisle at the Family Dollar and uploads bitter YouTube videos about how he could have been something if not for his humble roots."

"I don't think his roots are entirely to blame," Dad says. "If he couldn't hack it, that doesn't fall entirely at the feet of Henley."

"I agree," I admit. "And I do think Henley is a nice place to live."

"Then why not celebrate it?" Mom asks. "Why drag it through the dirt? Why not stick with the clean image? It's not entirely untrue."

"Because dirt is part of being human," I tell her. "And I think there's greater beauty in a whole truth rather than sectioning off the easily palatable parts. I mean . . ."

I spin my fork, aware that I'm contradicting myself and unsure how to claw my way to clarity. "It's like this," I say. "Henley is a nice place, but nothing is perfect. As an aspiring journalist, I can do what I've been doing—highlight the positives and hope that all the world needs is love—or I can be truthful, present this town as a whole picture, and ask people to appreciate it for what it is, not what we pretend it to be."

"Well said." Mom nods. "I'll need you to write that down for me so I can repeat it when the phone calls from my knitting circle start coming in."

"Look," I plow forward. "All I'm asking is to be able to do exactly what Dad does every day, look at the darkness and find the shades of gray."

That one hits, and I let them marinate in it for a second.

Dad is one of the only defense attorneys in Markham County that will fight instead of roll over and plea down. He's won the hearts of plenty of people by defending the less fortunate, but there's an equal amount that won't speak to us for the same reasons. Being nice in Henley comes with a couple of *supposed to's*—you're supposed to be nice . . . but only to the people you're supposed to be nice to. Mom had to drop out of her book club last year after Dad defended the man who had broken into the organizer's house, taking everything right down to the kid's piggy bank.

But when Dad took on the case of Abe Lytle, even I have to admit that pleading insanity might be a better move than going for not guilty. Lytle came from a long line of proud military men and women. He'd signed up and shipped out at the age of eighteen only to return broken, driving his young wife back into the safety of her childhood home. She took their kid with her and filed for divorce—and full custody. Abe panicked, certain that he would never see his son again.

On an emotional tear, he'd decided the surest route to keeping his family together was kidnapping his child. He'd forced the school bus off the road, then pushed his way on board, waving a gun—but the driver wasn't going to let him anywhere near a kid—his, or anyone else's. When Lytle dragged Lawrence Horvath from his seat, the man's T-shirt came up, exposing a white belly that snagged on the steering wheel as Lytle threw him to the ground outside.

From there, the videos usually cut to the phone footage, the black-and-white of the bus feed now in full color as Horvath's teeth fly, and blood spills onto the highway. If you pause it just right, you can see Cody Lytle quietly staring out the window, watching his father beat his bus driver nearly to death.

Dad defending Lytle cost him a few other clients—paying ones. I'm not going to let my parents lecture me about staying on the good side of the right people in Henley when Dad takes bigger risks, and the only response from Mom is to pour a little more wine than usual.

"True," Dad says carefully. "The comparison between what you want to do with your podcast and what I do for a living is valid, but are you ready for the blowback?"

"I've been your daughter for eighteen years," I tell him. "Yes. And like I said, it's *historical*. I'm not going to be dishing dirt about classmates or faculty."

"No," Mom says stiffly. "You'll be trash-talking their grandmas."

"And people can be funny about their grandmas," Dad adds.

Their faces are still serious, but the mood has lightened, and I feel permission on the horizon. I finish up with a plea for some soundproofing panels and complete creative control of the upstairs linen closet, adding that one of my recent anonymous reviews commented that my sound quality could use a boost.

"For all we know, that was someone from Columbia," I tell them. "They're considering applicants right now, and I need to start churning out real content with high-quality tech."

Mom and Dad share another glance, a silent negotiation going on between them.

"I think this could be interesting," Mom says, the last top-off of wine adding to her enthusiasm. "But can you run episode ideas past your father and me first?"

"That's censorship," I tell her flatly. "No."

"Why don't you think of us as more of your corporate sponsors," Dad offers. "With a vested interest in the messaging?"

"Fine," I cave. "But you don't get to preview episodes."

"Deal," Dad says, ceremoniously reaching across the table to shake my hand.

"This could really be something," Mom says, warming to the idea now that she has some oversight.

"It's good optics," I say. "I've got a chance to exhibit true journalistic integrity, highlight some of the more interesting aspects of small-town life, illustrate my research skills and interviewing techniques, all while helping Bristal become the first Jamison with a diploma."

"A rising tide lifts all boats," Dad says.

"Exactly." I nod. "This isn't a door closing; it's a window opening."

"On the opportunity of a lifetime," Mom adds.

"Okay, are we done with the aphorisms?" I ask. "Because I've got work to do."

"I think we can put the ixnay on the aphorisms," Dad says.

"Please don't use weird nineties slang," I say, and then slap my hand over my mouth. Not because I hate pig latin, but because I just had an idea that is going to move this project from a rising tide that lifts all boats to a flood of listens—and maybe even some mainstream action.

FIVE

"Shit," I say, but quietly, since we're in the public library.

"Did you get what you needed?" Kenzie asks, looking over at me from the bean bag chair she'd commandeered in the teen room.

"No, actually," I sigh, plopping down next to her. "The *Henley Hometown Headline* never digitized. I'm going to have to go old-school and open filing cabinets down at the historical society."

"You look thrilled," MacKenzie observes, and she's not being sarcastic—I am positively glowing. "What are you looking for, anyway?"

"You know about the long stretch of bad days, right? From back in the nineties?"

"Ooohhh . . ." Kenzie's eyes get bigger. "That was, like, a real rough time."

A *real rough time* is one way of putting it. In June 1994 Henley had suffered a week for the history books. A tornado flattened most of the town, a flash food drowned every dog at the shelter, and the body of the only homicide victim that Henley has ever seen was found floating facedown in his trailer . . . and the coroner determined he'd been that way for a while.

"Wait," Kenzie says, sitting up straighter. "Are you going to solve Randall Boggs's murder?"

"I highly doubt that," I say, giving her a shushing motion. We are in a library, number one. But also saying Randall Boggs's name in Henley is kind of like spinning around three times in front of a mirror at midnight and inviting Bloody Mary for a heart-to-heart.

"Has it occurred to me that I might solve a cold case?" I admit to Kenzie. "Yes, of course. Am I realistic enough to know the odds? Also yes. Just throwing around the dirt and raising the questions will be enough to get some notice, I think."

"And the tornado?" Kenzie asks. "And the dead dogs? Are you covering everything or just the murder?"

I hedge for a moment before answering. I'd tossed bravado around the dinner table last night, but Mom isn't wrong. As soon as I start talking about murder, and the fact that both the police and the public weren't terribly invested in figuring out who killed Boggs, hackles will be raised. If I take the events of the entire week into account and spin it as bootstrap work ethics and a community coming together to rise from the rubble, it might earn me enough goodwill to let the more probing questions skate by.

"I'm going to cover everything," I say. "The good and the bad. Dad had a few issues of the paper from before the tornado hit, and it reads like heaven in the heartland. There's a definite slant to the reporting, and it's all designed to make us feel good and look wholesome."

"Like what?" Kenzie asks.

"Usual fare," I tell her. "The days before the tornado hit have the Sweet Corn Festival on the front page, and little clip-out coupons for taking a shot at the mayor in the dunk tank."

"Fun!" Kenzie says, actually clapping her hands together.

"Quaint," I correct her. "There was also a printed notice that the tank had been officially inspected by the health department after last year's Sweet Corn princess developed a case of giardia after being the dunkee."

"Giardia?" Kenzie's face squishes together. "What's that?"

"An intestinal infection caused by a parasite," I tell her. I'd discovered this last night after a quick Google search. "It's more commonly called . . ." I glance around the teen room, just to be sure we're alone.

"Beaver fever."

"Oh my God!" Kenzie squeals, and falls back into her chair. "The Sweet Corn princess came down with beaver fever? That's priceless."

"Definitely," I agree, "but it's not something I can use in the podcast. I'm already on thin ice with my parents."

"Then don't share that little tidbit with Bristal," Kenzie advises. "She'll probably take the microphone from you and claim it's an STD that's present in the entire water system."

"Ha," I say, glancing at my phone at the mention of Bristal. We're supposed to meet at the historical society in fifteen minutes.

"But seriously . . . ," Kenzie says, her voice drifting off into uncertainty. I'm used to that—being uncertain is kind of her trademark. But there's a new note here, and I'm not quite sure what it is. I glance up to find Kenzie looking at me with something that edges on concern.

"You're not doing these live, right?"

"No," I tell her. "Too many variables, plus Henley doesn't have the best internet. I'd rather have a smooth-flowing recorded show than a live, buffering stream."

"Right, but, I mean, tech stuff aside. I wouldn't trust Bristal not to say something that could get you into trouble."

"Oh, don't worry," I reassure Kenzie. "She will be heavily edited."

"Edited is good," Kenzie says. "But can you just, like, put her on mute? Maybe just let her push some buttons on the laptop and say you collaborated?"

"Why?" I ask, feeling my pulse jump a bit. I don't like being questioned, and Mom and Dad had flown their own hesitancy about Bristal last night at dinner.

"I don't trust her," Kenzie blurts out. "Lydia, she *hits people.*"

I put my hand on MacKenzie's wrist and try not to laugh. My friend is what Henley wants to be—sweet, kind, and good. All the way down to the core.

"I'll be fine," I say. "Bristal will add a good edge to the podcast, bring some new blood to the voice, and I seriously doubt she hits me."

"And if she does?" Kenzie pushes.

"My dad's a lawyer." I shrug.

"Uh, a defense lawyer," she points out. "That wouldn't exactly help you in that situation."

"It would," I tell her. "Because if Bristal hits me, I'm hitting back. Harder."

Kenzie gives my skinny arms a glance but doesn't argue further. Maybe she trusts that I've got the situation under control . . . or maybe she knows that when I say I'd hit back, I'm not talking about muscles and knuckles.

I've got my own way of hitting hard, and it can bring people to their knees.

Mrs. Gurtz is manning the desk at the historical society when I walk in and doesn't do a good job of hiding her dismay. It's almost five, and I'm sure she is ready to go home and feed all her cats. I organized a canned-food drive through our church this past summer. Mrs. Gurtz had given us four boxes of expired tuna, along with a story about how it really should be just fine and that the dates were more of a guideline than a hard-and-fast rule . . . but she didn't want to chance it with Mitsy, Yo-Yo, and Ranger. Instead of giving the needy families of Henley botulism, I opened and emptied each can, rinsed them out and recycled them, and then tossed the garbage bag full of rotting food into the historical society's dumpster . . . six days before I knew it was scheduled to be emptied.

I might recycle, but that doesn't mean I don't know how to do revenge.

"Lydia!" Mrs. Gurtz stands when she sees me, making a move toward the door either as a sign that she might be coming in for a hug, or to send me the message by flipping the sign over to CLOSED. I dodge the hug and ignore her when she gives me a pointed look.

"I'm searching for articles from the paper about the tornado," I tell her. "Any chance I could take them home for the night?"

"We don't really check out materials," she says, shaking her head. "It's a reference collection, not a lending one."

"That works out great," I say, pulling a chair out from one of the tables and plopping my backpack onto it. "Because I'm going to be referencing them in my podcast."

I'm giving her my showstopping smile, which doubles as my you-can't-stop-me smile, but Mrs. Gurtz is missing out on the exhibition, her eyes darting to the left, where the current editions of the newspaper is on display. She doesn't have to worry; I've already seen today's headlines.

BUS BANDIT IN COURT TODAY

I've been walking around pretending like I have blinders on since I was in third grade, when Lindsay Pascale dumped her lunch tray over my head because Dad was defending the man who raped her older sister. I'd finished my cardboard box of milk with pear juice in my hair, stalwartly staring forward and focusing on MacKenzie's face.

"I know you're on your way out," I tell Mrs. Gurtz. "If you want to leave me the key, I can lock up."

She takes me up on my offer, perhaps remembering the heavy funk of forty pounds of rotting tuna. She presses the key into my hand and shows me the series of stones sitting along the sidewalk with the saying *learning your family history is the key to knowing who you are*, each word chiseled on its own stone. The key is unironically stored under the rock that says *key*.

The heater kicks on, and I take a minute to revel in the smell, breathing in deeply. The library had smelled like baby burp and body spray, but the historical society smells like old paper and musty bindings, crumbling glue and a warm copy machine. It's going to be my little cave for the next couple of hours—and Bristal's, if she ever shows up. I run my hands over the vertical files while I scan the dates on the carefully handwritten labels.

The label for the drawer covering the summer of 1994 is smudged, an old coffee stain neatly bisecting the writing that says *Jan—June*. The tornado hit on June 13, Randall Boggs was murdered the day before, and the flash flood that took out all the residents of the dog pound occurred on the fourteenth.

I pull the June 12 issue, even though it's the same one I looked through last night in Dad's study. I don't want to put a ton of work in only to have to catch Bristal up once she shows. I glance at the obituaries, making note of the familiar last names—Ballinger,

Crow, Lawson, and Hendrix. I scan them briefly, but the obits offer up little of interest. Lots of dying comfortably at home while surrounded by loved ones after an extended illness. The one thing that does catch my eye is that Margaret Ballinger was scheduled to be "laid to her eternal rest" the next day, at two in the afternoon. If I remember correctly, the tornado tore through town around four, so I doubt Margaret's rest was all that eternal.

The issue for June 13 is unremarkable as well, having been issued that morning, before the tornado hit. The *Hometown Henley Headlines* still reads like a quiet bedroom community where nothing ever happens, and everyone is content for it to remain that way. In the upper right-hand corner of the front page, the day's forecast innocuously calls for some thunderstorms in the afternoon.

There's a note card inside the file cabinet stating that issues for June 14 through June 30 have been transferred to microfiche due to "high interest and heavy use." An explanatory comment underneath simply reads *The long stretch of bad days* in Mrs. Gurtz's heavy, slanted cursive. Despite the warmth in the office, a chill runs down my spine.

My phone vibrates with a text from Bristal.

What's up, nerd?

Looking at old newspaper issues, I text back. **Alone.**

I know, she answers. There's a tapping at the window, and I look up to see Bristal pointing at me, the word *nerd* all too easily read on her lips.

Creeper, I text back, to which she gives me an enthusiastic thumbs-up, both on the phone and in real life. I point to the front door to let her know I'm coming around to let her in. She nods and breezes in with a jet of cold air, watching as I lock the door behind her.

"So, what's up? Other than me being late, because yes, I know. So let's not start with that." She flops onto a rolling chair in front of the microfiche machine, casually spinning in it. I take the chair next to her, where the boxes of fiche stand ready to load.

"I was thinking about the long stretch of bad days," I say. "It could be a great direction to take the podcast in."

Despite all their differences, Bristal's reaction is very similar to Kenzie's. Her eyes get big and she says, "Ooooohhhh." But then she starts chanting, "Murder, murder, murder," and banging on the counter. I kick her chair away from the counter, bringing the chant to an abrupt end.

"You're not screwing around, are you, Chass?" Bristal asks, rolling back into position. "Henley takes a swipe at your future, and you go for the jugular of its shady past."

"Exactly," I say, somewhat surprised that she's seen right through me. I'm not going to hang my guidance counselor out to dry for failing me; the real problem here is that no one wanted to point out that he could no longer perform his duties, for fear of hurting feelings and cracking the patina of politeness. My response will be to earn my history credit by outlining that pattern—in the form of an unsolved murder that no one wants to talk about and didn't try terribly hard to solve. Was it because someone from Henley did the deed? Or because everyone quietly agreed that our corner of the world was a better place without Randall Boggs in it?

"Yes, we'll highlight the murder," I tell her. "But the tornado and the flash flood occurred in the same week. The coverage on them is intertwined, and it's going to take real research to parse out the details. Are you up for it?"

"Sure." She shrugs. "As long as you give me the murder episode. Also, I've been thinking that we should call the podcast something else."

I was about to argue with her about doling out Randall Boggs, but taking creative license with my title is a much bigger problem. I cross my arms and glare at her.

"I'm thinking, *Henley: Your Parents Had Sex and Now You're Stuck Here.*"

I look up at the ceiling and pinch the bridge of my nose. At least I know she's not serious. "We've got a lot of material to get through here," I tell her. "Can you stick with me?"

"Like a condom," she promises, pulling her chair up close. "But a good one, not a cheapy slip-off one."

The white boxes with the fiche reel have been handled so much they barely retain their shape, the corners are rounded, the closing flap hangs on by the barest of cardboard threads, and the yellowed label peels upward on both ends. I power up the microfiche machine, and Bristal wheels in closer to me as I pull up the June 14 issue of the *Hometown Henley Headlines.*

I take a deep breath, my pulse suddenly thready in my veins.

The long stretch is more than just a run of bad luck. People died. Local businesses went under. Henley was literally destroyed. Do I really want to mine personal tragedy for clickbait?

"Is it broken?" Bristal asks, pointing at the fiche, which I haven't spun yet.

"No," I tell her, shaking off my malaise. The fiche isn't broken; Henley is.

And having a conscience is overrated, anyway.

SIX

Destruction is one thing, and I've seen it before. From house fires to car wrecks to instant replays of nose-breaking punches, the internet has treated my generation to pretty much anything we want (and sometimes don't want) to see, all in hi-def.

But this is different.

This is my hometown, and as important as escaping it is to me, Henley is still my origin. And seeing it in shambles rocks me in a way I didn't expect. Old brick buildings from the 1800s are torn in half, exposing beams that have real hatchet marks in them, a reminder that human hands milled these logs, and the descendants of those humans are wandering the streets, dazed. Cars are buried under rubble, an entire bedstead—mattress intact and pillows in place—is perched in a tree, seemingly undisturbed despite the fact it's been elevated forty feet.

Beside me, Bristal draws in a breath. "Shit, dude."

The cross from the Methodist church has been driven clean through the post office, the one apartment building in town is destroyed, the belongings of the residents strewn through the streets, hanging from the single stoplight, or twisting in the trees as the breeze toys with them. In one picture, a little girl stands, holding her mother's hand, the fingers of her other hand gripping a sippy cup as she stares at a mannequin that has been decapitated by a stop sign.

Though there are captions, I don't have to look at them to identify most of the people. A strong Hemming chin is hard to miss, as is the sharpness of a Beckley nose. A man wearing a Gold's Gym T-shirt and covering his mouth while he looks at his mobile home—now resting on top of the laundromat—is definitely a Richardson.

Through the chaos I can spot some landmarks. The bank is still standing today, as is the water tower and the legion hall. I flick through for more shots and find a picture titled *A view down South Lincoln Street*. My street. Trees are uprooted and lying across the road, electric lines are down, and broken glass covers the pavement while clothes dangle from the tops of trees like scarecrows arrived too late for the job.

Peeking through the branches, I can just see the stone cornices of my house. The shiver down my spine returns, running a quick route from my brain stem to my coccyx. I shake it off and turn the dial back to the front page so that I can read the article.

"Why isn't there an emoji for pee?" Bristal suddenly asks.

"What?" I spin in my chair to find her lost in her phone, scrolling through texts.

"It doesn't make sense," she says, shaking her head. "We pee way more than we poop. I probably peed three times today, and I don't think I've pooped all week."

"You probably need to see a doctor," I tell her. "Also—the whole focus thing?"

Bristal glances up from her phone. "Aw, you're cute. You've got things like health insurance, don't you?"

"I'm pretty sure it's illegal not to have health insurance," I tell her.

"I do a lot of things that are illegal," she admits.

I give up on trying to read the article and instead opt for printing it out, making sure I get a copy for Bristal, too, since she's clearly not sticking like the condom she had promised to be. I retrieve our still-warm copies from the printer only to come back to Bristal pumping her fist.

"Found it!" she tells me.

"Something about the long stretch?" I ask, leaning over her phone.

"No, a pee emoji," she says triumphantly. "See, my research skills are rock-solid. You were right to want me on this project."

"Was I?" I ask tightly, dropping her pages onto her lap. "There's your homework."

"Is this my murder stuff?" she asks.

"No," I tell her. "It's the first day of tornado coverage, and I'm not entirely sure about giving you the Randall Boggs episode."

"Pause," Bristal declares, and puts her phone facedown on her chest. "I'll give you the tornado episode *and* the flash flood if I can have the murder. Also . . ." She drops her voice, her eyes cutting around the dark interior of the historical society. "I've got some dirt for other episodes."

"What?" I ask, dropping into my chair. I don't trust Bristal as far as I can throw her, but I can read people, and she went from purposefully casual to dead serious real fast.

"About fifteen years ago somebody tagged all the government buildings in town," she whispers.

"Yeah?" I ask, leaning in.

"Totally my dad," she says with pride.

"Should we really have him admitting to vandalism?" I ask. "That probably cost a few thousand dollars to clean up. Spray paint doesn't come off easy."

"Neither does anyone who crosses a Jamison," Bristal says. "The post office told him he couldn't use an old microwave as his mailbox. He said he could. It escalated."

I don't have a response for that so I flick to the June 15 issue, where the front-page headline states "HOPE SURVIVES IN HENLEY!" as Bristal continues to scroll through her phone. I'm scanning grainy shots of bulldozers and the serious faces of National Guardsmen who had been called in overnight when Bristal announces, "I also want the ODOT roadkill crew episode."

I pull my eyes from the screen. "Is that a thing?"

"Yeah," she says, not glancing up. "It'll be a Bristal episode. I already talked to my cousin Larry and got a ride set up. He's giving me a shovel, too. Also gloves."

"How are you tying roadkill and Cousin Larry to local history?" I ask.

Bristal smiles and looks up. "These animals were alive yesterday; today they're dead. That's history. And super local."

"It's really not," I tell her, giving up on on-the-spot-reading once again as I hit the print button and get up to retrieve the copies.

"Just let me do my thing," Bristal calls after me. "I'll get Larry to talk about old shit. He knows things."

"Okay," I say hesitantly, handing over Bristal's copies. "So like a ride-along on a local history tour?"

"With dead stuff."

"I reluctantly agree."

"Good, because when I say that Cousin Larry knows things . . ." Bristal spins a finger in the air and drops her voice again, but I'm not falling for it a second time.

"Oh, like what?" I ask and scroll to the June 16 issue. "Who let all the air out of the bus tires five years ago and they had to cancel school across the whole district?"

"Yeah, he totally knows who did that because it was my cousin," Bristal says breezily. "But no, seriously, he might have a thing or two to share about Boggs. They were neighbors, back in the day."

"Hold up, what?" I look away from the microfiche, giving Bristal my full attention. "Your cousin was Boggs's neighbor?"

"Yep," Bristal says. "Some of my family grew up out on Far Cry. But the stuff he has to say might need to be off the record, you know?"

"Yes," I say immediately, the full cloak of journalistic integrity falling over my shoulders. "I would absolutely protect my source."

"Okay," Bristal says, leaning back in her chair. "Let me see what I can do. No promises."

"All right," I say, my voice picking up a notch, unsteady with adrenaline. "But in general, I don't think it's a good idea to have anyone in your family admitting to crimes on the air."

"What about yours?" Bristal asks, tiling her head toward today's issue of the newspaper, and the headline that screams "BUS BANDIT IN COURT TODAY."

"Uh, my dad doesn't commit crimes, he defends people who do," I tell her.

"But Abe Lytle?" Bristal pushes back. "He shot up a school bus. That's pretty gross."

I push back from the microfiche and spin my chair to face Bristal. She might be able to get intel on Randall Boggs, but nobody slings mud on my family.

"He didn't shoot up a school bus," I tell her. "That gun wasn't even loaded."

"But he beat the shit out of the bus driver," Bristal says. "Pulled him off and pounded his face in right in front of all the kiddos. I mean . . . there's video."

"Look, I'm not really supposed to talk about Dad's work," I say, turning back to the fiche and hitting print again, even though I already have this issue.

"You don't have to talk about it," Bristal tells me. "Plenty of other people already are."

"Whatever," I say, going for the same casual air that Bristal has perfected. The thing is, mine is a sham. I don't think Bristal actually cares what people think of her—or her family.

"Don't worry, I don't think your issues are interesting," Bristal assures me. "My family is waaaaay more fucked-up than yours. Remember when somebody replaced the coffee creamer in the staff break room with Ex-Lax?"

"There comes a point when you shouldn't tell me things because I become criminally responsible and am considered negligent if I don't report it," I tell her.

"That was all me," she says.

"BRISTAL!" I scream. "Mr. Bentley had to go to the ER for dehydration!"

"Yeah, but at least he wasn't full of shit anymore," she says.

I print out the rest of the *Hometown Henley Headlines* from the long stretch, knowing that coverage of the Boggs murder will continue, interest fading only as it becomes clear that whoever killed him isn't going to be easily captured and that nobody was all that upset about him dying in the first place. Out on the sidewalk, I hand Bristal the rest of her copies, which she dutifully folds into a square and jams into her back pocket. I pull out my phone to check for texts, only to find one from Bristal with twenty-six iterations of her newly found pee emoji.

"Thanks for all the research help," I say bitterly, flashing the screen at her. "You're an inspiration." I veer toward South Lincoln Street, Bristal keeping pace beside me.

"I may not think microfiche is sexy," Bristal says, "but I was doing research, YouTube-style. I looked up old news footage from the tornado."

"Oh?" I say, pausing by a monument for the tornado victims to take her outstretched phone. To my surprise, Bristal leans down and starts pulling some of the weeds that have overtaken the geraniums the village council plants every year. I push play on the video and turn up the volume, walking alongside Bristal as I head for home. Her phone screen is cracked, adding to the feeling of destruction. I'm no longer just being told what people said, I hear their voices. And these people are desolate.

"We're just hoping she finds her way home," Betsy Hemming says, concern for her elderly mother stamped on her features, while a man behind her winds a wheelbarrow through a field of debris.

"It's like taking a spoonful of water out of the ocean," I say to myself, and Bristal straightens beside me, glancing over my shoulder.

"Check out this next bit," she says.

A young man appears on the screen, his entire head wrapped in a bandage, a bright red oval of blood already seeping through from his temple. One eye is swollen completely shut, the skin around it a deep purple, his nose bent at an awkward angle. He's wearing the Henley classic—a wifebeater and a pair of loose-fitting blue jeans. But his skin is nicely tanned against the white of his shirt, and even I can't deny that the outline of muscles there is worth a second look. He's motioning at the pile behind him, but his words are lost in the reporter's voiceover.

"Dover Jamison, eighteen, was staying with family in town when the tornado hit," she explains.

"They got air-conditioning, and I don't," Dover says helpfully. "Thought I'd be able to get some rest, but . . ." He shrugs, an aw-shucks move that seems to work some sort of magic on the blond reporter, who moves in closer to him.

"Was it worth it?" she asks, with a coy smile.

"Well . . ." Dover scratches at the bandage above his ear, the grin still spreading. "That AC unit is sitting in the nonfiction section of the library now, and the couch I was on at the time got moved down to Third Street, but hey—at least I didn't get hurt."

"'At least I didn't get hurt'!" Bristal echoes, clapping her hands together. "His face is barely attached to his head and he's just glad he didn't get hurt. That's a Jamison for you," she says, taking the phone back from me. "We're hard to kill."

"So, Dover would be your . . . ?" I spin my finger in the air, waiting for her to fill in the blank.

"Uncle," she says. "Most everybody is my cousin, but he's actually my legit uncle. Mom's brother."

"Most everybody is your cousin?" I repeat dubiously.

"I mean, like, we don't differentiate second cousin, third cousin, once removed, twice removed. All that stuff, you know?"

"Genealogy?"

"Yeah, that," she says dismissively. "It's just easier to say *cousin* for everybody. And also like my mom's uncles or aunts, we grew up with her calling them Uncle Steve or Aunt Joan, so all my brothers and sisters, we call them Uncle Steve and Aunt Joan. But they're really not."

"They're your *great*-aunt and -uncle," I clarify, pausing at the end of my driveway.

"Yeah, sure," Bristal agrees half-heartedly, gazing down the length of the drive, past the tall pines to the broad expanse of our front porch. "Being rich looks fun."

"We're not rich," I snipe back. "We don't even use the third floor; it's just one big ballroom."

Bristal cocks her head at me, the wind playing with her dark hair, her half smile barely visible in the twilight. "Do you even hear the words that come out of your mouth sometimes?"

I reconsider what I just said, and don't see a way to backpedal from it. "Good job with the old news reels," I say instead. "It looks like your uncle was right in the thick of it. Would he want to come onto the show?"

"I don't know," Bristal says. "How do you feel about airing an episode from prison?"

SEVEN

"Mom? I'm home!" I call out as I kick my shoes off on the side screened porch. Dad's car isn't in the garage, which doesn't surprise me, with the Lytle case being in court today. It's also a nice bonus for me, because without Dad at the table, we'll be indulging in some grazing and snacks instead of a proper sit-down of a supper. Mom doesn't always play the straight and narrow game as well as he might want her to, and I don't rat her out when we do Cheez-Its and Pop-Tarts for a meal. It takes me back to my childhood, when Mom would tell me to make sure to hide my Happy Meal toys so that Dad thought we still had some self-respect when he wasn't around.

"Up here!" Mom's voice trails down the grand staircase. It's wide enough to drive a car up and takes a lofty bend to the left at the top, some ancient oak that grew at just the right twisted angle now transplanted as our hand rail.

I grab a bottle of water and follow Mom's voice to the upstairs living room, suddenly very aware of the mental distinction. . . . We have a downstairs one as well. I imagine Bristal's reaction to that and decide to close my thoughts to her for the moment. I don't feel guilt that the Chass name means I live in this house. We didn't break other people's backs to get here; my great-great-grandparents worked their asses off, and I have this as a result. Still, I can't help but wonder what Bristal's house looks like as I plop onto the love seat and twist the cap off my water bottle. Mom mutes the television and the man on-screen telling us all about the amazing attributes of arctic foxes falls mercifully silent.

"How'd it go?" Mom asks. "Get anything good?"

"Nothing unexpected," I tell her. "Did you hear from Dad? How did it go today with Abe Lytle?"

"It was just the arraignment today," Mom says, reaching up to ease a kink out of her neck. "He pled not guilty, and most of Henley lost their minds. I wouldn't get on social media for the next few days, if I were you."

"I try to avoid it," I reassure her, but my mind is whirling. "But you know that video is already out there, right? The damage is done."

"Your dad will do everything he can to keep that from being shown in court, I'm sure," Mom says, reaching down to wiggle her fingers for Uneven Steven, who bats at them from underneath the coffee table. He's unhooked from his wheels and rolled onto his back, happily wrapping his arms around her wrist as she goes in for a tummy scratch.

I swear that cat is probably going to get my room when I leave for college.

"Shown in court or not, everyone's already seen it," I tell her. "And good luck finding a jury in Markham County that hasn't."

"He'll petition the court to have the trial moved," Mom says. "For that exact reason."

"But why?" I ask. "Why even bother with the whole thing? Why not just follow the lead of every other half-baked public defender and plea down, just this once? I know Dad likes to fight for the little guy, but this particular guy isn't very little, and the last I heard, Lawrence Horvath is still eating through a tube."

I might not let Bristal say a sideways word about my family, but when Dad's actions mean that the rest of us have to wade through a waist-high sea of shit online, I've got something to say about it.

Mom reaches down and pulls Steven up from the floor, cuddling him to her chest. We like to pretend that we did that cat a favor by adopting him, but the truth is that even with all the extra care and medical bills, he's still way cheaper than therapy for Mom. With Dad constantly working and me chasing down whatever extracurricular is at the top of the pile, I wouldn't be surprised if one day I come home to find Steven in a high chair and Mom cutting up baked chicken for him.

"You know how your dad views his work," Mom says. "He always puts himself in his client's shoes. And if he can understand their behavior, he'll defend it."

"How did he come to understand pulverizing an old man's face?"

"By thinking about how Abe Lytle felt in that moment. He

wasn't seeing Lawrence Horvath as a human being; at that point he was an obstacle separating him from his son. Abe thought he was going to lose his child, and he relied on the one thing he'd been raised to do, what he'd been groomed for, and the only skill that was ever cultivated in him."

"Violence," I say.

"Exactly," Mom agrees. "The public sees two minutes of Lytle's life. They don't know anything about the thirty years that came before that, and all the boxes that were checked in order to create the perfect storm that brought those two men to that moment."

"So that's how Dad defends him? He can't create any reasonable doubt that Lytle did what he did."

"No, but he can ask the jury to consider him as a whole human, not simply a criminal. He's a man who just got back from a military deployment, where physical violence is the law of the land. And he's a desperate father who is afraid of losing his child, after having already lost his wife."

"It won't be easy," I say, stretching out my legs and enjoying the dual pops of my knees as the tension of the day evaporates.

"No, and that goes double for you. Are you having any trouble at school?"

"Over Lytle?" I ask. "No, not yet. But I'm so fixated on this podcast right now I wouldn't notice if someone threw a burning effigy of Dad into my car."

Mom winces and pets Steven little harder. "How is the podcast going?"

"Pretty good," I say, producing a notebook from my backpack

and fanning the printed pages of the *Hometown Henley Headlines* in her direction. "Lots of reading material about the tornado."

"The tornado?" Mom perks up. "That's a great idea. Everyone has a tornado story. Will it bother you if I turn my show back on?" Mom asks, but I give her a desultory wave, my eyes already roaming over the June 14 issue.

TORNADO TEARS THROUGH TINY OHIO TOWN

June 14, 1994

By Jeff Johnson

(AP)

Four people are dead, 50 injured, and more than 100 still missing in the small farming community of Henley, Ohio, after a tornado tore through town in the late afternoon yesterday. Markham County sheriff Bob Foxglove said they are trying to account for the missing people before bringing in machinery to sift debris.

"Every possible responder in the tri-county area was here, everybody all at once. We had hurt people being sent every which way, and until we can determine who ended up where, we won't really know who is dead, who is missing, and who could still be trapped under this godawful mess."

Although the governor immediately declared Henley a disaster area and deployed the National Guard, most residents of the town claim it was unnecessary.

"I guess they're all worried about looting," Delilah Lytle said. "They don't understand that kind of thing just doesn't happen in Henley."

While Ms. Lytle's optimism might seem a touch naive, the streets of Henley were filled with residents who—once the shock had been absorbed—all pitched in and began working. For others, there wasn't anything to clean up.

"My house should be here," Gary Parsons said, while standing on the sidewalk and facing an empty lot where broken gas pipes and water lines erupt from the ground. "I live here," he says, gesturing futilely. "But there's nothing to live in."

"Our grocery store is gone, our bakery is gone, our library is gone, our police station is gone, the firehouse is gone," said Bailey Foxglove, 16, daughter of the sheriff. She's been called into service herself—now manning the phone lines in her own home, as calls to the police station are being rerouted there.

"I've got people calling looking for their husbands, or their wives, and even their kids," she says, wiping a tear away. "I just don't even know what to tell them. People call asking if anybody had seen their dogs or their cats, and all I can say to them is that we don't know. We just don't know."

Chaos is the word for what has happened here in Henley, with a long list of missing, and volunteers calling their names while carefully shifting rubble with bare hands. Meanwhile, emergency lights are being brought in as the search continues through the night for those who may still be counted among the living in Henley.

"'We just don't know,'" I repeat, looking at the words of Bailey Foxglove. I imagine her, sixteen and frightened, frantically answering phone calls and having no answers for the people on the other end.

"Hey, Mom," I ask, and she glances over at me, muting the television. "Do you know someone named Bailey Foxglove?"

"Foxglove, Foxglove, Foxglove . . ." Mom's eyes glaze over for a second as she consults the Henley directory in her head. "Sheriff's daughter, right?"

"That's her."

"She was a couple years ahead of me, I think," Mom says, scooting aside a candy bar wrapper on the coffee table to make room for her wineglass, and shifting Steven down to her lap. "Nice girl, always had her hair in a French braid."

"She still around?"

"I think so, but I haven't run into her lately. I can see if we're friends online," Mom offers. "I mean . . ." She grimaces, and her mouth pulls into a downward turn. "I'll have to reactivate my Facebook account."

"You shut down your Facebook?" I ask, my antennae going up. "Why?"

"Oh, you know," Mom says blithely, waving a dismissive hand. "Taking a break, self-care, other buzzwords."

"You're lucky you're married to a good lawyer, because you're a bad liar," I tell her. "You're on every local group, from recycling to saving injured wildlife. It's a platform for good deeds and maintaining the family presence. Why don't you tell me the real reason you'd give up your stranglehold on the Most Active Volunteer in Markham County award?"

Mom sighs and sets her wineglass aside. "A platform for good deeds, sure. But it's also an instant delivery system for nasty attacks."

"Attacks?" I ask, sitting up straighter. "Did someone threaten you?"

"Calling it a threat would be putting it strongly," Mom says.

I push my laptop across the coffee table. "Log in and show me. I'll decide what to call it."

"No," Mom says, shaking her head. "You don't need to know what was said—or who said it. If you—or your dad, or anyone with the last name of Chass reacts too strongly—we're punching down, and it invites the floodgates to open."

"There's a difference between punching down and standing up for yourself," I tell her.

"Maybe, Lydia," Mom says, pressing her hands to her temples. "But quite frankly, I don't even want to think about it. It was vile, and it set me back for a few days."

"So your solution is to forget about it?" I ask. "Pretend like it didn't happen?"

"Stop. Just stop," Mom says, a little anger slipping into her voice. "This happened to me, not you. You don't get to have an opinion about it, and I don't think you're being funny right now."

"That's because I'm not trying to be," I tell her. "I'm dead serious. There are procedures for online threats. You let the platform know, and then you call the cops."

"The cops?" Mom actually laughs. "That would be a little

much. This person can just claim they're joking, and then I'm a drama queen—and a vengeful one, at that."

"And we're back to being nice," I say. "Smile and nod in the face of personal threats."

"It's the right thing to do," Mom says.

"No," I correct her. "It's the *nice* thing do. The nice thing and the right thing aren't always the same thing."

"You should cross-stitch that on a pillow," Mom shoots back. "Market a whole line called Pessimistic Wisdom Products."

"Is this my signal to change the subject?" I ask.

"Yes," Mom says, reaching for her wine again. "Especially if you want me to contact Bailey Foxglove for you."

"That'd be great," I say, shifting easily. "Her dad had her taking all the emergency calls the day after the tornado. I thought she'd make for a great interview."

"Probably," Mom agrees. "I don't remember her well, but she was the president of the FFA and had all the clout and speaking skills attached to that."

Mom's not being facetious, either. Being the president of the FFA in Henley is like being the president of the United States to the rest of the world.

"If you could check up on that I'd really appreciate it."

"Yep," Mom says. "Anything else I can do?"

I hesitate for a second, remembering the conversation at the dinner table the night before. Mom and Dad hadn't had anything nice to say about the Jamisons, and I'm not sure that I want to give Bristal's uncle too much airtime. But there had been a certain bootstrap quality to Dover that spoke of grassroots determination, something I imagine I have a dose of myself.

"What about Dover Jamison?" I ask. "Do you remember him?"

"Do I remember Dover?" Mom's mouth is half buried in another wineglass, and her eyes are directed downward, her mumble less of a trick of physics and more of a hedge for time. The blush rising in her cheeks can't only be from the wine, and I briefly wonder if the muscles I'd spotted under his tank had captured her attention back in the day.

"I knew Dover the same way you know the kids in your class," she goes on. "I could pick him out of a lineup, but that's about it."

"And you'd have to," I tell her. "He's in prison."

"Mmmmmm . . . ," Mom says, mouth finding the glass again.

She's not giving me real answers, and while she'd lifted her brows as high as Botox will allow, I don't think there was any real shock in her expression when I informed her of Dover's current whereabouts. I recall the sly smile the eighteen-year-old kid had tried out on an adult reporter—and remember that it worked.

"Do you know what he did?" I ask.

"Oh, look. Your dad's home," Mom says as headlights swim across the walls, bent by the colors of the stained glass picture window.

"Good timing," I observe. "But you better hide that candy wrapper. And the empty bottle of wine."

"And you'd be smart not to mention Dover Jamison," Mom says, tipping her glass toward me. I'm not sure if she's covering my ass or hers, but I take the point—as well the edge she just gave me.

"You'll get a hold of Bailey Foxglove?"

She purses her lips at my continued jockeying but gives me a nod. "And I ordered some of that soundproof material for the upstairs closet," she adds.

"Nice," I say, already mentally assessing how long it will take to empty the linen shelves.

"Where are my girls?" Dad's voice floats up the stairs, and Mom and I exchange a glance.

"Up here," we sing out at the same time, our tones carefree and light, as she balls her candy wrapper into her fist, rolls the bottle under the couch, and I slip my notes—with a doodle of a boy with an alluring smile and a head bandage—into my backpack.

EIGHT

Things get dicey real fast when the organizer of the blood drive doesn't show up on time.

The organizer in question would be me, and the dicey part is manifold—I just received my first tardy ever, and I should probably take Mrs. Nathans, the senior class adviser, off the list of people I was considering asking for a letter of recommendation. She'd met me in the foyer, arms crossed, lips thin, with the look of someone who just woke up next to the wrong person in the morning.

Or, in my case, a different version of the person she'd expected.

"I'm so sorry," I tell her, rushing alongside her to the gym, tardy slip in hand. "I got sidetracked last night and—"

She waves me off, and I'm secretly glad I don't have to tell her that I stayed up until one in the morning, following link after link that Bristal sent me. Most of the clips had covered one or the other of the tragedies from the long stretch, but she'd slipped in a demonstration on how to use a dildo with the accompanying message—**this one is a must! Great descriptions and some good shots!** A trusting fool, I'd clicked on it. And now my suggestions algorithm is seriously skewed.

"The cots are set up, and the Red Cross people are ready to get started," Nathans tells me as we clip toward the gym. "You've got the spreadsheet of volunteers?"

"Yep!" I say, waving a sheaf of papers above my head. It's not the spreadsheet; it's the *Henley Headlines* issues I need to catch up on. But Nathans only nods, and I slide into my seat at the welcoming table, whip out my laptop, and print out the volunteer list while she critically inspects the linens on the cots. Last year she'd done an impromptu bacterial swipe on one and came back a week later with a petri dish full of happily replicating staph. We'd had to inform the Red Cross, and all the blood we'd gathered had to be disposed of—a fact that did not make it onto my résumé.

I dash over to the office to retrieve my printed sheets and give the donor list a quick once-over before I ask St. John to start calling them down. I'm surprised to see Bristal's name on the list, followed by a big red *X*.

"Do you think you could start calling down the first wave of blood donors?" I ask Eva St. John, giving her my highest-wattage smile. "Maybe start with eight, and I'll let you know when the beds empty out and you can send more."

"Sure thing," Eva says, absently scrolling the student list. "What kind of doughnuts you got down there this time?"

"Everything," I tell her. I had pulled a few kids serving in-school suspension to help carry doughnuts, and I even conned some of them into donating blood in order to get one.

"You're stuck here anyway," I told Brandon Childress, who got three days ISS for hiding a vape pen in the panels of the boy's bathroom ceiling. Insiders knew where to go when they wanted a hit, but Jake Milhaus had slipped off the toilet when he tried to put it back and got a concussion for his trouble.

Brandon talked a few of his cohorts into accepting the needle, but the Red Cross people turn away Jake Milhaus, who is still suffering from his fall. I try to push for them to accept him—he's looking at the doughnut table the way I do the short list for Pulitzers—but when the nurse shows me his application, even I can't deny that he's not a good candidate. His writing slants off to one side, and he spelled his name wrong. Besides that, he appears to have herpes.

Which reminds me—why was Bristal turned away?

"Please don't have herpes," I say to the sheaf of papers. I know it's a sexually transmitted disease, but I was just holding her phone last night, and I doubt she's the type to disinfect daily.

As if my very thought of her had conjured it, my phone lights up with a text.

Can't get into see Dover until next week. Guess he got in trouble for "using urine as a weapon" on a guard.

"Nice," I say under my breath. Then type, **I'm at the blood**

drive. You were turned away, just FYI. Don't come down here looking for donuts.

I give the gym a quick glance, but everything seems to be going
fine. Nathans is walking through the rows of cots, offering up a
sympathetic ear and tips for anyone who is struggling. I was rel-
egated to the welcome table my sophomore year, after I'd tried to
comfort a girl by telling her that her body held ten pints of blood
and that we were only taking one. Then I'd held up her bag to
show her how far along she was, hoping that it would give her
stamina to make the push for the finish line. Instead, she passed
out, and Nathans decided to put someone who was better with
feelings than facts on the bedside duties. I surreptitiously slide the
Hometown Henley Headlines to the top of my volunteer paperwork.

The *Hometown Henley Headlines* had issued only one page on
the fourteenth, the day after the tornado, and I hadn't failed to
notice that the lone article was from the Associated Press—not a
local reporter. The June 15 paper has more of a local flavor and a
familiar byline from the owner, operator, photographer, and single
reporter who ran the *Headlines* back in the nineties.

HOPE SURVIVES IN HENLEY

June 15, 1994

By David Swinton

Though our hometown is still reduced to rubble and soldiers
patrol the streets, many hearts rest easier today in Henley. An
overnight flutter of activity—that this reporter was directly

involved in—resulted in a great reduction of our list of missing. After calling local hospitals with the roster, and in some cases personally checking in on those who had not recovered consciousness and needed to be identified, the Hometown Headlines is happy to report that at this time, the number of missing people has been drastically reduced to only three.

It is with a heavy heart, though, that we share the names of the deceased:

I skim over the next paragraph, knowing full well who they were and how they died; the monument at the base of the water tower exists to remind everyone. A young couple and their infant had done what they were supposed to do—take cover in the basement. But the next-door fire station had collapsed, most of the second story toppling onto their roof, driving their house down upon their heads as they huddled below.

The fourth name on the monument is that of an elderly woman who everyone agrees probably just had a heart attack, but since she died on the day of the tornado and nobody can say for sure whether it was the tornado that caused it, the village council decided to go ahead and give her the honor of being listed on the monument.

Swinton picks up a thread from the AP article of the day before, commenting on the number of loose dogs in the area.

Linda Chance, the local dog warden, is asking that anyone who is missing their pets to please come check at the pound in person. As we all know, Linda is the only paid employee of the pound, and her volunteer staff are all helping family members in this tumultuous time. The dog shelter has been flooded with calls . . .

I wince at the poor choice of words, only too aware of what lies in store for the residents of the pound.

. . . and Linda is unable to answer everyone's question at this time.

"People call and ask if I have their dog, but all they can tell me is that his name is Brutus and that he's brown and would never bite anyone. I've got thirty-seven dogs in here right now. A lot of them are brown. Half of them are named Brutus. Most of them don't have collars, and every single one of them is scared to death. I've been out on five stray calls just today and got bit each time. So don't tell me your dog is brown and he won't bite. Get your [expletive deleted] down here and look for your dog yourself, if you care at all."

I cover a smile and hope no one thinks I'm tallying up pints and am maniacally happy about bags of blood. Linda is still the warden and has devoted her life to the county kennel. She has two ex-husbands and no kids, and her front office is filled with pamphlets about getting your pets spayed and neutered, tips on protecting them from parasites, and framed, hand-stitched sentiments like "If You're Aware of the Dog, You Don't Have to

Beware of It" and "A Man Who Will Kick a Dog Will Hit a Human."

I take a look at my notepad, adding Linda Chance to the list of people I'll need to talk to, along with Bailey Foxglove. I add David Swinton as well, and my pen hovers for a second as I consider the names of the dead from the tornado. Their family members have been since wrung dry of any information, as well as tears. Every year on the anniversary, they're asked to "say a few words," and those words have become repetitive. Everyone listens, and people still bow their heads, but every year the blood that was spilled feels a little thinner.

Which reminds me—I've already promised a Civil War monument dedication episode to my listeners, and if I do a quick switch to Henley's less glorious moments, I might lose some eardrums—which, according to my stats, I can't really afford. I need to find a way to honor the moment while providing a new angle, something that can serve as a transition into coverage of the long stretch and a more critical eye on my hometown.

I chew my pen for a second, lost in thought, and glance up to survey the gymnasium. Brandon and one of his buddies look a little gray, but they're with it enough to tease each other about the "little prick" the nurse had warned them was "coming." The jokes only devolve from there; I roll my eyes, happy to return to lines of newsprint rather than rows of cots.

The June 16 issue of the *Henley Hometown Headlines* looks like David Swinton was managing a migraine, massive blood loss, and an oxygen bubble to the brain all at the same time. The margins are uneven, the print is crooked, and the photos were pulled out of the developing mix too early. But, given that a one-man operation was covering Henley's only recorded murder right after the destruction of most of the town, followed by a flash flood and the tragic death of every resident of the county pound, I'm sure that David was just doing the best he could under the circumstances.

ALL ACCOUNTED FOR IN TORNADO AFTERMATH

June 16, 1994

By David Swinton

Although it's been a rough few days for Henley by all accounts, we're happy to report that the remaining two townspeople are no longer missing. Johnny Aldridge, 7, was located with his estranged father, who had neglected to let the mother know he'd picked him up for a surprise fishing trip before the tornado struck. Margie Hemming, 82, a long-time sufferer of dementia, was found by a local couple in the state park.

"She doesn't know what happened," her daughter, Betsy, says. "We were driving her home from the hospital, and she just kept asking me where we were. I tried to tell her this was Henley, but she said, 'No, no, it's not.'"

Admittedly, all our brains are addled these days. With

the discovery of the body of a local man, Randall Boggs, in his home late yesterday evening, rumors are whirling and tensions are high—much like the waters of the creeks, rivers, and streams, which have leaped their boundaries in the onslaught of—

Someone is at the table, and I raise my head, aware that something in the article isn't quite right. And I don't just mean syntax.

"How's it going?" MacKenzie asks. "Mind if I join you?"

I make a noncommittal noise in my throat as she plops down next to me and scan the article again. Margie and Betsy Hemming . . . maybe that's what had caught my eye. I shuffle through the papers in my backpack, pulling out all the issues of the *Henley Headlines* that I'd printed, highlighting some of the finer points. But the name Hemming isn't there, and I have to flip the spreadsheet of blood donors back over to the top when Nathans approaches.

"You can probably ask Mrs. St. John to call a few more," she tells me, taking a look at the half-empty cots behind her. "But maybe only five or six. The Childress boy is going to need a minute to recover."

"That little prick was too much for him," his buddy says as he slides past the table.

I leave MacKenzie at the table and ask St. John to send the next wave, then return to my seat, still pensive. I can feel my thoughts cycling. Something about that June 16 article has my attention, but I don't know what it is yet. I've been here before, waiting for a tiny detail or an errant thought to come full circle and present itself to me clearly. This usually happens around three in the morning, or, in the very memorable moment of my first kiss, when Brett Johnson had leaned in and I'd suddenly blurted, "decollate!"

He'd pulled back immediately and asked if something was wrong, to which I said, "No, I was writing an essay about the guillotine as a method of execution earlier and I was using the word *decapitate* so much that I was trying to find a different way to say the same thing. I knew there was a synonym, but I couldn't come up with it. And then you called, and my mind kept looking for the answer, and it just popped up. Anyway . . ."

I'd then pursed my lips and closed my eyes, only to open them a second later to see Brett putting on his shoes and making awkward observations about how late it was getting.

Having a brain like a terrier—it'll dig until it dies rather than give up the quarry—can really be a damper on my social life. But it also means that I can relax until it retrieves the answer and brings it back to the forefront of my mind. I just have to summon the patience to wait that long.

"Hemming, Hemming, Hemming," I mutter to myself, an echo of Mom repeating Bailey Foxglove's name last night.

"We're not even on the G's yet," MacKenzie says skeptically as she consults the donor sheet.

"That's not—" I begin, but my phone goes off with another text from Bristal, responding to what I'd sent earlier.

I can't come down and score a donut. I got OSS for hijacking the intercom.

That's right, I forgot Bristal won't be gracing us with her presence for three days because of that little stunt. But that doesn't mean she can't make herself useful.

Something is bothering me, I text back.

Don't worry. I think you're still technically a virgin if it was just a blow job.

I take a picture of the front page of the June 16 issue and text it to Bristal.

This pinged something in my brain, but I can't figure out what.

Maybe you'll have better luck.

I send MacKenzie to call for the next group of donors, and she's not even back from the office yet when I get a response from Bristal.

Hemming. Betsy Hemming. She was the one on the newsreel right before Dover, said she hoped her demented mother would be able to find her way home. Looks like old Margie managed it.

"Right," I say, chewing my lip. It's a good observation and explains why my mind had locked on to the last name, but wheels are still spinning, and I know that's not the full explanation.

"Lydia!" Nathans shouts my name just as a freshman over at the doughnut table does a face-plant into the muffin tower. I rush over, MacKenzie at my heels, and we roll her onto her back, picking pieces of blueberry crumble out of her hair.

"Is she hurt? Is she bleeding?" Nathans asks, leaning over the girl in an absolute violation of all CPR training ever. I firmly back her up, and the Red Cross people swarm in, propping the girl's legs up and taking her pulse.

"I'm sure she's fine," I tell Nathans. "She was just . . . *TWO!*"

I scream the last bit, my overjoyed brain latching on to what it had been searching for and biting down at just the wrong moment—again.

"Lydia?" Nathans asks.

"You can only have one doughnut!" I whirl and scream at Brandon, who is guiltily double-fisting a couple of jelly-filleds. "You can't have two! I don't care how low your blood sugar is right now."

"Lydia," Nathans says carefully. "There really are plenty, if he feels like he needs it."

"No one needs two doughnuts, Nathans," I snap at her.

"And, no," I keep going, letting all the venom of my internal monologue out, "there might not be enough doughnuts, because this idiot just pitched headfirst into three feet of muffins."

The idiot in question is starting to come around, and she looks up at me with a rage that might burn a little brighter if she had a few more red blood cells inside of her at the moment.

"Fuck you, Chass," Brandon Childress says lazily, his mouth moving around about half a pound of strawberry jelly. "My little sister was on that bus."

He's not the first person to say *fuck you* to me, and getting a lunch tray over the head in elementary school was way more embarrassing than this. But coming hard on the heels of Mom being threatened over Facebook, I don't have a retaliatory response locked and loaded. His words aren't sliding off my back the way they usually would; anger rises in my stomach, but it was preceded by something else—cold, hard fear.

"You!" Nathans says, trying to regain some control and pointing at Brandon. "Get back to ISS, and let Mrs. St. John know you're doing an extra day for how you just spoke to Lydia."

"'Kay," he says, snagging a sugar cookie as he leaves, apparently all his anger about his little sister mollified by about fifteen hundred free calories.

"I'm just going to take Lydia to the bathroom for a minute," MacKenzie cheerily informs Mrs. Nathans, then steers me by the elbow out into the hallway.

"You okay?" she asks as I lean against the wall, my breaths coming shallow and fast. "Brandon better get more than one day OSS for that."

She's worried about me, and I appreciate it. But it's not only Brandon's casual attack that has my blood pressure high. It's because I just figured it out, and like Archimedes hopping out of the bathtub to go tell the king what he'd discovered about volume and water displacement, nothing else mattered to me in the moment. Archimedes ran outside naked, and I screamed a seemingly random number in the middle of a blood drive.

"Two," I repeat to MacKenzie, putting my hands on her shoulders. "The June sixteenth article said the remaining *two* townspeople who were MIA had been found. But the June fifteenth issue said there were *three*."

"Neat," Kenzie says, with complete disinterest. She's not listening, and she doesn't care—but I know someone who will.

Unfortunately, that person is as high as a kite when I call her.

"Lydiaaaaaaaaaa," Bristal says, drawing my name out as long as she can. "What is up?"

"I figured out what was bothering me about that article," I say, taking her off speakerphone so that anyone else in the girls' bathroom doesn't know exactly how under the influence Bristal is at the moment. "The reporter said the two missing people have now been accounted for, but the issue before had the tally at three."

"Huh," Bristal says, mulling it. I don't know if I need to do the subtraction for her, or if she's got this. "Could've been a typo, do you think?"

"Maybe," I admit. "But I doubt it. Swinton might have been the only employee and was run absolutely ragged, but he was good at what he did. That's a pretty big slip, to not know the number of missing when it's the biggest moment in Henley history."

"So who was this third person?" Bristal asks. "And how do we find out?"

My mind goes back to Bailey Foxglove, sixteen years old and trying to answer the questions of every resident in Henley who can't find their loved ones.

"Two options," I tell her. "Remember the sheriff's daughter who was taking police calls? We can ask her, and, of course, we follow up with David Swinton, the reporter. What are you doing right now?"

"Now?" Bristal asks. "I'm smoking the devil's lettuce."

"Well, I need you to stop," I say, then flick through my messages to find one from my mom that came in this morning with Bailey Foxglove's contact info. "We're going to meet with the sheriff's daughter after school. Can you be sober by then?"

"Dude, it's cheap weed. I'm going to be fully functioning in like five minutes."

"Great," I say. "Because I'm going to need you to be sharp."

"'Kay," she says. "But can you bring me a doughnut?"

NINE

Bristal still has icing on her face when I pull into the gravel lot beside the shelter house at the park. There are a couple of young kids on the swing set, and I see a few pairs of shoes lined up beside the path that leads down the bank to the river. But there's only one person in the shelter house, and I double-check the blonde's profile with a pic from Facebook.

"That's Bailey," I confirm to Bristal as she pops her door open. "And here." I hand her a disinfectant wipe. "Check yourself."

"Good catch," Bristal says, taking a glance at the visor mirror. "Don't want to make a bad impression, even if I do have to introduce myself as a Jamison."

"Bailey, hello," I say as we approach her, and the woman puts down her phone.

"Lydia," she says, reaching out to shake my hand. "And you

are . . . ? Oh, never mind," Bailey says after giving Bristal a once-over. "You're a Jamison."

"The oldest," Bristal says. "And no, I'm not pregnant."

I flinch, not realizing that Bristal knew the saying about Jamison girls.

"Thanks so much for meeting with us," I say, keeping it light. "I was so glad when my mom said she'd found you on Facebook and that you'd moved back home."

"Yes, well"—Bailey's finely lined face pulls into a forced smile—"divorce does tend to send us running back to our roots."

"I'm sorry to hear that," I say smoothly, pulling out my notebook and pen. "Mom said your husband was military?"

"Yeah, and I'm here to tell you, don't let a uniform turn your heads, girls," Bailey warns us. "They can make a man look pretty, but they can't change what's inside. Just look at what Lytle—well, never mind." Bailey shakes her head, her eyes dropping. "Sorry. I know your father is his lawyer."

"Yes, he is," I say matter-of-factly, keeping my tone neutral.

"So, your mom said that you're doing a podcast about Henley?" Bailey says.

"Yes," I tell her. "I'm working on something about the long stretch. I read in the paper that you took all the phone calls coming into the police station after the tornado?"

"Yeah," Bailey says, and a little bit of the light goes out of her eyes. She's tall and well-built, muscular where my mom is soft, but the mention of the tornado has her slumping in her seat. "That was rough."

"Do you mind?" I whip out my phone and open a recording app.

Bailey nods her assent and sits up straighter, tugging on the front of her shirt where the buttons had gapped. I recite the date, time, and Bailey's name, then jump in with my first question.

"What was your own experience of the tornado, as a sixteen-year-old girl suddenly asked to field all the incoming emergency calls?"

"It wasn't easy," Bailey says. "People were frantic. We didn't have nine-one-one yet, so everybody wanted to talk to my dad. They all wanted up-to-the minute reports about what was going on. The Guard had blocked off the roads into and out of town, but some people just came in on foot to look for their loved ones."

"People didn't have cell phones yet?" Bristal asks.

"No." Bailey shakes her head. "Mary Jennings had one, and she loved to tell people about it. I worked at the Grill and Chill, and she would call and say, 'This is Mary Jennings, I'm calling from my cellular phone.'" Bailey pipes her voice high and wheedling, making air quotes with her fingers.

"Then she'd order a fish sandwich and a cup of coffee and want it to be ready when she got there. Like she had something more important to do than get home and smack her kids around."

"Uh . . ." I glance down at my phone, where the recording app exhibits a stream of the sound wave.

"Shit," Bailey says. "Can you not use that part? Or maybe erase it?"

"Statute of limitations," Bristal says. "It's six years for a felony, two for a misdemeanor in Ohio. Mary Jennings is in the clear. Besides, I got hit plenty as a kid and I turned out okay."

She follows this up with a belch, and Bailey sends me a pleading look.

"Mary finds out I said something, and she'll be on me like a tick on a coon hound."

Bailey's right. Only about half the justice in Henley goes through the courts; the rest is settled in backyard brawls and intense social media posts. But Bailey did agree to go on the record, and my app is rolling.

"We're really only interested in topics pertaining to the tornado," I reassure her, then smoothly pick up the thread where she'd left off. "You said the vast majority of people didn't have cell phones, so everyone was calling you?"

"Yes," Bailey says, her eyes shooting to the phone again, perhaps making a mental note to watch her mouth. "Dad had them reroute all the calls to the house, since the station was destroyed. Mom was out with the road crews, running a chain saw, so I ended up taking the brunt of everything."

"People were upset?" I ask.

"Well, yeah," Bailey says. "I know it's hard for you kids to imagine, but we didn't know where everybody was all the time back then. We couldn't track phones or text somebody or anything like that. If you wanted to find somebody who wasn't home, you drove around looking for them."

"And people couldn't drive into town because the Guard had blocked off the roads?" I repeat. That particular detail hadn't made it into Swinton's article, something I make a note of on my pad, underlining it.

"Yeah, so people walked in," Bailey confirms. "All the good it did them. Even those who lived in town couldn't find their own homes, or at least, their lots. Trees were down, buildings were gone. We navigate by certain things, you know? When you use the church steeple to tell you where you are on Main Street, and then the steeple's gone, suddenly Main Street looks real different."

"Points of reference were lost," I say, doing my own translation as I jot down some notes.

"What was it like to suddenly be responsible for the concerns of an entire town?"

"Hell," Bailey says quickly. "It was hell. You know that young mother that died, with her baby? Her mom was out of town when it happened and was flying back from California. I was the one that had to tell her." Bailey's face was a carefully held mask of control. "When she got into town she came straight to our house. I'd just found out. Mom and Dad weren't home. I . . ."

The mask slips, and Bailey's face falls into a grimace.

"Take your time," I tell her, dropping my voice low.

"I had a little . . ." She lifts her fingers, tapping the picnic table in front of her. "A little notebook next to the phone, with headings on the pages. I had one for the found, one for the missing, and one for the dead. They'd just uncovered them, that family. So I had their names and their ages listed. I didn't know what to put for the baby because he wasn't even a year yet, so I just put *baby*."

Her voice quivers, and she takes a deep breath. "When I told her, that woman, she just fell down. Like her body had quit work-ing. It was like watching a light go out."

I'm nodding empathetically, and while I do genuinely feel for the teenage girl that Bailey had been, forced into the position of informing a woman that two generations of her family were gone, something else has my attention.

"Do you still have that notebook?" I ask her, doodling on my own pad, as if what I'm asking is inconsequential. "It could be a great visual, really tap into the chaos of the day."

I'm imagining deep ink slashes through the names of the missing, as Bailey transfers them over to found—and one name that never made the trip.

"Back home, somewhere, probably," Bailey says, her compo-sure back. "I'd have to look through my stuff."

"The newspaper reported that there were—" Bristal begins, but I step in.

"I think that's about all we need," I say, turning off my re-cording app. "Thank you, Bailey, you've really helped capture the mood and the tone of that day."

Bristal kicks me under the table and gives me a nasty look, but I reply with the barest shake of the head. We say our goodbyes to Bailey, and Bristal lays into me the second she pulls the car door shut.

"What the hell? I thought we were going to ask her about the missing person that wasn't accounted for."

"That was my intent," I tell Bristal. "But did you see how hard she braked when she accidentally mentioned that Mary Jennings hit her kids? She didn't want to tell us anything we didn't already know, and she definitely didn't want to be on record bad-mouthing anyone."

"But you weren't asking her for gossip, you were asking about inaccurate data," Bristal fires back.

"Asking the *sheriff's daughter* about inaccurate data," I tell her. "If there really was a flub and someone went missing and was never recovered, she might not want to implicate her father. And if we can get a name of the missing person, that's more ammo when we go and talk to David Swinton."

"The newspaper guy." Bristal nods. "When's that?"

"Still waiting on a response to my message," I say, pulling out onto Main Street. Reflexively, I look at the bell tower on the Methodist church. It could use a coat of fresh paint, but it's clearly a new build, like everything around it. The Henley of today is blocky and modern, the clay-baked bricks and stone cornices of the past all broken, buried, or turned into shrapnel on June 13, 1994.

"She's right about the steeple," I say, idly sharing my thoughts with Bristal as I drive her back to her car. "Everyone in town could probably draw it from memory."

"Whether they go to church or not," Bristal agrees. "Which, I don't. Do you?"

"Go to church? Yeah, I mean—it's expected. I'm a Chass."

"I appreciate the irony," Bristal says.

"What do you mean?" I ask, bristling.

"If you asked anybody in Henley which one of us is dangerous, they'd say me, every time," Bristal explains. "I'm a powder keg with a short fuse that's already lit."

"True," I say, my eyes returning to the scabs on her knuckles.

"Meanwhile you're walking around wearing button-downs and singing in the choir, but you've got the nuclear codes," she says, tapping her temple. "You played Bailey Foxglove, backing off right when you needed to, then pushing for that journal—and she has no idea why you want it."

"Which is why I'll get it," I say, flipping up the visor. "It's just a matter of when."

"She'll go home and look right now," Bristal says.

"I made her feel special by seeking her out," I agree. "She wants to hold on to that feeling."

"Or," Bristal counters, "she wants to keep you happy because you've got her on record accusing somebody of domestic violence. Either way, you get what you want—which is something I think you're accustomed to. And you'll get it, by kicking guys in the nuts at recess, or holding something over the head of a housewife."

"Regardless—" I begin, but Bristal cuts me off.

"People can see me coming a mile away: scars, bruises, black eyes, the Jamison name and a bad mouth attached to it. But you? You sneak up on them. Your teeth might be professionally whitened, but they're sharp as hell behind that smile."

"We should set up a time to record an episode," I say, choosing to sidestep her less-than-flattering character sketch of me. "And plan everything else out. I need to get my episode about the Civil

War monument up, but I want to hear about how all your research into Boggs is going."

I say the last part carefully, trying not to make it super obvious that I'm deeply invested in her putting the screws to Cousin Larry. While I might have blown off Kenzie when she suggested that I might solve our one and only murder, the ember in my chest had been fanned into a flame when Bristal mentioned that her cousin had been Boggs's neighbor and might have previously unknown information.

But as usual, Bristal seems to know what I want and is dedicated to not giving it to me. "Civil War monument?" Bristal asks. "That sounds super sexy."

"I know," I admit, leaning back in my seat. "I've been thinking how to make it interesting, put some emotion into it. You know how Bailey got upset remembering how she had to tell the woman that her daughter and granddaughter were dead?"

"Yeah, that sucked," Bristal says. "What about it?"

"I've been thinking about grief, and how the passage of time makes it easier, dulls the edges," I say. "Bailey got upset thinking about the peripherals. It wasn't the mom and baby dying that choked her up, it was telling the grandmother. I was thinking that if I can tie each soldier to a living person—"

"BLAH," Bristal blurts out. "I admire your vagina-to-the-wall attitude, but you could toss up anything and Henley High is going to give us a pass. They're the ones that screwed the pooch, not us."

"I know," I admit. "But—"

"But Ivy Leagues," Bristal says.

"Not just that," I say. "I mean, yes, I want to do a good job because I need to pad my résumé, but I also just want to do a good job because I . . ." I lift my hands, trying to encapsulate the nature of my drive to perform.

"Because you love work," Bristal finishes for me. "Most people love fun, but Lydia Chass loves work."

I shrug. "You say potato . . ."

"I say—who wants a fucking potato when French fries exist?"

TEN

"Bristal! Come in!" Mom says on Saturday afternoon, the absolute joy at finding a Jamison girl on her front porch indistinguishable from the real thing.

"Thanks, Mom," I say, brushing past her before she can take Bristal on a well-meant but painfully awkward tour of the house. I manage to dodge the mom-clutches but even if that does do away with such phrases as a *breakfast nook* or the *three-seasons room* and the *summer kitchen*, I can't hide every inch of the house from Bristal. Of course, she latches on to the most obvious before we're even halfway up the staircase.

"Is that an honest-to-God, actual, real-life hunting mural?" she asks, head craned to the right as we ascend the stairs, the poor fox who has been evading predators since before my time dodging into what I can only hope is a lifesaving bush.

"Yes," I say, mentally admonishing myself for not bringing her up by the back staircase and then becoming embarrassed all over again that we even have one. I lead her past the guest bedrooms—all of them painstakingly decorated by Mom and awaiting guests. One even has a silver tea tray and set arranged at the foot of the bed, hoping someone might pop in for a bite. I jerk the door shut as we slip past, praying Bristal didn't spot it.

There's no hiding the fact that I have a balcony attached to my room, but Bristal is mercifully silent, simply throwing herself across my made bed along with her backpack, which sports a bead lizard with a cigarette glued onto its mouth and a patch that reads, "In My Defense, I Was Left Unsupervised."

"So," she says, her face buried in a mountain of pink and purple throw pillows. "What's first?"

"First, you roll over so I can hear you properly," I say, and she does so, taking a pillow and putting it over her face.

"Next?"

I grab my laptop and flop onto the bed next to her, pulling the pillow away and tossing it onto the floor.

"Next, you tell me everything you've learned so far about the Boggs murder."

At the mention of murder, Bristal's face lights up, and she pulls a square of paper out of her back pocket, which I recognize as her copies of the *Hometown Henley Headlines* I'd printed out for her.

"These articles had the bare facts, things you and I—and probably our listeners—would already know, just from living in Henley. Boggs was a sixty-five-year-old man who lived alone out on Far Cry Road. No family, no friends, no reliable means of income. Some neighbors kayaked over to his trailer after the flood to see how the old bastard was doing, and the way he was doing was pretty bad, because they found him dead-ass dead."

"I'm pretty sure David Swinton would have never described it that way in the local paper," I say, uncapping a pen and making some notes in my journal.

"No," Bristal says, running her finger down the page. "Swinton says they 'found the unfortunate Mr. Boggs to be deceased.' I got the *dead-ass dead* quote from Cousin Larry."

"So you already did some interviews?" I ask, impressed.

"You bet your bideted ass I did," Bristal says, then shoots me a look. "Seriously, do you have a bidet? Because if you do, I'm in. Or, it's in me. Whatever would be the right way to say that."

"The right way is to not mention it all," I tell her. "And no, we don't have a bidet. Who found the dead body? Was it your cousin?"

"Yep," Bristal says, flopping back onto the mattress again, this time choosing a round pillow, tossing it toward the ceiling, catching it, and tossing it again. "Together with a guy by the name of Dale Childress."

"Brandon's dad," I say, clicking my pen closed. "Glad you did that interview and not me."

"Yeah, I heard he told you to fuck off and that his little sister was on that bus that Lytle ran off the road," Bristal says, batting the pillow to the ground. "Then he ate a bunch of your doughnuts. If I'd had some advance warning, I could have injected them with Ex-Lax."

"Anyway," I declare, "back on topic—Dale Childress and your cousin discovered Randall Boggs's body?"

"Yes." Bristal nods, sitting up again. "And Larry said he knew something was 'dead-ass dead' before he even paddled up to the front door."

"The smell?" I ask, my own nose wrinkling.

"'Like a skunk that got eaten by a bigger skunk, then vomited it up, then ate the vomit, then shit the vomit out the other end,' is how it was described to me," Bristal says helpfully. "Dale said he pulled open the screen door, but that was about all he could take. Boggs was facedown in the water, and even though he was swollen 'like a dead cow pregnant with six calves,' he could see that he was missing the back of his head."

"'A dead cow pregnant with six calves,'" I muse, then notice Bristal's bright smile. "You can't say that on the podcast."

"Why not?" she protests. "It's a direct quote."

"Did you record the conversation?" I ask. "Or take notes?"

"Yeah, I took notes," she says, tapping her temple.

I groan and do a face-plant in the remaining pillows that Bristal hasn't thrown around the room already. "Go on," I mutter, my own voice now lost in cotton and goose down.

"Childress called the cops, and Foxglove and the coroner came out. After an autopsy they were pretty sure that Boggs was shot on the twelfth, but his body had been floating in rainwater, fast-food trash, and a decent amount of raccoon shit, so they couldn't really say for sure. What they could definitively say, though, was that somebody beat the absolute hell out of old Randall before they shot him."

"Really?" I ask, whipping open my notebook as I sit up, ears perked. "How did you get this information?"

"From this," Bristal says, tearing open her backpack and tossing a police file onto my bed. The manila folder falls open, and a wave of gruesome crime scene photos and original, handwritten police reports waterfall across my pink and white quilt.

"BRISTAL!" I exclaim, running over and slamming my bedroom door shut. "How the hell did you get that?"

"I traded it for some good info about where to find the local fentanyl stash," she says with a shrug. "Well, I wouldn't say it was good info, but the conversation ended with the cops knowing more than they did before, and I got this out of the deal."

"This is an open criminal investigation," I say, part panicked, part elated, as I'm torn between diving through the material and packing it out of sight. "They never figured out who killed Randall Boggs."

"And never will, either, because nobody gives a shit," Bristal says. "From everything Childress said, Boggs was a racist, sexist asshole. 'Nastier than an infected cut' were his actual words. Cousin Larry told me that he wouldn't have even gone over there to check on the old man if it hadn't been for the rumor about him having some sort of family treasure stashed away."

"Oh, really?" I ask, doodling a dollar sign. "Is this something the police followed up on? Is it mentioned in the report? It could be motive."

"You're going to have to dirty your little hands yourself," Bristal says, nodding toward the file. "But Larry was super straight with me. He said he and Childress already assumed that Boggs had gone tits-up. They hadn't seen him outside in days, and he'd never been in the best of health. They went to pick the place over before reporting it, and you know, maybe see if Boggs had any drugs laying around."

"Right," I say, chewing my pen. "Because a family treasure is a long shot, but from what I understand of Boggs, drugs weren't."

"Nope," Bristal says. "But when they saw that the old man had been murdered, they didn't want any part of it. Called it in, square and clean. Didn't touch a thing."

Intrigued, I play with the corner of one of the photos. Bristal wasn't lying. Fast-food burger wrappers and empty beer bottles are floating in the water that fills the trailer, standing at least a foot high on the kerosene heater—likely the only thing keeping the old man alive through the winters. I can just see the pale outline of a naked foot floating in the water.

"Go ahead," Bristal says. "Nobody is going to be missing that."

Despite my better intentions, I've got the photo out—and a dozen others—and two minutes later am tapping away on my phone, checking first to make sure I'm not uploading to the cloud.

"Did you look through this already?" I ask, fanning the pages out.

"Yep," Bristal says. "You can keep it, if you want, but the low-down is that Boggs was beaten quite badly; the coroner estimated that he would've died of internal bleeding if he hadn't been shot, execution-style. He put up a hell of a fight, though. His knuckles were busted on both hands, and there was skin under his finger-nails, but it didn't match any DNA in the system at the time."

"And I doubt they're in a hurry to run it now," I say, sifting through documents.

"There's no one screaming for justice on this one," Bristal agrees. "He was an asshole, and somebody killed him. Live dirty, die dirty."

"Is there anything here to corroborate drug connections, other than gossip?"

"They found MDMA in his trailer," Bristal confirms. "And a bit of that, a bit of this."

"'A bit of that, a bit of this'?" I ask, glancing up.

"A bit of that," Bristal says, picking up the folder and shaking it, until a little white baggie with a cat's pawprint stamped on it falls out.

"And a bit of this," she adds, digging around until she locates another bag, also with a white powder in it.

"Um . . . Bristallll . . . ," I say, my voice going up in volume as I draw out her name.

"Heroin," she says, holding up the first bag. "Five-Toed Cat, if we're being specific. And cocaine," she says, pointing to the second.

"You seriously brought *heroin* and *cocaine* into my house? And the cops just handed you this file?"

"Yeah, they definitely didn't know those were in there," she says.

"Oh my God, oh my God," I say, shoving everything back into her bag. "If my dad knew about this—"

"He'd represent you. I hear he's got a soft spot for the real hard cases."

"I want you to take all of this back to the police station," I say firmly, zipping up her book bag.

"After I make copies?" she inquires, one eyebrow raised.

I shoot an uncomfortable look at her bag. "Yes."

"So Boggs was beaten and shot," I say, wiping my lip where a bit of nervous sweat had formed. "But they still found drugs lying around the trailer?"

"Right," Bristal says. "So whoever did the old man probably wasn't there about the drugs. Which, if you ask me, gives Larry's idea about a family treasure a little more weight."

"But the simple fact that there were drugs present made people assume that it was a drug deal gone wrong," I say, thinking aloud.

"A drug deal where the drugs get left behind," Bristal repeats. "Which is, like, no drug deal, ever."

"I wouldn't think so," I agree. "But why did the cops just let it go at that?"

I thumb my phone, paging through the pictures I'd taken of the Boggs file. Everything is a horrific mess. Aside from the obvious trash, there are holes in the walls, and the one piece of stuffed furniture—a couch—looks like it had been slashed open.

"Whoever broke in was looking for something," I observe. I'm a journalist, I don't want to do a deep dive on a rumored family treasure—especially when it's at the disposal of someone clearly living hand to mouth. But I can't deny that something isn't right here.

"And it wasn't drugs, because those were lying right out on the coffee table," Bristal says, reaching over my shoulder to point out the very two bags I'd just stashed away. "Do you think heroin goes bad?"

"It can't go bad, it's always bad," I tell her. "And don't even think about doing some at-home experiments to test your hypothesis."

"Not my style," she says, whipping out her vape pen, which I immediately confiscate.

"You can't smoke in here," I tell her.

"Is it okay if I menstruate, though, because . . ."

"Oh my God, okay," I say, shaking my head. "Someone broke into Randall Boggs's trailer looking for something, but it wasn't drugs. They beat him up, but he wouldn't talk."

"Or he did, and they got what they wanted, shot him, and left."

"But what could Randall Boggs have?" I ask, sliding past pictures, each more depressing than the last. In the bathroom, the toilet is backed up, and a layer of filth rests in the bathtub. The bedroom consists of a bare mattress, exposed coils breaking through.

"The cops did put some effort in," Bristal tells me. "They thought the place had been tossed, but Boggs's parole officer said things always looked that way—right down to the holes in the walls. What tipped them off was the couch being slashed."

"But nothing was inside?"

"Some mice and a handful of change," she says. "Forty-seven cents, if I remember correctly. Like I said, though, there was just too much going on for Foxglove to get whipped up about it. Boggs was an eyesore on the community as it was, and Henley had its hands full with the tornado, the flood, and all the dead dogs."

"Henley never searched for his murderer, but the citizens made up for it by chipping in for a killer headstone," I say.

"Good opening line," Bristal says. "Except this episode is mine."

"Right," I say. And I have to admit, she's done a fantastic job researching. She even got her hands on a police file. Pushing the crime off as a drug deal gone bad—and letting the blame fall on unnamed nonlocals—solved a big problem during a time when problems was all the town had.

"So what do you think happened?" I ask her.

"I think the old man ran his mouth off a little too much about this family treasure, and somebody took him at his word," Bristal says. "When nothing turned up, he caught some lead for his lies."

"Or, there was something, and they took it," I chime in.

"Same ending for Randall," she says. "Can I call this episode 'Just Another Old Dead White Guy'?"

"No," I say. "Try harder."

"Well, there is this," she says. "Along with rambling about family treasure, Cousin Larry says Randall also claimed that he had 'an Indian princess' in his family."

"Native American," I correct her.

"I'm directly quoting," she tells me. "And he didn't use those words."

"I bet he didn't," I say under my breath. "If I had a penny for every white person that claims they've got Native American blood . . ."

"It would help you out with these," Bristal says, holding up one of my scholarship applications that had littered the bed before she arrived. "But you're super white."

"So white," I agree.

"What do you need scholarships for anyway?" Bristal asks,

brow furrowing as she fans the stack of pages. "Aren't you country-club rich?"

"Looks can be deceiving," I tell her, refusing to say more and holding out my hand for the papers.

"Not in my case," she says, tossing them at me. "One glance at where I live sums it all up." Bristal hops off the bed, going to my balcony door and looking out over the back lawn. "Is your mom in a cult or something?"

"No, why?" I get up and join her at the window, where Mom is taking Uneven Steven for his walk. Exercise helps him move his bowels, so Mom takes him for a walk every day by supporting his hind end with a loop of silk, while he trots happily along, leaving his breakfast behind him.

I explain this to Bristal, who watches, fascinated as Steven finishes his tour of the yard and Mom folds up his silk extension, cradling him in her arms as they head back to the house.

"Now, that," Bristal declares, "is a family treasure."

ELEVEN

The dedication of the Civil War monument is just as dead as the people it's commemorating.

I take pictures of the new spire, making sure to capture all the names of the townspeople who lost their lives inscribed across the four sides. Paving stones etched with the names of donors surround it, and I dutifully record them as well, silently grateful that Bristal isn't there to give me a hard time about the fact that the Chass paver is a little bigger than the others, in direct ratio to the amount donated. But the drive for that money had been years ago, when Dad had fewer enemies—and more paying clients.

Mrs. Levering is there with her class of fifth graders who are way more interested in their Gatorades than they are in Gettysburg. The high school band plays "The Star-Spangled Banner," then a solitary trumpet player breaks away to play taps. Its solemn tones are echoed from another trumpeter, hidden below the rise of a knoll. Hats come off and heads are bowed, but most of the hands I can see aren't exactly folded in prayer. Pretty much everyone is checking their texts while they wait for taps to finish up.

The mayor says a few words just as the breeze kicks in, sending dried leaves scuttling across the pavers, a little touch of death brushing against the shiny new stones. Maybe in another two hundred years someone will be launching a campaign to save the pavers, reetching the last names of those who gave money to remember those who gave lives, everyone pouring effort into making sure their own predecessors are remembered.

It's a morbid thought, and I stifle a shudder, thinking of all the places around town where the name Chass holds sway. The high school baseball diamond is named after us, and at least four rows of seats in the new auditorium have our name on brass plates. There's a Chass Street in town and Chass Corners out near Far Cry Road, an old dividing line between the country cousins and the family members who lived within the village limits. You can't walk through the cemetery without passing a Chass. I can see four from where I'm standing, their tombstones taller than the others. One even has an angel perched on top, her head hung in perpetual mourning for whoever lies six feet under her.

It's like being forgotten is the worst thing that can happen.

"There it is," I blurt, the gray funk that had gathered in my mind suddenly pierced by a ray of inspiration. That's my angle, that's how I make this interesting. I don't have to make people care about the dead; I just have to remind the living that they're going to die one day, too.

Nicely, of course.

The mayor is still talking about sacrifices, and the fifth graders are idly pulling up grass and sneaking it into each other's hair when my phone vibrates. I slip it out of my pocket to see a text from Bailey Foxglove. A series of pictures are trying to download, but the service in the cemetery is spotty at best. The gray downloading circles aren't any closer to being useful images by the time I'm back at the school, signing in along with the band kids in the front office.

"So how was it?" MacKenzie asks me at lunch. "Historically invigorating?"

I decide not to explain to her that she's going to die someday and instead just tell her about the fifth grader who wandered off from the group and fell into a freshly dug grave. When some adults had fished him out it'd been written all over his face that he totally gets it. My phone vibrates in my pocket, letting me know the downloads are finished.

I whip it out, scrolling through. Bailey has sent me a series of pictures, all close-up shots of the journal she'd kept next to the phone as she fielded calls from panicked residents of Henley. There are notes to herself—*Call back Les Hendrix, grandma's necklace found hanging from Willow Street stop sign. Fran Childress, missing cat, long hair, black, personality: "kind of bitchy." Dover Jamison, lost dog, German shepherd mix.* The message about Fran has a line drawn through, which I guess either means that the cat came home or its body was found. As for Dover's dog, I make a note to check with Linda Chance and see if the German shepherd was one of the unfortunate inhabitants of the dog pound as the water began to rise.

Everything is written deeply, Bailey's own tension translating into pressure on the pen. I can see a collection of dots and imagine her on a particularly long call—maybe with Fran Childress describing her cat—and Bailey tapping the pen impatiently.

On the second page Bailey's finger obscures part of the top left-hand corner, but I enlarge the pic and just make out *sshole* peeking from underneath. No doubt another note to herself, a brief rumination on the character traits of someone who had likely just given her an earful. She's covered who exactly was an asshole to her in 1994, probably worried that I'll announce it on the podcast.

The last few pics are what I'm really after, Bailey's lists of the missing, the found, and the dead. She wrote the header in all caps, and these pages hold no doodles, no idle ink marks, no extraneous thoughts. This is serious business, and she knew it.

The list of the missing goes across four pages, each of them with a line drawn through the names, then copied over onto the found page. Bailey hadn't settled for checkmarks or notations; she'd fully transcribed their names over onto the right list, moving the feared dead over to the living, transferring relief, and the promise of continued breath along with them.

Except for five.

The names of the young family who died are listed together on the first page of the missing, their names conspicuously not crossed through: *Jimmy Beckley (23), Jessica Beckley (21),* and

Beckley (baby). On the third page I spot the name of the elderly lady who had died of a heart attack: *Laura Richardson (72)*. These are names I've only seen in the black and white of newsprint, or chipped into stone. Written in Bailey's loopy script, the blue ink faded with age, makes my heart skip a beat. These aren't stale names or fuzzy memories. These are the freshly dead, newly mourned, and I can see the impact of it where Bailey's hand had quivered as she wrote *baby*.

The last name is on page four, standing out starkly in the middle of the list, the only name not crossed out and inscribed among the found.

Denise Halverson (?)

I glance up and spot Bristal on the other side of the cafeteria, eating with Beck Parsons and Lainie Crow. Beck is wearing an oversized sweatshirt that can't hide her four-month pregnancy, and Lainie is using a black Sharpie to sketch something on her arm; probably an extension of the badly chosen barbwire tattoo she got last year to match her boyfriend's. When he broke up with her, she'd paid someone to convert it to vines and roses, but I imagine when she looks at it all she sees are the sharp edges.

I shoot Bristal a text, letting her know that Bailey came through, and I share the pics with her. She reaches for her phone, then looks up at me. A response comes quickly.

B: Somebody's an asshole

L: You saw that too?

B: I can always spot an asshole.

L: Check out the sixth picture, fourth page of the missing.

"Got something good?" MacKenzie asks.

"You know anybody named Halverson?" I ask, and she chews on her salad, pulverizing a crouton into a pasty mess that I'm treated to a great view of when she lands on her answer.

"Don't know that one," she says, shaking her head. "Sure it's not Halbertson?"

It's a good question. There are plenty of Halbertsons in Henley, and it's possible that Bailey was mentally overloaded and wrote the name down wrong, or maybe misheard it. But that question mark after Denise's name doesn't indicate confusion on Bailey's part about the name; she didn't know how old Denise was . . . which means that whoever called her in as missing wasn't totally clear on that point, either.

B: Who the hell is Denise Halverson?

L: That's what we're going to ask David Swinton.

L: What are you doing after school today?

B: I've got to drive Beck. She's getting an ultrasound.

B: I can do tomorrow.

L: I'll see what I can set up. Tell Beck I say good luck.

I watch as Bristal relays the message to Beck, who glances at me and gives a small wave. I return it, hoping that I have my face arranged the right way to convey positive thoughts about teen pregnancy.

"What's that about?" MacKenzie asks.

"Beck has an ultrasound today," I say, slipping my phone back into my pocket.

"Uh . . . you know how she got pregnant, right?"

"I assume a male ejaculated inside of her—"

"Gross, Lydia, really?" MacKenzie says, shoving her food away.

"You asked." I shrug. "I thought you would've remembered from sixth-grade health, but . . ."

"Stop," she says, her mouth going into a thin line. "You know what I meant. Beck lives in Ash Park."

The smirk falls off my face at the mention of the trailer court down by the stream at the edge of town. Commonly called Trash Park, the name refers to the people who live there but also to whatever clutters the driveways and sidewalks. I've heard that the kids that don't have shoes aren't allowed to go outside, for fear of stepping on used needles.

"Mom told me last time they went in there to serve a warrant, they couldn't find the guy because somebody tipped the whole park off that the parole officer was coming. They've got a system set up; when the law comes, they switch trailers. My mom can only serve the warrant to someone after they identify themselves. If the person who comes to the door isn't the recipient, they can't be served," MacKenzie says, her face tight.

"I'm impressed," I say. "That's really industrious."

"It's not funny, Lydia," MacKenzie snipes at me. "Mom got hepatitis when one of those assholes spit on her, and a children's services employee brought home bed bugs after doing a well check at Trash Park."

"How'd the well check go?" I ask.

MacKenzie sneaks a glance at Bristal's table but looks back down at her food when Beck raises her head.

"Nobody there is doing well," she says.

"What's that got to do with Beck being pregnant?" I push.

MacKenzie twirls her fork around in what's left of her salad, the last, withered pieces of greens and some limp carrots swimming in ranch dressing. "Kids get trafficked out there for drugs."

"Whatever." I shake my head. "I've heard that before."

"Which makes you believe me *less*?" MacKenzie asks, her eyebrows going up.

"Actually, yeah," I tell her. "Because if that is going on and everybody knows, it would be stopped. Period."

"Wow," MacKenzie says, tossing her fork aside and finally giving up on her salad. "I don't know where you find sand deep enough to bury your head."

My temper, which had been warming, reaches my voice. "What the hell is that supposed to—"

"A lot of bad things happen in Markham County, Lydia," MacKenzie says, leaning in across the table to stare me down.

"They just don't happen to us."

TWELVE

I spend the evening emptying the linen closet and taking down all the shelves, then stapling the soundproofing material on all four walls, the ceiling, and the back of the door. My movements grow more muffled as I work, the black acoustic foam triangles soaking up everything. Dad has to knock twice before I hear him.

"Sorry," I say when I pop open the door, but he shakes his head.

"Don't be, I'm glad to *hear* this stuff works," he says, peering around me to get a look.

"Bad dad joke, bad dad!" I tell him, shaking my finger in his face as if he were a misbehaving puppy. "What's for dinner?"

"Your mom abandoned us," he says. "So I'm thinking—"

"Not sushi," I tell him. "I won't eat raw seafood in a landlocked state."

"We've got Lake Erie," Dad says, crossing his arms and waiting for my rebuttal.

"Catch me a tuna out of Lake Erie, and then we'll talk," I counter.

"Point taken," he concedes. "Pizza?"

"There we go." Both of my parents operate on the assumption that the other one is judging their parenting, which means that I can get junk food out of Mom when Dad isn't around, and carbs and fried food out of Dad when Mom checks out for the night with her friends.

Thirty minutes later we're camped out with our individual greasy boxes around the fire in the backyard—all the easier to toss our incriminating trash in when we're done.

"Looks like the closet is shaping up nicely," Dad says, wadding up his napkin and throwing it into the flames. It dances briefly, then disintegrates into ash. "When's your next episode?"

"Sooner rather than later, but I'm stalling," I admit. "I've been trying to think of a way to make the Civil War monument more interesting, and I landed on the idea of tying each soldier to a family alive today."

"Shouldn't be too hard," Dad muses. "We don't exactly get fresh influxes of new faces that often in Henley."

"No," I agree, pulling out my phone to check my notes. "I only found a few last names I hadn't heard of—Mattix, Dovecoat, and Fender."

"Can't say I know those, either," Dad agrees, twirling the long neck of his beer so that the flames dance across the glass bottle.

"Right, so I thought about taking it the opposite direction," I say.

"Meaning?"

"Today at the cemetery it was like nobody really cared. I mean, I'm a geek about this stuff and even I wasn't all that interested," I confess. "But I got to thinking about the monument, how we replaced the old one with a new one, bought pavers to commemorate those that donated money for it, and how maybe someday we'll be worried about preserving those stones. It all feels kind of futile."

"'Time and tide wait for no man,'" Dad quotes. "Or woman, mind you." He tilts the bottle toward me. "But what do you mean about taking it the opposite direction?"

"What if I focused on Mattix, Dovecoat, and Fender?" I ask. "Three family names that aren't here anymore. These men could have been only sons, or childless men. They died, and that's why their names are gone. The Civil War monument is about honoring the dead, but all the living want to do is see their own names in stone. Mattix, Dovecoat, and Fender are really, truly dead. Shouldn't we care about them the most, instead of the least?"

"I see what you're getting at, and you're not wrong," Dad says, still twirling his bottle, his eyes following the play of the flames. "But isn't that a little dark? And you're right—the living do care about their ancestors, or at least, their own last names. What if somebody gets offended?"

"Um, remember that whole thing about me taking the gloves off?" I ask, tossing my pizza box into the fire. "I'm not using the measuring stick by which all things are judged in Henley—what if somebody's feelings get hurt? Everyone knew Benson was a drunk, and people don't want to talk about it. So we pretend like it didn't happen, just like all the shit that goes down in Trash Park."

"Lydia!" Dad snaps. "You weren't raised to talk that way."

"No, I was raised to be nice and pretend like everyone else is, too."

We both go silent, and the fire snaps as a log collapses. The sparks settle before either of us speaks, and Dad is the first to break the silence.

"What did you mean about Ash Park?"

"It's . . ." I sigh, not trusting myself with the words. But I can't lambast everyone else for looking away from ugliness if I can't speak about it to my dad, in our own backyard. "MacKenzie said today that she thinks Beck Parsons got pregnant because she was being handed around the trailer park in exchange for drugs."

"She thinks this or she knows this?"

I shrug. "That's kind of my point. I mean, if something that horrible was really going on, someone would stop it—right?"

I meet Dad's eyes across the fire, and he suddenly looks very old, the creases around his mouth shadowed deeply, the lines in his forehead starkly black.

"Right?" I ask.

"Lydia," he begins, "the world is a very complicated place—" He holds his hand up to stop me when I would speak, and I fall silent. "And it can be a very dark place."

"So it does go on, and nobody stops it?" I press.

"I can't say that it does or doesn't," Dad admits. "But I know how hard it is to get children out of the care of their biological parents, even when the situation is dire. The courts are set up to keep families together, not apart. And unfortunately, that's not the best solution for the unlucky few."

"The unlucky few," I repeat, my voice dull.

"I know it's hard to hear, and even harder to think about," Dad says. "But the truth is that no matter how many police there are, no matter how hard the justice system works, no matter how many teachers and guidance counselors and pastors and parents and task forces exist, someone will always fall through the cracks."

"That's the truth?" I say, glancing up to meet his gaze.

"That's the truth," he admits, nodding. "If what you heard about the Parsons girl has any shred of fact about it, she has to be the one to come forward and say so. It can't be you, it can't be MacKenzie Walters, and it sure as hell can't be her mom. Josephine should know better than to say stuff like that in front of her daughter. It violates confidentiality."

"Don't say anything," I plead, forcibly reminded that my dad's work brings him into the courthouse and in the path of county parole officers on a daily basis. "I'm sorry I brought it up."

"I won't, but don't let MacKenzie develop a habit of running her mouth," Dad warns. "This is how rumors like that get started. One person has an opinion, they share it with someone who throws their two cents in, and pretty soon it's a known fact and the pitchforks come out."

"Maybe some people need to get pitchforked," I offer.

"Maybe," Dad says. "But remember—you're talking to a defense lawyer. It's my job to keep pointy objects away from my clients."

"Yeah, your clients," I mutter, my mood going even lower.

He's quiet for a moment, watching me in the low light of the dying embers of the fire. "Are you catching flack at school?"

"Kind of," I say. "Brandon Childress said something at the blood drive, but mostly it's been pretty normal."

"Your mother's been having some problems, too," Dad tells me. "I guess she said hello to Norman Walton at the market the other day, and he acted like she wasn't even there."

"Let me guess, he had a grandkid on that bus," I say, tossing my paper plate into the fire. It catches, adding a little light to the first circle before flaming out.

"At this point, everyone in town claims to have had a relative on the bus," Dad says. "Despite the fact that the video shows there's only eight kids, max."

"Nine if you include the Denney guy who was filming," I correct him.

"You watched it?" he asks, and all I can do is shrug. "What did you think?"

"It was pretty awful," I tell him.

"And it's hard to imagine why I want to defend Lytle?" Dad asks, prodding me.

"I mean . . . yeah, a little," I admit. "Mom talked to me about it. She said something about how you are good at putting yourself in other people's shoes, and how Lytle wasn't looking at the bus driver as a human being in that moment. He was just an obstacle in between him and his kid."

"And you don't want to get in between a parent and their child," Dad agrees. "But there's more to it than that, Lydia. Yes, I can see why Lytle would behave the way he did. I can't forgive it, or excuse it, but I can defend it."

I think of warm blood on the hot highway, screaming children and the sound of flesh against fists. "I don't see how."

"You know I don't condescend, so take this as it's meant; you will understand when you're older."

"Oh, c'mon. Really, Dad?"

"It's not that you're not smart enough to get it, and you know I respect you," he goes on. "It's because you haven't been alive long enough to make any really big mistakes."

He doesn't know that I had illicit drugs in my bedroom over the weekend, and I decide not to inform him.

"*Really* big mistakes," Dad repeats, hitting down hard. "I know that we've raised you in a certain way—some things are good, and some things are bad, and you identify them as such. But the world isn't black-and-white, Lydia. The more experience you have moving through life, you'll see that most situations have fuzzy edges and gray areas."

"So it's okay to haul someone out into the street and pulverize their jaw?" I ask.

"It's not, and it never will be," Dad says, shaking his head. "The action is wrong. But the person committing it is a breathing, thinking, living, feeling human being. And I can tell you that most of the time where there's violence, there's fear—and it's not only being felt by the victim."

"Lytle was scared he was going to lose his son. I'll give you that," I say. "But did he have the right to batter Lawrence Horvath and traumatize a bus full of kids?"

"Eight kids," Dad corrects, the defense lawyer kicking in.

"*Nine*," I shoot back, and he concedes the fact with a nod.

"No," he admits. "Lytle didn't have the right, but he did have a *reason*. It's my job to convince the jury that extenuating circumstances drove him to behave in a way that he normally wouldn't. Trust me, Abe Lytle is not a bad person. Good people can do terrible things, Lydia. The longer you live, the more you see it. That's all I'm trying to say."

A silence settles over us as I digest that. Freshman year MacKenzie had let Brian Phillabrant go up her shirt in the back of the band bus on the way home from a football game. That was a Friday night, and everybody knew about it by Saturday morning. MacKenzie had lain facedown on my bed, her tears soaking my duvet as she moaned about her romantic exploits being fodder for the town gossip mill. Her mother had even heard about it, and Josephine had called the band director, insisting that he make sure she sat with me for the rest of the season.

Mortified, MacKenzie had bewailed her fate, and I had reminded her that we live in Henley. "If you're thinking about doing something you wouldn't want your mother to know about, you probably shouldn't do it," I had archly informed her.

"Welcome to the world of moral quandaries," Dad says, smiling at me when I glance up. "Also, you'd make a horrible poker player. Everything you think is on your face."

"Your pizza is on your face," I say, trying to lighten the mood, but there's still a heaviness on my chest.

"I know that right and wrong aren't always that easy to define," I admit. "I just need to figure out how to decode that area in between."

Dad snorts. "Your grandpa had a really easy way of explaining it."

"How's that?" I ask.

"'You can be wrong, or you can be a Chass,'" Dad says, his eyes going hard in the firelight, his mouth tight.

Grandpa Chass died last year, and while the line at the funeral home was long, most of the eyes were dry. He hadn't been a mean man—just a hard one. One of my first memories of him was at my own fourth birthday party. He said that I could have cake or ice cream but not both. I'd told him that it was my birthday, and I would do what I wanted. We'd sat across from each other at the table, stuck in a stare-down as a bowl of ice cream grew warm in front of me, the candle on the cake next to it burning down. He waited for me to make my decision so that he could pull the other away. I waited for him to fold. Mom said the only thing that ended the standoff was that we both eventually took a nap. She found us that way, him leaning sideways in his chair, snoring, me facedown on the table, strands of my hair floating in the melted ice cream, the birthday candle a puddle of wax on top of the cake.

She's always told it as a funny story, a little anecdote to illustrate the Chass personality. But now, looking at Dad in the firelight, I have to wonder what it was like to sit across from Grandpa every day and to be told that he could be wrong—or he could be a Chass. I've always felt the pressure to do the right thing, but I also feel the supportive love that underpins it, the unspoken understanding that I am human, I will make mistakes, and they will love me anyway. I don't know if Dad ever had that, and maybe that's why he works so hard to defend people who mess up . . . even if their mistakes fall more into the category of assault with a deadly weapon.

I think about the Chass gravestones at the cemetery, the angel looking down over Grandpa's grave, her molded stone tears held in place for eternity, as a substitute for real tears of mourning that did not fall at the funeral. I'd stared that man down as a small child, the steel inside of me reflected back in his gray eyes. Mom's laughter had always been shaky after she told the story, and included a sideways glance at me that I could never quite interpret. Bristal had mentioned me kicking Lyle Hunter in kindergarten as a reminder that I'm not the wilting flower everyone thinks, and my subtle maneuvering of Bailey Foxglove had only confirmed to her that I am not averse to pulling any strings necessary in order to win. I have to wonder—is that wariness buried in Mom's side-eye? A quick check-in to see just how deeply the Chass steel is embedded in me—and how far I'll go to get what I want?

"When you and Mom say I'm just like Grandpa, it's never

meant as a compliment," I tell him. "But he was a Chass, all the way. Why did he get to step on toes, but I've got to play pin the smile on your daughter?"

"Fair question," Dad says. "I don't know if you're aware of it or not, but there's this thing called sexism—"

"Yeah, I'm aware," I say, tossing a wadded-up napkin at Dad. "Thanks for clearing that up."

Mom's headlights swing across the driveway, and we both shift in our chairs, easing the tension that had developed.

"Save me from your mother and destroy the evidence like a good daughter, okay?" he asks, tossing me his beer bottle.

"If by destroy you mean recycle, I've got you. But she's going to smell it on your breath."

"Not if hers is worse," he says, giving my hair a tug as he walks past me.

"Good night," I call after him, watching as the final sparks settle into coals, and thinking about the cracks of the world, which the unlucky few could fall through.

THIRTEEN

David Swinton hasn't aged much since I approached him as a third grader and told him that I was going to be a journalist. On that day, he bent down to look me in the eye and said, "I believe you." Now, I'm a full six inches taller than him, but I still feel slightly intimidated when he stands to greet me and Bristal when we walk into the library. This man kept the *Hometown Henley Headlines* running all by himself for years, right up until a news conglomerate bought him out in in the early 2000s. David knows every man, woman, and child in Henley by name, and is friendly with all the right people in Markham County as a whole.

If anybody is going to know the name Denise Halverson, it's him. Which is why I need to execute this meeting perfectly.

"Lydia, it's good to see you," David says, giving my hand a

quick, professional handshake. "How's your dad doing? Still defending the despicable?"

"He prefers to think of it as being a beacon of hope for the downtrodden," I say easily, settling into a folding chair while he greets Bristal, who eyes him dubiously and responds in monosyllables.

We have the library basement all to ourselves; decorations from last years' summer reading program—which had been luau themed—are stacked in the corner, along with boxes that are marked for recycling. The librarians had borrowed produce boxes from the food pantry for storage, and I can see a row of yellowed, cracked spines through the air holes. Books that are irrelevant, obsolete, or falling apart have been culled, awaiting their new lives as fresh paper, with different words printed on them. I think about Bailey Foxglove's notations in her journal, and wonder if someone else's thoughts are captured in the margins of those books, a phone number, a grocery list, or underlined passages and some brief flash of illumination as the reader made a discovery or got excited about an idea.

Now those ideas are collecting dust and waiting to be pulped.

"Nice spread," Bristal says, drawing my attention to the tables that David has set up. They're strewn with newspaper clippings and photos, all of them pertaining to the tornado. She begins taking pictures of everything, double-tapping her phone and moving hastily around the tables, barely pausing. She downed two energy drinks and drained her vape pen in the parking lot, and I imagine her camera roll as a modern impressionist masterpiece: everything blurry, nothing to hold on to.

"This is great!" I say, plastering a smile on my face as I try to summon some enthusiasm. It's a treasure trove, but I'm focused on the name Denise Halverson, and the ominous question mark that followed it.

"This is the front-desk bell from the old Fairlawn Hotel," David says, lifting a brass bell. "It was recovered from the creek in 1997, when a few kids who were searching for crawdads found it. I cleaned it up and gave it to the historical society."

He rings it, the clapper hitting the sides with a high-pitched tone that might have sent bellhops running in the 1920s but makes me want to make a break for the emergency exit.

"That's so cool!" I say, keeping my smile in place.

"If you ring that again, I'm going to break your nose with it," Bristal says.

"Fair enough," David says, resting the bell back on the table. "It's got a certain edge to it, I know." He takes a seat, and we arrange ourselves opposite him, Bristal tapping one finger nervously against her hip.

I start recording, and we get the known stories, the old facts. I already have microfiche copies of the issues of the newspapers that David brought, but I listen politely as he walks me through each page, pointing out a familiar face here or an interesting angle there.

"A lot of people like to talk about the things we lost that day," Swinton says. "But we forget it could have been worse. If the tornado had come through two days earlier—on the eleventh, during the Sweet Corn Festival—there would've been a lot more casualties. I took a lot of pictures the day of the festival, and they make for great before and after shots.

"I pulled this one aside in particular," David says, fishing a picture out of a stack and handing it to me. I try to keep my face politely interested as I scan it, not sure what it is I'm supposed to be reacting to.

It's a wide shot near the railroad tracks, where uprooted pine trees lay on their sides, hopelessly horizontal, while a car is balanced neatly on its nose in the background. A dog with its tail between its legs is sniffing at something, and a child's bike hangs from the sagging electric lines. Nothing is as it should be, and everything speaks of chaos and danger, but I don't know why David Swinton wanted me to see this until he hands me another one.

"Before," he says. It's the same shot, but taken during the Sweet Corn Festival, with food trucks and vendors lined up along the tracks. Still, I don't understand why he thinks it will be of particular significance to me—then my eyes land on a group of teenagers standing together. I pull it closer, squinting, but this photo was taken before the digital age, and the harder I try to look for details, the more things blur together.

"Is that my dad?" I ask.

"Bingo!" David snaps his fingers, and I hold the photo at an angle, trying to decipher more. My dad is standing with another boy with his back to the camera, and a girl with black hair holds a cigarette, her mouth a dark, round blur as she exhales smoke.

"I didn't know my mom used to smoke," I say, flipping the

photo over to look at the back. David's clear, precise handwriting indicates the date and location.

June 11, 1994, Henley, Ohio N/S Railroad Tracks, Sweet Corn Festival

"Don't tell her I ratted her out," David says. "It was the nineties. A lot of people smoked."

Bristal takes the photo from me, gives it a curious glance, then snaps a pic of it, this time zooming in and concentrating on holding her phone as still as possible in her shaky hands. Leave it to Bristal to carefully document my mom's bad habits from decades ago while brushing over actual historical importance with disdain.

"Anything else I can help you with?" David asks, leaning back in his chair. I double-check that my recording app is running and make a show of giving everything on the tables another glance.

"Actually, there is one thing I was curious about," I say, tapping my index finger against an issue of the *Hometown Henley Headlines*, forever embalmed in lamination. "The June sixteenth article said the remaining *two* townspeople that were MIA had been found. But the June fifteenth issue said there were *three*."

"Huh . . . ," David says, pushing his glasses up his nose and leaning in over the paper. "Must've been a typo. Everything was bananas for a couple of days, and I was my own editor. This is exactly why a pair of fresh eyes is so important. Sometimes we can't spot the problems in our own work."

"Right," I agree, turning the issue of the *Henley Hometown Headlines* so that I can read directly from it. "'The *Hometown*

Headlines is happy to report that at this time, the number of missing people has been drastically reduced to only three.'"

David nods as I read his own words back to him.

"What was that like?" I ask. "I talked to Bailey Foxglove. She said it fell to her to tell a family member that their loved ones were dead."

"Carol Vosher," David says automatically, nodding. "She was Jessica Beckley's mother, grandmother to the baby."

"Right." I nod in confirmation. "You know everybody, don't you?"

"Yeah, I mean . . ." David laces his fingers behind his head with a touch of pomposity. "When you've been covering everything from high school sports to the paving schedule for the county roads all by yourself for fifteen years, you get to know people. It used to be you had to know their phone numbers, too. We couldn't tell Siri to dial for us. Back in the day, you had to be a walking directory."

"So you were good with numbers?" Bristal chimes in.

"For sure," David says, rocking his chair onto the back two legs. "It wasn't like it is now. No offense, ladies. But people had to carry information in their heads back then, not their pockets."

"Cool," Bristal says. "What's the phone number for the library?"

"555-763-2515," David rattles off without even thinking. Bristal taps on her screen, then tilts the phone toward me so that I can see he's right.

"How about the county courthouse?" I ask.

David gives us another correct number, then another, as Bristal interrogates him about a local pizza joint, the Methodist church, and finally the only bar in town. He easily provides the info, growing more confident with every answer. Bristal is setting him up perfectly, and we couldn't have planned this better.

"That's impressive," I tell him, after he's recited the directory of half the businesses in town. "Weird that you would've mistaken a two for a three when reporting on something as important as the missing from a natural disaster."

The grin disappears, and all four legs of his chair come back down to the ground.

"Does the name Denise Halverson mean anything to you?" I ask.

"Halverson . . ." He taps his fingers against the table. "You sure you don't mean Halbertson?"

"I'm sure," I say. "See, I've got Bailey Foxglove's journal from when she was taking the sheriff's calls. I confirmed with her, and the last name is Halverson."

It's a small lie, but beads of sweat are forming on David's forehead, and I'm not going to loosen the coils on this trap now that it's sprung. I turn my phone so that he can see the pics of Bailey's journal, scrolling through them and pausing on the name in question.

"Denise Halverson," I repeat.

David clears his throat and glances around the room, which remains empty except for us. "You still aiming to be a journalist?" he asks me, and I nod. "You familiar with shield law?"

"Yes," I say, reaching out to turn off my recording app.

"I'm not," Bristal says. "What does that mean?"

"It's a lot of things," Swinton answers. "But in our case what's relevant is that it protects journalists from having to reveal their sources."

"So he can talk to me with the assurance that I won't tell anyone where I got the information."

"Neat trick," Bristal says.

"Now," I say as I lean forward. "Tell me about Denise Halverson."

FOURTEEN

"She was a foster kid," David says, leaning forward now, all the lines in his body tense. "Came to live with Erin Hendrix a few months before the tornado came through. She was kind of like a tornado herself, come to think of it. Didn't tear down any buildings, but she left plenty of wreckage behind her, that's for sure."

"Wreckage how?" Bristal asks.

"Well . . ." David looks at Bristal, then back to me. "You know Erin, right?"

"Yeah, I know her," I say. Erin Hendrix volunteers at the food pantry out of the Methodist church, and I've seen her sneak extra cookies into boxes when a minivan full of kids pulls up. Once, we got an entire truck full of oranges, and she'd driven an hour into the city to buy as many juicers as she could find. The church parking lot had smelled like citrus for days, and we'd all had sticky hands and cramped wrists. But there was fresh orange juice in every fridge in town, and she'd even boxed up the rinds and thrown them into fields for the birds.

"She really cares," I say. "She cares a lot."

"She cares too much," David says, looking at me pointedly over his glasses. "Erin gives everybody the benefit of the doubt, then takes their problems onto her own shoulders."

"That's what happened with Denise?" I ask.

"I think so, and I'm not alone in it," David says. "I know people can't be blamed for how they're raised, but this girl—"

He breaks off, looking at Bristal. "You're a Jamison, right?"

"Not pregnant," she says automatically, garnering a smile from him.

"It was a Jamison that palled around with her," David says, and I make a swift note with my pen to follow up on that.

"Denise wasn't easy to get along with, I'm guessing?"

"That's one way to put it," David says. "But it was more like she didn't *belong* than she couldn't *get along*, know what I mean?"

"Maybe," I say dubiously.

"I don't know where she came from, exactly," David goes on. "But it was obvious nothing good had ever happened to the girl in her whole life. Erin told me that Denise flat out asked her how many times a week she was expected to give Paul—"

David stops talking, but Bristal starts.

"A handy? A blow job? What?"

"Whatever he wanted," David says, a little color rising to his face. "I guess that's how things had operated where she'd been before. She got room and board, but the room wasn't exactly private, and nothing was free."

"But Paul Hendrix wasn't taking her up on it?" I ask.

"No, of course not." David shakes his head. "But she still locked her bedroom door. Erin told me that after Denise left, she went in to clean up her room and found the bed completely made, except all the pillows were in the closet, along with a stash of food."

"She'd been sleeping in there, in case of a surprise visitor," Bristal says, in a knowing voice. "And keeping food back for herself if she got cut off."

"Yeah," David says. "I guess so. Which, I mean, it's horrible to consider what would drive her to think she had to do those things, but she never said a word of thanks to the Hendrixes, either."

"You said she left?" I ask, scribbling furiously in my notes, now that the app is turned off.

"Yeah, split town," David says. "She got picked up with a bunch of kids down at the riverbed—your folks ever tell you about that?"

"Drinking spot," I say.

"Still is," Bristal adds.

"I'll pretend I didn't hear that last part," David says.

"We're pretending like we don't hear a lot," Bristal says sharply, nodding toward my phone, the face of which is black and blank.

"Fair enough," David continues. "So, Denise and a bunch of kids were down at the riverbed on June tenth. It had been especially dry that summer, and kids were driving right down the banks, parking their cars in the dry bed, and drinking. Most of the time, Foxglove would just ignore the things that went on

135

down there. I mean, everyone in Henley had their first beer under that bridge, so it's not exactly a big secret. But with it being so dry, and the heat piling up thunderheads during the day, it upped the chance of flash floods."

"More than a chance, it turned out," I say, idly doodling a dog in the corner of my notes. In my illustration, his ears are pointy and his tongue hangs out to the side in a comical smile. Irritated with myself, I scratch it out. "So the sheriff cleared the kids out, for their own good?"

"That was the intention," David says. "Foxglove didn't even go in there with his flashers on. Just parked the cruiser above the bridge and shone the spotlight down on the kids, told them to hide their cans and get their asses home. Most everybody took it as the favor it was meant to be, except for Denise Halverson."

"Did she have some words for Sheriff Foxglove?" I ask, when David falls silent.

"Bad words?" Bristal adds.

"Uh . . ." David glances at the phone again, as if to reassure himself it's not on. "More than words. She hit him."

"She *hit* him?" I repeat, my pen going lax in my hand.

"Assault on an officer," David confirms. "I guess she had a few drinks in her already, but the friendly warning didn't sit so well with her, and things escalated. She got a free ride home in a cop car. Erin and Paul weren't too happy, and they grounded her. Which didn't last long. Denise went out her bedroom window the next day."

"They reported this?" I ask, my pen back at work.

"They did," David says. "On the morning of June thirteenth."

"The day the tornado hit," I say. "And she just got lost in the shuffle, didn't she?"

"Completely lost," David agrees. "By the time we'd accounted for everyone, a couple of days had passed, and one of those days was Denise Halverson's eighteenth birthday."

"So she became an adult," Bristal says. "Not a runaway."

"Not a runaway, not a missing child," David says. "Legally, there were no grounds to go after her, and we hardly had the resources as it was."

"Not with the murder of Randall Boggs and the flood on top of it," I say. "So she was just gone? Did anybody ever see her again? Did she have any friends looking for her?"

"Like I said, she palled around with a Jamison," he says, nodding at Bristal. "But I can't say I remember which one. There are a lot of you."

"Yeah we're good at existing," she says.

"And nobody looked for her?" I ask, pushing. "Nobody cared about this lost teenaged girl?"

"She didn't care to be cared *about*," David says, his voice taking on an edge. "Paul and Erin tried—they did. But everything was upside down for a while after the long stretch. I mean, you should've seen the telephone poles in town. They were covered with missing posters for dogs and cats, people looking for their wallets or the wedding ring they'd taken off to mow the yard before the storm rolled in. We didn't have—"

"The internet. Phones. Compassion," Bristal supplies, twirling her finger in the air.

He ignores her last jab. "Back then you lost something, you had to make a poster and hang it up in the town square, hope somebody found it, hope they knew you were looking for it, and hope they would give it back to you."

"The Hendrixes put up posters?" I ask.

"Sure, all the good it did," David says. "Denise Halverson was gone."

"And everyone assumed she ran away?"

"It wasn't just an assumption," David says. "She'd been telling everyone as soon as she was eighteen she was gone. So she did exactly that, and we had our hands full here in Henley, taking care of our own."

"Which she wasn't," Bristal tacks on.

"And you changed the number of missing in the paper?" I ask, coming back around.

David falls silent, his fingers toying with the edge of the laminate covering the June 15 issue of the *Hometown Henley Headlines*. "I didn't feel right about that, exactly," he admits. "But at first Erin was hoping the girl would come home, and Denise was supposed to be under an unofficial type of house arrest, on account of hitting Foxglove. She was trying to keep her out of trouble, still looking out for her."

The three of us fall silent, and the library's heater kicks in, rumbling to life in the closet behind me. The vent above us pushes hot air onto the table, sending a few loose photos to the floor. I bend to pick them up, careful to only touch the edges.

"Thanks for talking to us," I say.

"I didn't talk to you," David says. "Not about Denise Halverson."

"Understood."

We skip the handshakes as we say goodbye, and Bristal whips out her vape pen the second we're in the parking lot, shaking it in irritation once she realizes it's empty.

"What'd you think?" she asks, jerking her chin toward the library.

"I think it's messed up," I admit as she leans against her car. "But I don't know if there's any wrongdoing, exactly. It makes me think about something my dad said last night."

"What's that?"

"He said occasionally things get missed, even when everyone involved has the best intentions. Sometimes people fall through the cracks."

"Funny thing about those cracks," Bristal says. "Most of them are teenage-girl shaped."

FIFTEEN

Saturday morning I'm sitting crisscross applesauce on the floor in the linen closet, my computer in my lap and Bristal's knees touching mine as she runs her fingers over the black foam triangles.

"I had an acid trip that looked just like this," she says, and I'm very thankful that the soundproofing works and my mom didn't hear that.

"I need you to focus," I tell Bristal. "We've got to record a new opening for the podcast, and I need to have the monument ep edited and published by Monday morning."

"Technically you don't have to," she contradicts me. "The publishing schedule is an arbitrary goal that you set for yourself."

"Set for us," I remind her, giving her knee a nudge with mine. "It's to keep both of us on task."

"By which you mean me," she says, shoving back. Her kneecaps are bonier than mine, and I wince. "But don't worry, Lydia Chlamydia, I'm going on that little road trip with Cousin Larry and ODOT this afternoon."

"Right, the roadkill episode," I say under my breath.

"AKA the best episode," Bristal says.

She's quiet for a minute while I pull up the recording software, and I glance up to see that she's staring at the ceiling, her mouth gone slack.

"Bristal?" I ask, suddenly worried that she has some sort of medical condition I don't know about. The last thing my dad needs right now is a Jamison girl going comatose inside a sound-proofed closet at his house. Actually, that sounds like a really horrible public relations nightmare.

"Bristal!" I say again, reaching over and tapping her shoulder.

"Sorry." She shakes her head and her eyes come back into focus. "It's just if you stare really hard at the tip of one of these triangles, things get funky fast."

"I need you to—"

"What are we going to do about Denise Halverson?"

I sigh and close my laptop, aware that we're not going to get any work done until we address the elephant in this small, cramped room. "I don't know," I admit. "I tried to find her on social media."

"Me too," Bristal says. "I checked Facebook first, since it's for old people. But I didn't find any Denise Halversons that are the right age."

"I looked, too," I tell her. "But if she got married and didn't list her maiden name, there's very little chance of finding her."

"Right," Bristal agrees. "I tried looking just for women named Denise that live in the area, but then I thought that was probably stupid, because she literally got the hell out of Henley thirty years ago after only being here a few months."

"She's not going to list it as where she's from," I say.

"So what do we do?" Bristal asks.

"I don't know if there's anything we can do," I tell her. "I ran this down in the first place because I wanted to get all the facts straight for the tornado episode. I spotted inaccurate data, and I wanted to know why. Now I know, and I'm just not convinced it's worth following up on. We've got an actual murder to cover, remember? And your lead about the family treasure could be a real angle. I don't want to waste time running down dead ends."

Bristal's face had been getting harder as I spoke, the dim light inside the closet shadowing her deep eye sockets. Her jaw muscles are pulled tight and ticking, the edges of her lips flattened into a thin line of anger.

"Because it's easier? Because with Boggs you already know something has gone bad, you just have to jiggle the body some more and see if something shakes loose? You're just like Foxglove and everyone else back in the nineties—you don't care enough to look for this girl and find out what happened to her."

"Because I'm not convinced anything did," I shoot back.

Bristal makes a show of banging her head against the foam walls. "I swear, I spend much more time with you, Lydia Chass, and this is not the only padded room I'll ever be in. A girl flat-out fucking disappeared and nobody gave a shit."

"Paul and Erin did," I argue.

"Oh yeah." Bristal smacks her forehead. "I forgot. They made posters. I bet they didn't even buy stencils for the lettering."

"Erin has a shit ton of stencils," I tell her. "She uses them all the time for the food pantry signs."

"I made you say *shit*," Lydia says, with a grin. "And fuck the food pantry. You know that's not my point."

"Whatever," I mutter, and open my laptop, my fingers dancing across the keyboard as I set the audio controls. "Are you ready to record this or what?"

"It's a girl," Bristal says suddenly.

"What?"

"Beck's baby, it's a girl," she repeats, her voice flat and odd without the edge of anger that she usually carries.

"Oh . . . well, congrats," I say.

"That's part of the reason I want to know about Denise, okay?" Bristal says, raising her eyes to mine. "Beck got fucked, and it sounds like Denise did, too. I just don't want to see how many generations of girls Henley can keep chewing up and spitting out."

"Okay," I say, my own anger suddenly drained. A silence settles over us, and I look down at my audio controls. Everything is set and ready to go, the reason why Bristal and I are sitting here in a linen closet, knee to knee. But it doesn't feel important right now.

"Was Beck trafficked for drugs in Trash Park?" I blurt.

"Trash Park? I don't think I know that name," Bristal says, her face a mask of mock confusion. "Let's see . . ." She whips out her phone, tapping an address into a mapping app. "Oh wait, I found an *Ash Park*. You know . . . *where I live?*"

"Right, yeah, no," I stammer, the blood rushing to my cheeks. "I mean, it's on Trillium Lane, right? So I was thinking about Trillium Lane and Ash Park at the same time and it all got tangled up on my tongue and it came out as Trash Park. Isn't that weird how that happens sometimes? Like your mouth gets ahead of your brain and it all comes out messy like that? I think there's a name for it. I'm sure there is. Something like being dyslexia but not quite the same?"

"It takes a lot less oxygen to just apologize," Bristal says.

Crap. I close my eyes, wishing the soft, squishy walls of the recording closet would close in on me.

"Here, I'll walk you through it," Bristal says. "Repeat after me—I, Lydia Chass, was wrong."

"I was wrong," I say, willing the words past the lump in my throat.

"Wait, hold on, this is for posterity," Bristal says, and I open my eyes to see her checking her phone. "Okay, start over—I, Lydia Chass, was wrong, at three twenty-three p.m. Eastern time—"

"Oh my God, just stop," I say. "I'm sorry, all right? Really, actually sorry."

Bristal nods, accepting the apology. "But no, to answer your question. Beck got pregnant the old-fashioned way: she fell in love; he didn't."

"That sucks," I say, meaning it.

"What sucks more is that you thought she was being passed around like a party favor," Bristal says.

"It's what I heard, okay? And I asked out of concern."

"Maybe you did," she says. "I'll give you that, because I think you're actually a decent person. But the truth is that I hear a lot of things about where I live, and most of them are wrong."

"Okay," I say as my laptop screen goes dark, sliding back into sleep as our discussion continues. "Like what?"

"You know all the fires?"

"House fires?" I ask, but I can't feign like it's a true question. The fire department is called out to Ash Park a few times a week, and while the official blotter might read that there was a kitchen fire, everyone assumes it's a meth lab mix-up.

"A few of those were arson," Bristal says calmly. "Some of the respectable residents of Henley would rather we weren't residents at all."

"Were the police told this?" I ask, but Bristal snorts.

"No, people in Ash Park don't invite the cops into our homes. Beck called nine-one-one in fifth grade after we got that long talk about how the police are our pals; remember that?"

"Yeah, I remember." The Henley police force had come into the school with Popsicles and rubber bracelets, encouraging all of us to say something if we saw something. "Why'd she call the cops?"

"Her mom's boyfriend at the time was working her over, had already broken her mom's nose and was putting a good dent in her skull when Beck made the call. They showed up and arrested him, but they also nailed Beck's mom for truancy. Beck hadn't been to school in a while because her younger sister had pneumonia and her mom didn't have sick days to use, so Beck ended up playing nurse. I'd taken her one of those bracelets the officers handed out, and Beck did what she was told was the right thing to do—called the cops."

"It *was* the right thing to do," I say. "He could've beaten her mom to death."

"Maybe." Bristal shrugs. "But all Beck knew was that she called the cops for help, and she ended up sitting in the back seat of a cruiser, holding her baby sister and being interrogated by CPS. They got put in foster care, and the kids got split up. Beck didn't even see her little sister for three years, and by the time she started kindergarten, that little girl didn't even know her last name was Parsons anymore."

"That's horrible," I say.

"Yeah, it is. And that's one of the reasons why people who live in Ash Park don't call the cops. We take care of our own shit."

My eyes go down to her knuckles. The scabs are gone, to be replaced by thin, silver scar tissue. I reach out and hesitantly touch them, the pad of my finger sliding over the sharp edges of her hands.

"Is that why you have these? Taking care of your own?"

"Yep," Bristal says. "There's a fire bug in town, and he thinks burning down places that don't matter is the safe way to get his rocks off. He found out otherwise."

"Who was it?" I ask.

"If I told you, that'd be straight-up gossip, no different than you believing Beck's mom would trade her own daughter for crystal," Bristal says. "Instead, why don't you put those investigative skills to work and keep your eyes open for someone with a two-week-old broken nose and a thousand-yard stare, because I put a beating on that asshole, and I guarantee you there was at least a grade-two concussion involved."

"Bristal!" I shriek. "You can't just go around beating people up—"

"Well, I did," she says. "And there haven't been any more fires where I live. But I'm not letting you change the subject—are you ignoring Denise Halverson, or are you going to pony up and stick your tits out for a fellow female?"

I close my eyes and consider. The applications for all my top-tier schools are still stuck on *Processing*. I need to get solid content on the air, fast. Bristal's right—Boggs is low-hanging fruit. With a murder already documented, all that's left to do is turn over old rocks and prod the insects there. Digging for information about Denise Halverson is going to be time-consuming, maybe to the point of never finding answers—a dead end to the otherwise interesting narrative. I think of Beck and her baby bump, her holding her little sister in the back of a cruiser.

"I'm sticking my tits out," I say, swiping my fingers across my laptop screen to wake it up. I focus on the question that has been haunting me ever since I stood in the graveyard that day, surrounded by the dead while the living went through the motions of honoring them.

"What's the worst thing that can happen?" I whisper.

"My vagina growing shut," Bristal says without hesitation.

"That's not—oh my God, Bristal! That's not even a thing."

"I bet it is," she says, whipping out her phone.

"No, stop. I'm ready to do this, and I can't lose steam," I say. Then I hit record, clear my throat, and solemnly intonate the opening line of the first episode of the no-longer nice and fully reloaded season of *On the Ground in Flyover Country*.

"The worst thing that can happen is being forgotten."

SIXTEEN

Excerpt from podcast episode "Faded Away, Forsaken, and Forgotten"
of On the Ground in Flyover Country

Welcome to *On the Ground in Flyover Country*. I'm Lydia Chass, inviting you to join me and my new cohost, Bristal Jamison, as we explore the past and traverse the present of our hometown. This week, I'll be covering the dedication of the new Civil War monument, located in Fairlawn Cemetery. Tune in next week when Bristal takes the wheel for a tour of the responsibilities of your local ODOT crew.

The worst thing that can happen is being forgotten.... This is what I was thinking as I stood with the other participants for the memorial service and dedication of the new Civil War monument last week. Thoughts collided as I marveled at our inability to grapple with our own mortality. We insist on honoring the noble dead—as we should—but what message was I, a local girl, supposed to take away with me from that chilly afternoon?

The name Chass is everywhere in town, and the new monument is just another example. But other names can be spotted in Henley: the St. John's aid station, which is set up every year at the county fair, isn't a nod to piousness but rather a remembrance of William St. John, Henley's sole physician, who did house calls on horseback in the 1800s, and great-great-grandfather to Eva St. John, whose voice will greet you if you call the Henley High School front office.

Childress Lane and Horvath Street stand as markers where those families built the first permanent residences in Henley when it was established in 1827—houses that are gone now, destroyed by the tornado of 1994, one of the first in a series of events locally known as the long stretch of bad days, which we'll be covering in detail in future episodes.

Mention the name Ballinger and you'll be treated to the history of a local man who played minor league baseball and famously was called up to pitch for the Yankees for one inning in 1965. Talk of the Whitesides, and you'll be told that they make the prettiest women and even better apple pie. The Richardsons are known for diligently farming their same family fields for nine generations, the Lytles for signing up and serving, losing a soldier in every American military entanglement since the French and Indian War.

All these names can be spotted on the Civil War monument, on the pavers that surround it commemorating those who donated, and etched even more deeply into the tombstones that sprinkle the green grass of Fairlawn Cemetery.

But there are other names—ones you won't see posted around town or hear in the mouths of the living. They aren't on the pavers that surround the monument, either, because there are no descendants in Henley. Mattix, Dovecoat, Fender, and Halverson—these are names that have been forgotten and no longer reside within living memory. Though they may be etched in stone on the new memorial, there are no bones that carry their names in Henley, nor blood to continue their line.

This is what I brought home with me from the dedication and memorial.

Yes, there was also the shiver of recognition that came with seeing the name of my ancestor—Charles Chass—on the new spire. He survived the Civil War and came home to the house on Lincoln Street, for which I am, of course, eternally grateful. I'm equally relieved to know that Harold Walters, the great-great-great grandfather of my best friend, MacKenzie, returned to Henley. Without him, I don't have her.

Who else am I missing? What Mattix or Dovecoat could have been in my life? What Fender or Halverson? We honor the dead, but ultimately we are honoring our own, and giving thanks for the fact that we, ourselves, exist. Living in a small town means we know each other on an intimate level.

Our parents went to school together, teachers often see three generations of the same family before retiring. We go to each other's weddings and funerals, nod to one another on Sundays, and cross paths when grabbing a pizza, or walking into a football game.

Henley is often so close-knit that we can't see the holes, the places where someone might have been. Often I hear people mourning what Henley used to be: the old historic buildings, lost cornerstones and the nostalgic feel of peering out through wavy glass windows. I never knew this Henley, though I can see it in grainy photos and postcards from the past. The staid pencil sketches of our pioneer families can tell me what Abraham Henley looked like but not how his voice sounded, or if he was the sort of person who kicked his dog (an ancient measuring stick for the decency of a man, I'm told).

And what of that name? Abraham Henley founded this town, but you won't find his surname on the Civil War memorial, a paver, or anywhere outside the signs welcoming you into—and bidding you farewell from—the village. The reason why isn't because Abraham died young, or heroically in the war, leaving behind a childless wife. In fact, Abraham fathered twelve children and lived until he was eighty-eight, passing away in his sleep on Christmas Eve in 1890.

The reason why you spot the name Henley only at the village limits is because Abraham had only daughters. They move among us today, wearing the faces of a Beckley or a

Hemming. You can spot the high hairline of a Henley in a Levering or a Foxglove. The dozen Henley daughters brought forth sixty children altogether—bearing the names of Foxglove, Childress, Chance, Parsons, and many more, all of them familiar to local tongues. But our ancestors who carried the name of our hometown rest in Fairlawn Cemetery under stones that pronounce them to be a Milhaus, or a Lawson. The Henley daughters are now only the wife of—or mother to—someone else.

Women are easily lost in the record of time. Our names change, our faces aren't captured. If you look at the old stones in Fairlawn, you'll see that half our founding population are commemorated only through initials: J.F., wife of John; or A.S., mother of Hiram. If I cannot hear the voices of our founding fathers in their pencil sketches, how much more has been lost that we don't even know the names of the women?

Last week we bore witness to the dead; today I ask you to remember the forgotten. The following are the names of each of the Henley men who died in the Civil War. Remember them, and honor them. Then, if you have a chance, stop by the historical society and ask Mrs. Gurtz to help you locate the soldier associated with your family—then find out the names of their mothers, their wives, and their daughters.

Discover them. Remember them.

Then ask yourself who else you may have forgotten existed.

SEVENTEEN

"I have done my friend duties," Kenzie announces as she flops down next to me at lunch.

"You posted on the ep?" I ask, and she nods.

"Thanks." I glance up from my phone and the comment section from the newest episode. A text from Bristal appears, and I look over to her table, where she's giving me thumbs-up.

Halverson nod is perfect.

"Did you see your other comments, though?" MacKenzie asks. "Not everyone is happy with you."

"I know," I say, my lips twitching slightly. "I'm kind of thrilled." Another text comes in from Bristal.

Ouch. Maybe don't read the comments.

I smile and text back. **As the creators, it's important that we process the feedback of our audience.**

Cool, Bristal responds. Then adds, **I'm going to create an app that blocks any of your texts that sound self-righteous. It will be called BitchWidget and I will make millions.**

"You've got a nice one here from Mrs. Levering," Kenzie goes on, reading it aloud. "'Great coverage, Lydia! Thank you for caring about our ancestors and the wonderful history of Henley! I look forward to your next episode.'"

It's a nice comment, sure, but it does make me wonder if my fifth-grade teacher missed the point. My thumbs fly across my phone as I hit upon a comeback for Bristal.

I'm going to create an app that filters all your bad words. It will be called SwearCare and I will make billions.

"Well, this one is not so great," MacKenzie says.

"Read it," I say, not glancing up from my phone.

"Um, no," Kenzie refuses, handing me her own phone instead, and pointing at the offending commenter.

cuntryboy69: fuck you and fuck your dad.

"Oh, dang," I say, understanding why Kenzie didn't want to read it to me. I hand her phone back and keep scrolling through my own, spotting one with a littering of heart emojis.

BigMacKenzie: BFF Shout out!!

"Nice," I say, looking up. But Kenzie's going through comments, too.

"Here's one that says you don't know what you're talking about, that there are plenty of Halbertsons still around."

"Yeah, I see it," I tell her. Luckily, I don't have to do the work of correcting the poster. Somebody else already has done it for me.

"Nice," I say under my breath, just as another text from Bristal comes in.

"Halverson?" Kenzie asks, scrunching her nose at her phone. "What's that all about?"

I bite my lip and read Bristal's text, which has a screen cap of the comment from navaronne1976 and says—**somebody is picking up what we're throwing down.**

I respond with, **they're not the only one**, and send along my own screen cap of a comment that just posted a second ago.

whorevath1977: Halverson. Haven't heard that name in a
long time.

"Somebody didn't take kindly to you trying to recast the Lytles," Kenzie says, turning her phone so that I can see.

SweetieCorn94: Nice try on calling the Lytle's patriots. More
like thugs.

I shrug. "It was worth a shot at reminding people that the Lytles have a long history of serving their country. Some people aren't going to like it. Whatever."

I try to be casual, Bristal-style, but a new comment pops up on Kenzie's phone that takes the breath out of my lungs and sends dark spots across my vision.

whorevath1977: Tagging Erin Hendrix.

"Oh, shit," I say, my hand going to my chest, where I can feel my heart galloping.

"Lydia? What?" Kenzie asks, reaching out to grab my wrist. She glances at the new comment, but of course it means nothing to her. MacKenzie doesn't know who Denise Halverson is, or why I would care that someone is running to Erin Hendrix—not that I shouldn't have expected it. The only thing that travels faster than news in Henley is STDs, but resolving to tear off the Band-Aid and being responsible for exposing someone else's wound are two different things.

I pull away from Kenzie's grasp and shoot a text to Bristal. **Bathroom, now.**

"Lydia? Are you okay?" MacKenzie asks as I get up.

"I'm fine, I've just got to . . ." I lock eyes with Bristal, who gives me a little salute on her way out of the cafeteria. Kenzie follows my gaze.

"Oh, okay. Got it," she says stiffly. "Emergency podcast meeting with the new, trashier best friend."

"It's not like that," I say, but she just waves a hand at me as I backpedal. "I'll explain later."

Bristal is waiting for me in the bathroom, leaning against a sign that reads NO VAPING while she vapes. "I saw," she says. "Erin Hendrix is about to get a serious blast from the past."

"Yeah," I say. "And it's my fault."

"Fault?" Bristal's brow furrows. "More like this was your goal. You wanted to talk about things people refuse to acknowledge, and you found a flat-out missing person cover-up. You should be ecstatic not . . ." Her eyes follow me as I lean against the wall and slide downward.

"Not on the floor," she finishes. "Dude, you okay?"

"I think so," I say, pushing my palms into my eye sockets. "What does a panic attack feel like?"

"I don't give a lot of shits, so I don't really know," she says. "But get up before my foot gets you up. You did good work. You found this girl that everyone had forgotten."

"You don't understand," I moan, hands still covering my eyes. "I go to church with these people, and Erin is a super nice woman. I should've talked to her before I aired the ep. I bet her phone is blowing up right now and she probably has no idea why."

"Better to apologize later than ask permission first," Bristal says, pulling out her phone. "We're getting listens. There's a bump in your downloads. These are all positive things."

I pull my hands away from my face and look up at Bristal. "Positive things," I repeat. "You're right. Solid content. Good stuff. Interaction and listens and maybe even some Ivy Leagues taking notice."

"Speaking of good stuff," she goes on. "I got some great stuff out of Cousin Larry for the ODOT ride-along. The audio isn't awesome because I was using my phone, and the windows were down because he was smoking and I was vaping."

"Bristal!" I cry, coming to my feet at the thought of bad audio. "I hope it's usable. And you shouldn't vape," I remind her.

"Your mom smokes. I have photographic evidence," she says, then flashes me the 1994 pic of my parents at the Sweet Corn Festival from Swinton's interview.

My phone goes off in my pocket, and I grab it, any good vibes that Bristal had been trying to float to me totally obliterated.

"Crap," I say. "My mom just texted."

"She need you to pick up a pack of cigs?"

"No," I say flatly. "Erin Hendrix just called her. And I'm in a lot of trouble."

EIGHTEEN

Mom and Dad are sitting at the dining room table when I walk in the back door, and my stomach bottoms out at the sight of them. Mom's mouth has the tiniest downturn on each side, which usually happens right before she starts yelling. Dad has on his courtroom face, not giving anything away. The last time I saw them like this was when I came home fifteen minutes past curfew, and I got a long talk about my responsibilities and how I would understand when I have kids of my own.

Now I'm wondering if I'll live that long.

"Hey," I say. "Can I get something to eat first—"

"Lydia, sit down," Mom says firmly, and any appetite I had disappears.

Comments had been coming in on the first episode hard and fast all day. Some of them shared Mrs. Levering's enthusiasm for the young people of Henley being interested in their roots. But more than a few had been aggressive, and some downright inflammatory—like the one that told me to go eat a bag of dicks so that I could understand what men have given for their country.

I didn't understand how chowing down on penises is going to help me appreciate male valor, but Bristal had taken the reins and responded in kind, with the comments section blowing up into an all-out gender war that I eventually shut down by turning off commenting. But the flames had spread from the podcast site onto social media, with links popping up on the Markham County Block Watch Facebook page. By the time I got home, *On the Ground in Flyover Country* was the topic of conversation in Henley, and Dad left work early to convene a family meeting.

I sigh and pull out a chair, bracing myself.

"Lydia," Dad begins. "Your mom and I have been getting phone calls all day."

"People are upset," Mom adds.

"When you and I talked about this the other night, I told you I wasn't sure that it was a good idea to—"

"To tell the truth?" I interrupt, my temper flaring. "What did I do wrong, exactly? Please explain this to me."

"It's pretty simple," Dad shoots back. "People don't want to be told how to feel by an eighteen-year-old girl."

"Oh, really?" I ask, crossing my arms. "Does this go back to that sexism thing you mentioned the other night?"

"Do you know how many people called me today?" Mom asks. "Do you know how many times I got an earful about my daughter?"

"I can guess," I say, whipping out my phone. "Probably about the same amount of times I was called a bitch today. Does that bother you? Either of you? Or are you more worried about what people think?"

I look from Mom to Dad, questioning. They exchange a glance that only married people can share, communicating more with it than I can translate. Dad clears his throat.

"No, it's not okay that you're being attacked. But you struck first, Lydia. You called out the entire town as sexist and condescended to them about forgetting their female ancestors."

"Funny thing," I say. "I bet if I were a guy it would be called *educating*, not *condescending*."

"And," Dad goes on, "your jab about the Halverson girl didn't go unnoticed."

"Good," I say. "It wasn't supposed to."

"It upset quite a few people," Mom says again.

"Oh no," I gasp, clutching my chest. "People are upset? We can't have that! Just like we can't say that the guidance counselor has addiction issues or that the real reason the St. Johns don't host female exchange students anymore is because Hank got a little too friendly with the one from Sweden."

"Shut up!" Dad suddenly roars, slamming both hands down onto the table.

Mom yelps, and the wooden bowl in the center jumps, the plastic apple rolling out and falling to the floor. I watch it fall, incapable of meeting his eyes as my stomach opens and my throat closes.

"Brent!" Mom gasps. "Don't—"

"No, I'm sick of it!" Dad yells, his finger in my face. "You want to talk about feelings? Do you have any idea the emails I get? The text messages? The letters under my windshield wipers? I go to work every day to defend the actions that someone took against someone else, and they *both* live in this town. I've got to glad-hand and smooth-talk my way through every conversation I have, Lydia. Everywhere I go in Henley is the court of public opinion, and my daughter just threw herself onto that pyre, doused it in gasoline, and practically begged someone to strike the first match."

I'm quiet, staring down at the floor. Uneven Steven wanders in, his wheels squeaking as he inspects the errant apple. He gives it a half-hearted bat, and it rolls under the table. Mom scoops Steven up and unhooks his wheels, curling him against her chest. He nuzzles under her chin, his purrs filling the tense air of the dining room.

"Dad," I say, the word almost lost, my mouth dry. I try again, wetting my lips. "I didn't mean to—"

"Whatever you meant doesn't matter," Mom says, wiping a wet cheek against Steven's furry coat. "Intention means nothing, and perception is everything. People listened to that podcast, and they heard you telling them what to think and how to feel. They didn't like it."

"And I know how ugly this town can be," Dad adds, his anger flushed out now. "There's no reason to expose yourself to it for the sake of a goddamn school project."

"It's not just about that," I say, taking a deep breath. Dad's anger is spent, and Mom's got her therapy cat snuggled in tight. If there's a time to cut through the cake to the gooey center, it's now.

"It's about Denise Halverson."

Steven stops purring and lets out a small *mew*. Mom's knuckles are white, her fingers digging deeply into his orange fur. Dad leans back in his chair, the blankness of his courtroom face back on display.

"You said Erin Hendrix called," I turn to Mom. "What did she want?"

A bubble grows in my flattened stomach, a rising panic as I say Erin's name. As much as I want to rail against the heavy criticism the episode is gaining, there is a part of me that understands exactly what Mom and Dad are talking about. Community is everything here, and social capital can mean much more than income.

"Mom?" I ask, the bubble making it to my throat. "Is Erin mad at me?"

"No," she says. "But . . ." Mom glances to Dad, who nods. "She wants to talk to you."

"Really?" I lean forward, everything inside of me suddenly rearranged as I go from being knocked down a few pegs to pulling myself up again to regain lost ground. "Has she ever heard from Denise? Does she know if she's okay? What happened to her?"

"This is exactly what we're worried about, Lydia," Dad says. "The Halverson girl is a sore topic, and if you go poking at old wounds—"

"Why is it a sore topic?" I demand, plunging back in. "Why wouldn't everyone band together to find her back in 1994? Why weren't there search parties? Why didn't people care more about this girl turning up missing?"

"People cared," Mom says. "But it's hard to care about someone you don't know—and who burned their fair share of bridges—when your house is gone and everything you own is scattered across the county."

"Burned bridges—like punching the sheriff?"

"Who have you been talking to?" Dad says, sitting straighter. "This is exactly what we mean, Lydia. Once you start sticking your nose—"

"This isn't gossip, Dad!" It's my turn to blow up, my anger popping the bubble of anxiety that had nearly made me choke before. "This isn't meddling, and it's not about minding your own business. A girl *disappeared*, don't you get it? She vanished, and nobody looked for her."

"People looked," Mom says, her mouth a grim line that Steven reaches up to touch, his fuzzy paw patting her face, as if to reassure her. She kisses his pink pads, then tucks his foot back under her chin. "Don't make this into something it isn't."

"Then explain to me what it is," I say, my voice equally hard. "Because I'm having a hard time understanding."

"It's not easy to hear, I guess," Dad says. "And not easy to say, when it comes down to it. But the truth is that the Halverson girl wasn't from here, she didn't belong here, and she didn't stay here. She left when everything was in chaos, and Henley didn't have a moment or a dime to spare for anyone who wasn't our own."

"Which she wasn't," I tack on.

"No," Dad agrees. "She wasn't."

We're all quiet for a moment, but the tension is gone. It's been replaced by a low, thrumming sadness, something that Uneven

Steven picks up on, his ears swiveling back and forth, looking for the source.

"What's your next episode about?" Mom finally asks.

"ODOT," I say, shrugging. "Bristal is in charge of it. She rode along with one of her family members. A guy named Larry."

"What? Old Scary Larry?" Dad asks, his mood immediately lifted. "You'll have to make sure you edit that. His language might be a little much for the sensitive ear."

I bite down on my tongue, holding back a reply that all of Henley seems to have a sensitive ear, one that only wants to hear the positive and leave darker topics in shadowed corners.

"Speaking of editing," Mom says. "Your dad and I want to listen to your next episode before you air it."

"Excuse me, what?" I ask, in a tone that would send Bristal's yet-to-be-invented BitchWidget flying into the red.

"We think it would be best if we have a say in what you publish," Mom continues. "Your dad is in a tenuous position right now."

"I hope you don't mind if I point out, once again, that this is censorship."

"Censorship or common sense?" Dad asks, perking up as he senses a good-faith argument brewing. "Don't bite the hand that feeds you."

"Or the hand that rocks the cradle," Mom adds.

"Or I could just admit that ignorance is bliss and make the rest of the episodes about idioms," I say.

"I would listen to that," Dad pipes up.

"Of course you would," I say. "Is the interrogation over? Can I eat something now? Because I'll have you know that everything that just went on here was in direct violation of the Geneva Conventions."

"You're not starving," Mom chides, but she latches Steven back into his wheels and heads to the kitchen, calling back over her shoulder. "Peanut butter and jelly sound good?"

"Sounds great," I agree. "Strawberry is better than grape."

"You heathen," Dad says, pushing back his chair. "I'm returning to the office, but remember that we want to listen to the next episode. I'm really looking forward to hearing what the Jamison girl and her cousin Larry have to say about roadkill."

"I bet you are," I say, not quite able to hide the acid.

"You're doing good work, kiddo," Dad says, patting my shoulder as he walks past me.

"I know I am," I say as I dive into the sandwich Mom puts in front of me. And while I'm sure my parents are relieved to know that Bristal's episode won't cover anything more controversial than potholes, I can't imagine how they're going to react to the Randall Boggs episode.

If Henley can't stand talking about a runaway, how are people going to react to an episode dedicated to our one and only murder?

NINETEEN

I've been to Erin Hendrix's house plenty of times, for church youth parties, like on New Year's Eve, when we would drink sparkling grape juice out of plastic toasting glasses that came in two pieces, the bases falling off as we clutched them by the stems and staggered around, pretending to be drunk. Last year Bob Denney had done the best impression, resulting in a well-meaning phone call to his parents inquiring about their own imbibing.

I'm used to being in Erin's house when there are a lot of people, either for knitting circles, book clubs, or scrapbooking swaps. This house is always full of laughter and talk, the brightly painted walls echoing the women's voices of Henley, or the light-hearted giggles of the church youth. I've never been here when no one else was and had never appreciated the reason why Erin probably packs the rooms full whenever she has the chance.

This is the house in its normal state, quiet, lonely, and more than a little sad.

"I'm sorry, again," I tell Erin, getting up from the couch to take the tray with lemonade and cookies as she returns from the kitchen.

"No, really." Erin waves me off as she takes a seat on the couch next to me. "It was a relief. Nobody wants to talk about Denise, ever. When Sherry Horvath called me, it was like I'd been waiting to hear someone else say her name for thirty years."

"Mmm," I say, sipping my lemonade and making a mental note of the person who had ratted me out. Sherry Horvath, Lawrence the bus driver's wife. Big surprise.

"So, what do you want to know about Denise?" Erin asks, leaning back.

"Mostly I'm just curious about how something like this could even happen," I say, hoping she won't be disappointed that I'm not here to do a character sketch of her long-lost foster child. "I was told that she disappeared on the eleventh?"

"Yes." Erin nods, not asking how I know that, which is a blessing. "But we didn't report it until the thirteenth, because . . ."

"Because Denise was already in some trouble for hitting Sheriff Foxglove," I supply, hoping that the fact I'm already aware of the girl's checkered past will put Erin at ease, since she won't have to speak ill of Denise herself.

"In retrospect, it was stupid," Erin admits. "We should've called right away, maybe she would've still been in town, or somebody would have spotted her. After the tornado hit, all bets were off. Everyone had their own problems, and it was a while before everything calmed down and Foxglove even followed up with us."

"And she'd turned eighteen in the meantime," I add.

"Exactly. Foxglove said there wasn't much they could do but . . ." Erin fades away again, clearly not wanting to say anything bad about Henley's law enforcement.

"I understand," I say. And I do, given that Mom and Dad are going to go all FCC over my upcoming podcast episodes.

"So how did you even come to know about Denise in the first place?" Erin asks, pulling a cookie from the tray. They're home-made, not store bought. I imagine the children she had wished for, the unmade voices she'd hoped would fill these rooms, their throats never formed.

"I came across her by accident," I tell Erin. "There was an inaccuracy in the data of the missing from the tornado, and I sniffed it out."

I can't say how, exactly. David Swinton had invoked shield law before speaking to me, but if Erin presses, I can always point to Bailey Foxglove's journal notes.

"Well, I'm glad," Erin says. "It's nice to know that someone cares."

"Have you ever heard from Denise?" I ask. "Do you have any idea what happened to her?"

"No," Erin says, shaking her head. "It's not surprising, really. We only had Denise for three months, and well . . . it wasn't ex-actly a wonderful time in our lives. The poor girl walked through life believing everyone was out to use her for something, or to put one over on her. And with good reason, I guess. I didn't ask too many questions, but it was obvious Denise had been hurt in more ways than one."

"And she expected more of the same?" I ask, using my words carefully.

"She certainly didn't believe that Paul and I were sharing our home just out of the kindness of our hearts. I asked her to do her part, of course, help with the dishes, do her own laundry. But she'd been the oldest of seven in the house she'd come from before, and expected to parent the other six. As for Paul, well . . ."

She breaks off, blushing.

"I'm guessing she was expected to be a parent to the other kids and take on the wifely duties as well?" I ask delicately.

"Yes." She nods. "Something like that. Nobody had been kind to this girl, ever," Erin says, putting her lemonade back down, untasted. "She didn't know what to do when someone was motivated by something pure, like care or concern."

"So she's never contacted you?" I press. "Never reached out since 1994?"

"No, why would she?" Erin asks. "Kindness was foreign to her, and she thought Paul and I were both monsters inside. She was just waiting for us to show our true faces. She told me as much, before she ran off."

"Three months in and she still didn't trust you?"

"No," Erin says. "I think Denise could have stayed with us her whole life and still been waiting for the other shoe to drop. She trusted no one and liked even less people."

"Someone told me she hung out with a Jamison," I say, latching on to the tidbit. "But you claim she didn't like anybody."

"Well . . . ," Erin says, brushing some cookie crumbs off her knee. "It was a Jamison."

So, not really a person? It's a thought that goes unspoken, but I feel the cool lemonade warming in my stomach as my irritation spikes.

"Do you remember which Jamison? A boy or a girl?"

"Oh, a boy, for sure," Erin says. "Denise liked boys. That girl doing the podcast with you is a Jamison, right?"

"Bristal," I confirm, fighting the urge to tack on that she's not pregnant. "Does the name Dover Jamison mean anything to you?" I ask.

"Sounds about right." Erin nods. "Is that Bristal's dad?"

"Uncle," I say, quickly tapping out a text to Bristal.

At Erin Hendrix's place. She says Dover knew Denise.

A response comes in immediately.

Cool. We can ask him about her when we visit him in prison.

I've got that all set up, btw.

"She never reached out to you, but have you ever tried looking for Denise?" I ask Erin.

"Not at first," Erin said. "Foxglove told us there wasn't anything we could do, and when I talked to CPS they weren't exactly helpful. They said she was an adult now and we could file a missing person's report, but there wasn't a whole lot to be done."

"Did you file that report?" I ask.

Erin shifts uncomfortably, then rearranges the couch pillows behind her back. "We didn't want to cause any trouble."

Trouble—the second worst thing in Henley, coming in right behind hurting someone's feelings. Last year Janice Pascale had slipped and blown out her knee in her backyard during a snowstorm, then crawled over two acres to her daughter's house rather than call the ambulance, even though she'd had her cell phone on her. When asked about it in church, she'd smiled and said she didn't want the neighbors to be upset by the sound of sirens.

This is Henley. And while any other journalist worth their stuff would press Erin about not filing a report, I have to admit, I understand completely.

"We trusted that Sheriff Foxglove would have the word out and his eyes open," Erin goes on. "We told him what she'd been wearing and all that kind of stuff."

"What was she wearing?" I ask, tapping the pen against my notebook.

Erin smiles for the first time, and there's a brief flash of tears in her eyes. "Funny, I remember exactly. Denise wore a lot of black, all the time. That's all her wardrobe was, and I wasn't about to tell her what to wear, or anything like that. I offered to take her shopping, and she'd grab something black, then throw it in the cart and glare at me, challenging me to tell her to put it back.

"But one time—when the JCPenney was over in Gradiron—remember?"

I don't remember. JCPenney is as dead as Randall Boggs, but I nod anyway.

"I took her there, and she was eyeing this blouse. . . . I'll never forget, because it was so unlike her—white-and-gray pinstripe, with little blue roses. Very delicate. I had gone to the ladies' and when I returned she was rubbing the sleeve between her fingers and pulled her hand back when she saw me, like she wasn't allowed to touch something so nice. I pretended like I didn't notice, but I went back the next day and bought it for her."

Erin falls quiet, running her finger along the edge of the food tray. "Size medium," she says, and those two words seem to puncture whatever balloon she's been holding her grief in. Tears start to fall, and I look away, giving her a moment while I check my phone and see another text from Bristal.

> **Hey can I come over? Got the stuff for the ODOT ep, want to use the acid room.**

I stifle a giggle, aware that this moment with Erin is the last place to be amused by anything, and respond to Bristal.

> **I'm not home, but go ahead. Mom is. She'll let you in. My laptop's on my desk.**
>
> **Recording software is pretty simple to figure out.**

The bubble with an ellipsis in it shows up, and Erin excuses herself to get a tissue. I nod and take the opportunity to cram a cookie in my mouth. It's good, still warm from the oven, with an obvious overuse of butter and big chunks of chocolate.

> **Cool. I'll probably bum a cig from your mom.**

For the second time, she sends me the picture of my mom smoking, my dad turned in profile.

> **Go for it. She doesn't smoke.**

Bristal doesn't respond with words, only the pic again, this time cropped to just my mom's blurry face, and the cloud of smoke coming from her mouth.

"Sorry," Erin says from the doorway. "I don't know what got into me."

"Emotions," I say, after the last swallow of gooey chocolate delight slides down my throat. "We all have them."

"Well, some more than others," Erin says, as if embarrassed of her tears as she thumbs the last errant one away. "Would you like to see Denise's room?"

"Sure," I say, and follow her down the hall, though I'm not sure that it will serve any investigative purpose. As I had suspected, it's been stripped of any sense of habitation; an old PC sits in the corner, and the closet is empty of all but three wire hangers, one of them bent and twisted.

"You're confident she went out the window?" I ask, peering out of it.

Even though the Hendrixes live in town, their lot is heavily wooded. Denise could have easily slipped out without being seen.

"Yes," Erin confirms. "She kicked the screen out. Paul found it in the yard in the morning, put it right back in, of course."

I wander around Denise's room, trying to imagine a teenage girl here, young, morose, troubled, intent on leaving. My hand rests on the old PC, a boxy thing with a monitor that could fill the back seat of my car.

"Did Denise use this?" I ask.

"No, we bought it later, once the internet was a thing. I thought maybe it could help us find her."

"Good thinking," I say, more to make her feel better than anything else. Bristal and I had both combed social media and come up with zilch.

"The thing about that shirt . . . ," Erin goes on, her eyes going to the empty closet. "I knew that's what she was wearing, when she left. It was the only thing missing."

"What?" My ears perk up, my notebook flips open. "The shirt with the blue roses?"

"Yes," Erin says. "She was wearing it, and that always made me a little bit happy. That's what she took when she left—something I bought her. Something nice."

"Right, yes. Of course," I say swiftly, my heart racing in my chest. "Well, thank you, so, so much!"

I'm bright and perky again, thanking Erin for the cookies and her time and her memories. I all but thank her for her thoughts and prayers as I make my way to the front porch, hands itching to text Bristal. My phone vibrates in my hand before I'm behind the wheel, with a text from Mom.

Your weird friend is here. She asked me for a cigarette.

It's followed by a confused face, but I flip right past Mom's text and type out a message for Bristal.

Home soon. Stay there. Just talked to Erin H.

Denise Halverson didn't take anything with her when she left

Bristal answers immediately.

Which means she wasn't planning on going far

"Yep," I say aloud as I start my car. "But she never came back."

TWENTY

I breeze past Mom and burst into my bedroom, but Bristal is no-where to be seen. My laptop is missing, though, so I put my ear up against the linen closet door, but the soundproofing material is seriously effective; I can't hear a thing. I crack the door and peek in, to have Bristal wave me through as she pulls a pair of headphones off.

"Just finished uploading," she tells me. "ODOT episode is a go, and I'm pretty much done with the Randall Boggs one, too. Give me the scoop on the Hendrix chick."

I close the door behind me and settle in across from Bristal. "She didn't put it together, but when she told me that Denise went out that window with only the clothes on her back, it had my alarms ringing."

"True," Bristal admits. "But she could have arranged to meet with someone and was traveling light."

I nudge her knee, surprised that she's not going with the darkest possible explanation. "You really think a girl that's never had anything would leave behind everything she owns?"

"No," she says. "But I'm trying not to jump to any conclusions. Work with me, here. It's difficult being the responsible one."

"Whatever, this stinks and you know it."

"It does, like week-old period," Bristal says.

"Ewww," I say, glancing at my laptop. "You didn't say anything like that on your ep, did you?"

"Um, no?"

I sigh and lean back against the wall, the puffy foam triangles soft against my spine. "I got in big trouble with my parents for dropping Denise's name in that first episode. People were upset." I put that last word in air quotes, and Bristal rolls her eyes.

"They're going to be downright livid if we announce that we don't think she just up and disappeared."

"Right," I agree. "I don't think I can even talk about this with my parents without the roof coming off the house."

"We can talk to mine," Bristal says. "And Uncle Dover."

"Good idea." I nod. "When?"

"We're popping over to the prison on Saturday," Bristal says, checking her phone. "Which, by the way, you'll have to drive. I don't think my Neon can make it."

"No problem," I say. "And your parents? When can we sit down with them?"

"Whenever," Bristal says, shrugging. "What else did you get out of Hendrix?"

"I know what Denise was wearing," I tell her. "A gray-and-white-pinstripe blouse with little blue roses on it. And we know that she hung out with Dover, so that's something to follow up on. We need to check social media again, and not just Facebook this time."

"'Kay," Bristal says, tapping out a note on her phone. "What else?"

"What else? God . . ." I want to fall forward, collapse, and cry, even if just to clear my sinuses. "I need—and I mean I *need*—to get that tornado episode put together. We haven't even talked to Linda Chance about the dog pound yet. And I'm thinking about shutting down the comments section altogether. We don't need a new civil war breaking out like it did on my actual Civil War episode. I'm glad we're not being graded on the content of comments, because people can be downright nasty, and you were right—I shouldn't have looked. Besides that, if this whole thing about Denise Halverson really blows up, we could be in a bad place. Nobody wants to be the first person to say something, but Swinton did mention shield law so—"

"I'm never asking you 'what else' again. Like, ever," Bristal says. "You just depressed the shit out of me."

"Sorry," I say.

"Refresh me on shield law," she says. "That's the thing that means you can't just say that David Swinton dished to you about the Halverson girl, right?"

"I *can*, but I don't have to," I clarify.

"That's cool," Bristal says. "So I don't have to tell anybody that Dale Childress and Cousin Larry were totally going to rob Randall Boggs but things were too corpse-y for them to try?"

"Something like that, sure," I say, going with her loose interpretation.

"Which reminds me," she continues. "I want to go out to Far Cry Road."

"What for?"

"Boggs's trailer is gone," she says. "But I went door to door, and it's a rough patch of a place. My grandma and grandpa used to live out there, Dover and Mom's parents. They moved into town when Mom and Dad set up in Ash Park, to help with me and the rest of the pack; Jamison girls are kind of like Pez dispensers when it comes to babies," she says, looking dubiously down at her own midsection, as if daring it to grow.

"But from what I could see after doing the interviews for the murder episode, nothing much has changed out there. I think having a long sit in Boggs's old driveway might help really set the mood for the episode."

"Okay," I say, surprised she's that into it.

"Also, there's totally a bigfoot out there."

"So that's why," I say. "You want to do a bigfoot episode."

"Hey, man," she says, both hands going up in the air. "All I'm saying is that some weird shit goes on out in the sticks. Do you even know how Far Cry Road got its name?"

"Yes, because it's a far cry from town," I tell her.

"Okay, yes, that," she admits. "But also, the weird noises."

"Weird noises?" I repeat.

"Yep," she says, clearly satisfied with herself. "I used to hear them sometimes, when I'd stay with Grandma and Grandpa before they moved. It'll keep you up at night, I promise."

"What's it sound like?" I ask, interested in spite of myself.

Bristal only shakes her head. "I'm not even going to try to do it," she says. "You've got to hear it for yourself."

"I'm in," I tell her. "Think we can hang out with your parents for a little bit first, see if they've got anything to share about Denise?"

"We can try," she says, nodding. "When?"

"What have you got going on tomorrow?"

"Nothing. Neither do you. I checked your calendar," she says, tapping my laptop.

"Snoop away," I tell her haughtily. "I've got nothing to hide."

"I know," she says, wrinkling her nose. "I was expecting some German dungeon porn at least. But I think your dirtiest deeds are probably not folding your underwear."

"I just toss them in the drawer," I say, dropping my voice low.

"What about socks?" she asks, matching my tone.

"Don't even match the pairs," I sniff.

"Demon! Begone!" She makes a cross with her fingers and wards me off with it.

We're giggling like insane people when my mom cracks the door. "Girls? Sorry, I didn't want to interrupt—"

"Oh, you're not," I reassure her. "What's up?"

"I was wondering if Bristal wanted to stay for dinner?" Mom asks.

"Cool, yeah, I like food," Bristal says. "Thanks."

"No problem," Mom says, backing out of the closet and closing the door behind her.

"Here are the rules," I say as soon as she's gone. "You can't talk about Denise Halverson; that is strictly off the table. My parents are upset enough about that topic as it is."

"Got it," she says. "What about Boggs?"

"I think that's okay," I tell her. "But don't mention Abe Lytle or the school bus situation."

"What about the heroin and cocaine I brought over the other day?"

I cross my arms. "You know better."

"Yeah," she admits. "But I still like watching that little muscle in your jaw twitch."

TWENTY-ONE

"So murder is totally a thing that happens," Bristal says lightly, popping a piece of cheesecake in her mouth post-dinner.

"Nice, great segue," I tell her.

"Why? What were we talking about?" she asks, genuinely confused.

"Whether eating veal is a moral choice," Mom informs her, and if I'm not mistaken, adds a little eye roll to her statement, along with a nod toward Dad and me, who had—admittedly—done a deep dive into our arguments and counterarguments.

"Yeah, we can't afford veal, so I don't know about that," Bristal says. "But any cow I eat has technically been murdered, so murder is totally a thing that happens. To cows, and to people named Randall Boggs."

"Your use of the word *technically* implies that you think a cow is a living thing with rights, otherwise you would simply say it had been killed," Dad says, leaning forward on his elbows, obviously eager for Bristal's rebuttal and moving on to his next opponent.

"How about it's dead, and I don't really care how it got that way?"

"Fair enough," he says. "But what were you going to say about Randall Boggs?"

"Uh . . ." Her eyes cut to me, but I'm gauging the mood. Mom is my barometer, and her hand is steady as she lifts her third glass of wine. Boggs is a safe subject; I give Bristal a nod.

"His murder is the only one we've got," she says, making homicide sound like a precious metal. "But it's an unsolved case, and a cold one."

"It's a sad thing to say, but I don't think the old man was missed much," Dad says, leaning back in his chair now.

"Now or then," Mom adds.

"Live dirty, die dirty," Bristal says, and both my parents nod.

"Why the interest in Boggs?" Dad asks.

"That's one of my episodes," she explains. "And I just think it's odd that our only murder is also unsolved."

"I can understand your thinking, but you've got to consider the statistics," Dad says. "A lot of homicides go unsolved, but that's not a headline you'll see in the paper."

"Not the *Hometown Henley Headlines*," Mom murmurs into her wineglass.

"Any paper," Dad doubles down. "The public likes to believe that justice will always be served. Informing them of how often that doesn't pan out isn't in their general interest."

A cold ball is forming in my stomach, a reminder of Dad's comment the other night about the gray areas of life, areas people wander into and never find their way back out of.

"How many?" I ask, and Dad pulls out his phone.

"You want a number, or a percentage?"

"A number," I say.

"From 1980 to 2019, in Ohio, over ten thousand murders went unsolved."

A high whistle escapes from Bristal, and Mom sits her glass down harder than necessary. "I don't know if this is really good dinner conver—"

"Dinner's over," I say sharply. "What's the percentage on that?"

"That's a sixty-seven percent clearance rate," Dad says, pinching his phone to zoom in on the chart. "That's actually not too bad."

"Not too bad?" I demand. "That's thirty-three percent of murders going unsolved! Randall Boggs is one of those numbers. That is unacceptable."

"Maybe you should be a cop, then," Dad tells me. "Go make the world right."

"Maybe you should stop defending the people that commit crimes," I snipe back.

"I'm sorry, Bristal," Mom says, pouring herself another. "I think this was supposed to be a good-natured debate, but it's turning into a family fight."

"This is a fight?" Bristal asks. "Nobody's thrown anything yet."

"Don't worry," Dad says, holding a hand out to Mom in a staying gesture. "I'm not going to take the bait."

"Sorry," I say. It's terse and sounds anything but genuine, yet Dad stills nods his acceptance.

"It's okay," he says.

"I really am surprised at those statistics," I admit.

"I'm not," Bristal says. "Think about it. Somebody gets killed, who probably did it?"

"The husband," Dad says.

"Or the wife," Mom adds, tipping her glass toward him.

"Possibly their daughter," I tack on, raising my Diet Coke.

"Exactly my point," Bristal goes on. "Boggs didn't have any family. No spouse, no kids. Nobody had anything to gain from him dying, so there was nothing for the cops to really go on in terms of motive."

"You said yourself that no one liked the guy," I counter.

"Yeah, but I don't like a lot of people, and I've never murdered anyone," Bristal says.

"Here's my card, just in case," Dad says, pretending to dig in his pocket.

"Regardless," I hop in. "Boggs wasn't just shot; he was beaten. There was something more complicated going down in that trailer other than a drug deal. It was personal."

"It sure looked that way," Bristal agrees, and Dad immediately jumps on her wording.

"Looked?" He leans forward again. "Have you seen photos?"

"Uh . . ." Bristal shoots me a panicked look, then crosses her arms in front of her face. "Shield law!" she yells at Dad, then turns to Mom, arms still crossed, and screams, "Shield law!" again.

"Am I doing this right?" she asks me.

"No," Dad tells her. "But it's amusing."

"You don't have to say it," I tell her. "Shield law stands without being invoked. And you don't have to actually shield yourself." I reach across the table and push her arms down.

"Lydia's right," Dad says calmly. "You don't have to reveal your sources, and I know you're not my daughter, but I want both of you to be careful."

"We are," I say confidently, lying through my teeth.

"Both of you," he repeats, looking at Bristal, who only nods, her arms twitching like she wants to bring them back up again.

"I read the comments on your last episode of *On the Ground in Flyover Country*," Dad goes on. "You girls really caught it in the teeth."

"I gave back as good as I got," Bristal says, her chin coming up.

"Be that as it may, I hope Lydia informed you that her mother and I would like to review each episode before it airs."

"Which is censorship," I add.

"It's parental concern," Mom says.

"It's censorship masquerading as parental concern," I restate, for Bristal.

"Ohhhh, okay, so . . . about that?" Bristal eyes shoot to mine, and my stomach drops. "I don't think I technically knew about the censorship-slash-parental-concern angle."

"Oh my God," I say, pushing back from the table and grabbing for my phone. "Is it already up? Did you *publish*?"

"I . . . Okay, so here's what happened," Bristal says, looking around the table. "I scheduled it for future release—"

"Monday," I say, stabbing at my phone as I wait for our site to load. "We publish on Mondays. That's what we agreed on."

"Yep, we totally did," she says. "And that's what I scheduled it for. Except, I saw there was a typo in the show transcription. I said something about County Road 33 being an *accident-prone area*, but the AI fumbled it."

I glance up from my phone. "What did the transcript say?"

"Uh . . ." Bristal glances in between my parents. "The transcript read that County Road 33 is an *accidental porn* area."

Mom spits out some of her wine, and Dad doesn't even bother hiding his laughter. "Well, that'll send the kids out that direction."

"And not just them," Mom says.

"You fixed it, right?" I ask, scrolling through the transcript. "Please tell me you fixed it."

"I did," Bristal says, and I exhale in relief. "But when I went back in, it must've wanted me to set it up as a scheduled episode again."

"And you didn't?"

"No, I thought it would keep all the settings, so I just hit publish."

"Well, it didn't," I tell her, turning my phone around so that she can see the newest episode of *On the Ground in Flyover Country*, which apparently is titled "There Are Potholes Out Here Bigger than My Dick."

"Oh, whoops," she says, taking the phone from me. "It must've wiped out the title, too, and reverted to the one I was using as a placeholder."

"Your placeholder title is 'There Are Potholes Out Here Bigger than My Dick'?" I ask.

"Well, it's not my dick," Bristal says. "It's Cousin Larry's."

"I always heard he was packing," Mom says. "Why do you think we called him Scary Larry?"

"You're not helping." I turn toward Mom, inwardly seething. Some of my irritation must be on the outside, too, because Dad raises both hands in a placating gesture.

"All right, so it's up," he says. "Why don't we all go into the living room and listen to it together? That way there aren't any surprises when our phones start to ring."

"Upstairs or downstairs living room?" Mom asks.

"I vote downstairs," Bristal says. "Also, I want the bedroom with the silver tea set when I move in here after getting kicked out of my house."

"Deal," Mom says, and bumps fists with Bristal while draining the last of her wine.

TWENTY-TWO

Excerpt from podcast episode "There Are Potholes Out Here Bigger than My Dick" of On the Ground in Flyover Country

Welcome back to *On the Ground in Flyover Country.* This is Bristal Jamison, and I'm hosting this week's episode as I take you on a virtual tour of all the best—and worst—that Markham County highways have to offer. Also covered—my cousin Larry's anatomy, which is often used in comparison to whether something is as big as, or smaller than, his special appendage. We're also going to talk about dead stuff, how far the intestines of a possum can stretch (hint: longer than Larry's dick). Stay tuned to the end for some special gardening tips on how to grow a pickle that is larger than Larry's.

And by the way—we've turned off comments for this

episode, because you all had to go and be dicks last week. If you've got something to say to me about this episode, or really anything at all, pony up and say it to my face. I'm on probation, so I can't hit you . . . technically.

There are 380 miles of county roads here in Markham County and 337 miles of township roads. And if you bother to check in with the Markham County Block Watch Facebook page—and you really should; it's a great place to post your lost pet or pictures of suspicious people you caught on your driveway cam. Once they've been identified, you can get into a fight with their family members. It's the go-to place on a slow weeknight, if you don't count PornHub.

But seriously, if you take a glance at the Block Watch page, you'll see that every resident of those 717 miles of roads thinks that their section of road is the worst. And approximately 680 of those miles can put up a pretty good case for being the ugliest patch of asphalt around.

Take County Road 50 as an example. Running east west and stretching seventeen miles, it's the most traveled road in the county. Often called the Drunk's Highway due to five different bars being located along the way, it's also the hot spot for local law enforcement.

"They hide in the turnarounds by the railroad tracks. Pay attention to the crop rotation, too. Corn's high enough to hide a cruiser by mid-July, and the weekend of the Fourth is like payday for the po-po."

That's my cousin Larry. You'll be hearing from him on

and off during this episode. So—trigger warning for Cousin Larry. It's an all-encompassing heads-up.

"You see how most of the potholes are on the south side of the road? People think that's because most of the population lives in the western part of the county, and the drunks are coming home driving too fast. But that's not it. This here whole thing used to be one lane, all cobblestone, and when they widened it to two lanes, they didn't bother tearing up the original, just used that cobblestone as a base.

"They probably don't teach you this in school these days, but the earth is always moving, settling, freezing and refreezing. All kinds of stuff goes on down there—it's kinda like your mom's pants, if you know what I'm saying. Anyways, the south side of the road gets all tore up because the base is those original cobblestones, so you've got thousands of little shifting, moving parts. But the north side of the road, it's got a laid base—also kinda like your mom. Anyway, that's how come 50 is the way it is."

And there you have it, folks, that should cover the required historical aspects of this episode. Can I graduate now?

"But there are plenty of drunks, don't get me wrong on that. I live out on 50, you know, and one time this fella ran out of gas right at the end of my driveway. Needed to fill up his can to get on home. I didn't have any on me so I offered to drive him back, and on the way he tells me this whole story about how his cat just died. Something about how he lost the remote to the TV and went to look under the couch, but he couldn't see under it on account of it being so dark, so he just flipped the sofa right on over, and it landed the cat. He was in a bad way about that cat. I really felt for the guy."

Cats don't only die in living rooms in Markham County. The Markham County ODOT crew sets aside the first week of each month to do roadkill cleanup.

"It takes about three days to cover the entire county. Me and Mike Walton take the dump truck and some shovels. If there's a deer or something bigger like that, it's a road hazard and we've gotta clear it right away. Sometimes the dump truck is full of gravel or something, so we just take a truck with the lift gate. Once, the county's truck had a flat tire and we had to use Mike's, and his wife got a little salty about it.

"With a deer or like a bigger coyote the shovels won't cut it so we just both gotta grab a pair of legs—one guy on the front and one guy in the back—you just kinda get 'em swinging and give it a toss into the truck. Sometimes the legs have been knocked clean off and that gets tricky. You gotta stand there with your shovels and make some decisions. We always take a chain saw along, just in case."

Larry says roadkill is just another part of the job, and that you get used to it.

"I mean, yeah, sometimes you see things that set you back a bit. Like raccoons, the male raccoons are just kind of boy whores, but a female raccoon mates for life. So a lot of the time you'll see more than one dead raccoon, on account of the female won't leave her man, and she gets hit, too. You see it with the babies a lot, any kind of animal. The mom gets hit, and the kids don't know what to do, so they just hang around and get clipped. One time I scraped a whole possum family up off Township 20. That mom had a gut on her, intestines longer than my dick."

Some useful tips from Larry on how to cut down on that roadkill:

"There's never just one deer. Ever. You see a deer crossing the road, you stop, because there's another one coming.

"Don't ever feel bad about hitting a bunny. There's plenty of 'em.

"Buzzards take some time for liftoff. They are some big, lazy bastards. Don't think they'll just get out of the way in time. I've seen plenty of windshields blown out. Feathers and blood all over the place.

"Don't be a dick and throw your litter out the window. First of all, that's a five-hundred-dollar fine. Second of which, I find out it was you, I'll come beat your ass. That McDonald's trash draws in all kinds of stuff. I've seen flat squirrels holding fistfuls of french fries. Beer, neither. I bet if I Breathalyzed half those dead raccoons, most of 'em were drunk when they went down."

Nationwide data suggests astonishing annual death rates for roadkill: forty-one million squirrels, twenty-six million cats, twenty-two million rats, nineteen million opossums, fifteen million raccoons, six million dogs, and 350,000 deer.

But Larry has a message for anyone worried about their furry friends:

"If it's a dog or a cat that's got a collar on it, we take it off, send it over to Linda Chance at the pound. That way nobody's got to wonder what happened to their pet. For a while we would take a picture if it was a dog or cat without a collar, post it to the Markham County Lost Pets page, thinking somebody might be able to identify it. But then a moderator blocked us so we can't do that no more."

If you've lost a pet in the past forty years, the county's been using a mass grave for all unidentified roadkill since 1981.

"We just kinda dig a hole, do a dump once a week, cover it up once things get too spicy, dig a new hole, go back to the old one a few years later. Some archaeologist in the future is going to come across it and wonder what the hell happened here."

Animal apocalypses aside, Larry loves working for ODOT.

"It's the only place you can still smoke on the job."

No data has been provided for nicotine addiction in raccoons.

A couple of last words of wisdom from Larry, who aside from being a county employee, enjoys long stretches of shooting his pellet gun at buzzards and organic gardening.

"Don't ever go into your garden when you're on your rag. It wilts the pickle plants."

No data has been provided for male cousins and their understanding of euphemisms.

Thanks, everyone, for tuning in to this week's episode of *On the Ground in Flyover Country*. My cohost, Lydia Chass, will return next week for the first in our series covering the legendary long stretch of bad days.

I'd like to close by remembering the animals whose brief lives and splatterific deaths I witnessed during my ride-along on the highways of Markham County...

Randy the Raccoon, Samantha Squirrel, Tom Cat #1, Tom Cat #2, something that might be a toad, Pam the Possum (no length of intestines given), and the innumerable insects—

TWENTY-THREE

I power off the Bluetooth speaker and fix Bristal with a stone-cold glare.

"What the hell was that?"

"Lydia!" Mom chastises me. "You can't talk to—"

"Yeah, Mom. Actually, I can," I say, spinning on her. "Our listens are up, my applications are still in review, and any one of those sets of ears out there could be attached to someone who is making a decision about where I can or can't go to college—and Bristal is treating it like stand-up."

"And it was pretty funny." Dad looks at Bristal. "Quite well done. I can't say how the language will go down with the school staff, but if it comes in front of the school board, I think I can make a case for artistic license and capturing local color."

"Are you serious right now?" I say, switching my glare to Dad. "Henley might be all over this, but Harvard won't."

"If it matters—" Bristal begins, but I cut her off.

"It doesn't. It doesn't matter," I tell her.

"Well, now, hold on a second," Dad says, rising from his chair. "Bristal has a right to defend herself. This is a group project."

"Whose side are you even on?" I screech. Tears are pricking at my eyes now, the anger arching toward hysteria.

"I don't see why there have to be sides," Dad says.

"It's an argument, Dad! Yes, there are sides. And you're supposed to be on mine!"

The tears are coming now. I'm standing in the middle of the living room, my cheeks wet, hands on my hips. I can see my face reflected in the living room window, the darkness outside nowhere close to matching what I feel in my gut.

"Look, Lydia, I didn't mean to piss you off," Bristal says, her voice weirdly subdued. "But you gotta admit your monument episode was kind of a bummer."

"A bummer?" I yell. "It's about the Civil War, *Bristal*, which was a bummer for a lot of people. So, I'm sorry if I couldn't find a way to make it more amusing. I guess I'll have to get more dicks in there next time."

Bristal's face twists like she's trying to hold something back but can't. "That's what she said—sorry!"

Mom snorts, and Dad covers his mouth but can't hide his laughter. Rage spikes, and I'm at a loss for words, anger clogging my throat and murder on my mind.

"What the hell?" Mom says, but she's not looking at any of us; she's staring out the front window, where a spire of fire is rising on the front lawn. It's joined by two others, igniting in quick succession and moving closer to the house.

"Everyone outside, now!" Dad yells.

The bay window shatters, and a brick sails into the living room. I scream and hit the floor, but Mom is up in a moment, running through the house and yelling for Steven.

"Rebecca! No!" Dad yells, sprinting after her.

I look up to see Bristal, unfazed, staring out what remains of the window.

"I see him!" she yells, one foot up on the ledge as she hurls herself through the glaring hole, knocking the rest of the glass loose from the frame.

"Bristal!" I scream, but she's gone, and a heavy plume of smoke sails in through the window, choking me. I crawl on all fours back through the kitchen, where Dad finds me, grabs me by the shoulders and forces me outside. Mom is right behind us. Steven wide-eyed and ears flat, has his arms around her neck, holding on for dear life. The three of us spill out into the driveway as Dad yells into his phone, "Five-five-five Lincoln Street; yeah it's me, Debbie. We need the fire department. Looks like four, maybe five isolated fires on the front lawn."

"Six," Mom says, her mouth a grim line as she surveys the tall pyres. "What the hell are they?"

"Where's Bristal?" Dad demands, spinning on me.

"She went out the window," I tell him. "She said she saw

somebody, and she just took off. I couldn't stop her." I cough as a breeze blows a thick, noxious cloud in our direction.

"Smells like an accelerant," Dad says.

"Bristal!" I yell into the darkness, but my voice is covered by sirens from the fire station, two blocks over. "Bristal!"

"It's okay, baby," Mom says, cuddling Steven to her chest. "I don't think the house is going to catch," she says, eyeing the fires on the lawn, which are fading.

"No," Dad agrees. "But don't go back inside just yet. The whole first floor is probably full of smoke. You don't want to breathe this in."

"Bristal!" I scream again, and she emerges from the smoke, one hand curled to her chest.

"Jesus Christ!" Mom says as the fire trucks come down the drive, a police cruiser joining them, flashers on. The flickering blue and red lights illuminate the side of Bristal's face; there's a long cut along one cheek, and the eye above it is swollen shut.

"He got away," Bristal says, clearly disappointed. "I got some licks in, but he was bigger than me."

"Did you get a look at his face? Any idea who it was?" Dad asks, but Bristal only shakes her head.

"Sorry, no."

"Oh, honey, you don't have to apologize about a damn thing," Mom says, transferring Steven to hang over one shoulder as she takes Bristal by the chin, turning her face in the dying light of the fires. "You should see a medic."

"Nah, it's just a black eye. I've had worse," Bristal says, but I point to the leg of her jeans, where there's a slice in the denim, and a growing stain of blood around it.

"You cut yourself on the way out," I say, and she looks down at her leg.

"Oh . . . shit . . . ," she says, her voice fading out. "Guess I didn't see that. Sure didn't feel it."

"Sit down, right now," I say firmly, and grab Bristal just before she falls. Mom opens the car door and deposits Steven on the passenger seat as I ease Bristal to the ground. His furry face pops up in the window as he continues to monitor the situation.

"Sorry," Bristal says again, her eyes a little unfocused. "Sorry."

"Mom's right, you don't have to apologize," I say, looking her over for any other injuries. "What the hell were you thinking?"

"I was thinking—*get that fucker!*" Bristal says with a weak smile.

"Mom!" I yell as she goes around the side of the car. "Check with Dad, make sure there's an ambulance on the way. And . . . what the hell are you even doing?"

"Turning on the heat for Steven," she calls over the hood of the car, the headlights flashing as the battery comes on.

"It's, like, forty degrees out here," I yell at her. "He's not going to freeze!"

"Well . . ." She disappears for a second as she fiddles with the dashboard of the car, then pops back out. "He likes to listen to audiobooks, and I don't want him to be too stressed out."

A melodic British voice emanates from the car, and one of Steven's ears flicks backward.

"I love your family," Bristal says.

"Shut up," I tell her. "Also, thanks."

"Yep," she says, her one good eye sliding closed.

"Mom, stay with her," I say as I see the ambulance pulling in at the end of the drive. I run past the firefighters and cops, give a nasty look to the neighbors who are gathering on either side of the lawn, and grab the first medic who gets out of the ambulance.

"We've got one injury—a decent cut on the leg and some blood loss," I tell him. "She's up by the house and probably needs oxygen. She should also be checked for a possible concussion and a contusion on her left cheek."

"'Kay," she says, motioning her partner to follow her as they head back toward the house.

There's a gush of water from the fire hose, and the first fire disappears, then the second. Steam rises from where they stood, and Dad wanders into the yard, covering his nose as he approaches them. I jog over, hand over my face as we inspect the first one. It's a warped and twisted piece of metal, but it's easy to determine that it was originally an octagon. Another blast from the hose extinguishes the last of the fires, which all appear to be the same thing.

"Stop signs," I say to Dad, coughing as a whiff of singed metal hits me in the face. "Somebody stuck a bunch of stop signs in our yard and set them on fire."

"I guess the message is pretty clear," Dad says, nodding. "Only question is—is it meant for me, or for you?"

The sheriff turns on his spotlight, illuminating the entire yard brightly. Six burned signs tilt at crazy angles, still smoking, large patches of yard burned and dead underneath them. The low-hanging branches of an old oak are twisted and smoldering, and glass covers the front porch.

"If it's for me, it didn't work," I tell Dad.

"Yeah," he says, resting a hand on my shoulder. "Me neither."

TWENTY-FOUR

Steven has finished his audiobook, and Mom has downloaded the second one for him by the time we get the all-clear to go back inside the house. Mom grimly grabs a broom and begins creating piles of shattered glass. I pull down the curtains and toss them in the washer, even though I know we'll never get the smell out of them. There's a fine, dark film on the walls from the accelerant-laced smoke that I'll have to go at with a bucket of bleach water and a sponge. Dad surveys the scene and announces that he's going to go get duct tape and a tarp to cover the front window.

"You *did* tell the police about the Facebook threat, right?" I ask Mom.

"Yes," she says. "But I'm not telling you who sent it. For all we know, this is totally unconnected."

"Right," I say. "You're threatened, and then your yard is burned. Unrelated."

Mom whacks the broom over the trash can, and the tinkling sound of glass follows. "They didn't threaten to set anything on fire," Mom says. She's evading, but her eyes cut to Steven, and I gasp.

"They said they were going to hurt Steven!? I'm surprised you didn't—"

"They said if your dad didn't stop defending Lytle, I'd have as many legs left as my cat," Mom blurts, then covers her mouth with a hand. "Don't repeat that."

"Okay, well . . . not to be a jerk, but technically you already *do* have the same amount of legs as your cat."

"Yep," Mom agrees. "Which is why I didn't take it very seriously, and I'm not sure the cops did, either. They know who sent me the message, and they said they will check it out. But I think that person was just letting off some steam."

"You're sure Bristal was fine?" I ask. Mom had driven her home once Bristal was finished giving her statement to the cops about the man she'd chased—and caught, only to get a black eye for her trouble.

"She insisted she was," Mom says, shaking her head. "I can't believe she refused medical attention."

"I'm pretty sure she doesn't have health insurance," I tell Mom, running a finger along the wall. My skin comes away greasy and dark.

"I guessed that might be an issue," Mom says. "I told her we'd pay for everything, but she said she's allergic to charity."

"That sounds about right," I say, and bend to hold the dustpan as Mom pushes glass into it. In my pocket, my phone buzzes with a text from Bristal.

Everything okay over there at Domestic Terrorism Lane?

"I can't tell you how awkward it was taking a girl home and having to explain to her mother why she has a black eye, a gash in her leg, and smells like fire," Mom says.

"How'd that go?" I ask, standing up. I get a good whiff of myself and realize that I'll probably never get the smell of smoke out of my hair, either.

"She didn't even blink," Mom says, shaking her head. "She just asked Bristal what color she wants her stitches to be this time. Then she dug up a sewing kit, and I got out of there."

We're fine, I answer Bristal's text. **But how fucked was that?**

Fucked like the only girl bunny in the garden

"What's so funny?" Mom asks as she dumps the last dustpan full of glass.

"Bristal," I say, waving my phone at her. "Or, you know, it could just be that it's two in the morning and I'm in shock."

"No, she's funny," Mom says, sliding into a chair at the dinner table and resting her chin in her palms. "You shouldn't have been so hard on her about the lighthearted approach she took with her episode."

"Mom," I say sternly. "That's not up for discussion, whether Bristal took a punch for our family or not. This is my future we're talking about, and I can't have it turned into slapstick."

"Have you seen where she lives?" Mom asks.

"Bristal? No, I mean . . . I know it's in Ash Park," I admit.

"Uh-huh," Mom says. "And I just drove back from there. Her sense of humor might just be Bristal Jamison's only coping mechanism, so maybe take that into consideration."

"That and vaping," I mutter as another text from Bristal comes in.

Was that directed at us, or at your dad? Is this about Abe Lytle or Denise Halverson?

I don't know the answer to that, so I take a second before answering, turning my attention back to Mom when she clears her throat. "What?" I ask.

"I know a lot has gone on tonight," she says. "But did you ever actually apologize to Bristal?"

"For?" I ask, glancing down at my phone when it buzzes again. I scroll past the twenty or so texts from MacKenzie. After I'd assured her that I was fine and there was no reason to come over and bring snacks, she'd dropped into a long, rambling stream of texts that I'd stopped reading an hour ago.

My money is on Halverson. The more we learn about this, the worse it looks. 1) She took nothing with her, even though she was supposedly running away.

"For overreacting to her ODOT episode," Mom says. "I take your point about wanting to be looked at as a serious journalist, but you can't deny there was skill involved in what she produced."

"Dick jokes, Mom," I remind her. "She made dick jokes. That's not skill."

2) We can't find any record of Denise being alive today

"There was some low-hanging fruit," Mom admits. "But over-all, that was a clever episode, and very entertaining."

"Entertaining? Really?" I bristle. "If that's all you're looking for, you need to delete your CNN app and download TikTok."

"Well, there's a place in the world for both of those things, isn't there?" Mom says, too brightly for having just had the front of her house blown in. "What's wrong with incorporating different elements in your podcast?"

I consider explaining to Mom about marketing, how I need to brand *On the Ground in Flyover Country*—and myself—in a certain way, make it clear what this platform is and how it will be used. But then I remember that Mom has lived in Henley her whole life and been married to Dad for half of it. Dad had to live up to Grandpa's idea about what being born a Chass means; Mom had to prove that she deserved to marry one—she knows exactly what marketing is. But while she might have a point about my freak-out, I've got a different bone to pick.

"While we're on the topic of Jamisons and Dad isn't around, care to say more about Dover?"

"What?" Mom looks up, eyes suddenly sharp and bright.

"He hung out with Denise, Mom," I tell her, crossing my arms. "Erin told me. So I'm curious about him, and I feel like you're leaving some things out."

"Exactly what am I leaving out?" Mom asks.

"How would I know that?" I ask. "All I know is that you clammed up awfully hard when I dropped his name the other night, and now you're rushing to Bristal's defense and worried about what her mom will think about us. So I'm curious—what was Dover to you, back in high school?"

"A mistake," she says, and I'm alarmed to see tears in her eyes.

"Mom?" I ask, the edge gone from my tone. "What happened?"

"Your dad knows *none* of this," she says sharply, looking up at me.

"Noted," I say, taking my own seat.

"Okay, so," Mom takes a deep breath and swipes tears from her cheeks. "Dover was rough but not unattractive."

I nod, well aware of the fact.

"Pretty hot, actually," Mom says, gaining some steam. "And I'd noticed. So had a couple of other girls and we were curious about him. We'd just read *The Outsiders*, and I got it in my head that he was a roughneck with a heart of gold or something . . . I don't know."

She shakes her head, clearly still pissed at the younger version of herself. "Long story short, I went to a party, got drunk, got flirty with Dover, and woke up minus my virginity—and the guy I'd gone into the bedroom with."

"Mom!" I say, my hand going to my chest. "Did he . . . did he—"

"Rape me? No," she says, shaking her head. "I can't lay that on him, but we definitely had different ideas about what sex meant. I tried to talk to him about it afterward, and he made it clear he had no interest in me past my underwear."

"I'm sorry, Mom," I say, watching her as she bends down to snag Steven from the carpet, cuddling him against her chest.

"How sorry?" Mom asks, eyes sharp as she watches me over

Steven's orange fur. "Because you just interrogated me about one of the most humiliating experiences of my life right after my front window got blown in."

"Mom, I—"

"And I cheated on your dad," she adds, and I realize that the bottle of wine sitting on the counter is probably empty. "So now you know. Congratulations, junior reporter."

"Hey," I say, my own hackles rising. "I didn't ask for you to—"

"And I didn't ask to have my yard set on fire!" Mom suddenly yells, and Steven screeches in her arms, his ears laid back. "You think you're the only one affected by your dad's actions? Or that he's the only person worried about yours? I've got shit coming at me from all sides, because of my husband and my daughter. I can't go buy a goddamn gallon of milk—"

Steven hisses and bats at her face until she releases him. He slides down into her lap, staring up in disbelief at this angel turned demon.

"Nothing happens in this household without one of us paying a price out there," Mom says, waving a hand toward the broken window. "And I mean that quite literally. I hope you took us seriously when we told you to apply for scholarships because—"

She cuts herself off this time, her hand going to her mouth.

"Because what, Mom?"

She shakes her head, but I'm on my feet, my own anger burning.

"Because *what?*"

She looks up at the ceiling, her words so small and lost I can hardly hear them.

"Because we've been living off your college savings for months."

"What?" I ask, my voice creeping up an octave. *"How?"*

"How?" Mom sits up again. "It takes money to live, Lydia, and your father's been slowly leaking clients for years. When he took on Lytle, a lot more bailed. Now we've got a hole in the side of the house, and I don't know if it's because my husband doesn't ask enough questions, or if my daughter won't stop asking them."

"Maybe rethink that," I tell her acidly. "Your daughter asks questions so that she can have a career and make a living. Your daughter asks questions so that she won't have to rely on a man. Your daughter is asking questions so that she won't become a washed-up, worn-out Henley housewife."

That was a lot. That was low. Mom's stare levels with mine, and I'm about to break down and apologize when Dad's car turns into the driveway, the sound of the gravel crunching under the wheels startlingly clear with no glass in the front window, and her gaze goes steely.

"Not. A. Word," she tells me, one finger in the air.

"No," I say, shaking my head. "Don't worry."

It's the closest I can get to an apology right now. My phone vibrates again. I glance at the screen to see two more texts from Bristal.

My money is on the attack tonight being connected to Denise Halverson.

But also, I'm super poor, so I don't have a lot of money.

I grab my phone and leave the room to dial Bristal, ready to tackle at least one of the massive apologies I currently owe.

"Hey," she answers right away. "You didn't have to call, I was just getting my thoughts out."

"And they're interesting," I tell her. "But we didn't really dig all that hard trying to find Denise alive. Just because someone doesn't use social media doesn't mean they're dead."

"Nah," Bristal says, her voice wavery. I wonder if she's self-medicating after the at-home stitching session. "Denise would be on Facebook, throwing down on some Karens."

"You don't know that," I tell her. "If you really want to dive into this, we'll have to have something much more solid than your gut instinct on the internet behavior of someone you've never met."

"I'm down," Bristal says. "Whatever you need me to do. Just don't make me look at microfiche."

"So that would be step one," I say. "Thanks for your help and vested interest."

"No, I mean . . ." Bristal is quiet for a second. "Like, my eyes can't track when the pages are moving, and all that. It gives me a migraine. When I get one I have to lie in the dark for six or seven hours to even be able to function."

"Why didn't you say so?"

"Eh . . . you know, pride. Revealing your weaknesses. All that stuff."

"You are *not* weak," I say automatically, remembering the swollen flesh around her eye, and the blood filling her shoe.

"We still on for Far Cry Road–slash–bigfoot stakeout tomorrow night?"

"Ugh," I say. "Sorry, but I doubt it. Mom and Dad are probably going to have me on lockdown after our front yard turned into a five-alarm." And also, I strong-armed Mom into telling me her deep darks, so there's that, too.

"So?" she says. "Sneak out."

"Ummmm . . ." I glance into the living room, but Mom and Dad are out of sight.

"Seriously?" Bristal says. "You've got a balcony and you've never snuck out? Do you even have a vagina?"

"I have a vagina!" I assert, then check again to make sure nobody is anywhere within hearing distance. Low voices come from the kitchen, and I assume Mom and Dad are having their own hard-truth session.

"What about the interview with Dover?" Bristal comes back at me. "You know you need that material for the tornado episode."

"Ummmm . . . ," I say again. Bristal is smart to dangle the carrot of Dover Jamison in front of me. And while nothing Mom had to say about him was flattering, it didn't dampen my interest in him. If anything, I'm even more invested in this person who treated girls as disposable . . . and then one in his immediate circle disappeared.

"C'mon, Lydia Chlamydia. Go over that balcony!" Bristal's voice sails from the phone, interrupting my thoughts.

"How am I supposed to get down?" I ask.

"I'll catch you."

"That's the dumbest thing I've ever heard," I tell her.

"The dumbest thing I've ever heard is someone having an upstairs and a downstairs living room," Bristal says as I head for my room. Of course she picked up on that.

"Fair," I admit. "But seriously, what if I fall?"

"If you dangle, the drop will only be eight or nine feet. Your driveway has a slight downward angle. Put your car in reverse, but don't start the engine and don't turn the lights on. Make sure you cover the dome light with your hand when you get in. You'll roll all the way down to the road, where you can fire it up and come find me out at Far Cry."

"It's kind of alarming that you already had that figured," I tell her. "But why can't you just come pick me up at the end of the driveway?"

"This is for your own good, Chass," Bristal says. "Be a rebel. Sneak out."

"Fine," I say as I throw myself across my bed. "You've got it. I'll spend the afternoon with my good, nice, kind friend MacKenzie, and then I'll sneak out after dark to a murder location to meet my other friend—you."

"You hanging out with Kenzie tomorrow?" Bristal asks.

"Yeah," I tell her. "She thinks I almost died and is just about losing her mind."

"Cool," Bristal says. "Tell her to say hi to her mom for me."

"What?" I ask.

"She'll know."

TWENTY-FIVE

I glance up as MacKenzie flops onto my bed the next afternoon.

"Bristal told me to say hi to your mom for her," I dutifully relay the message.

"Yeah, she's Bristal's probation officer," MacKenzie says.

"Ohhhhh," I say, putting two and two together—a little slow, I might add. Last night's events might have had more effect than I realize—the fires both inside and out of the house. I'd found a chance to apologize to Mom, but she'd only shaken her head, given me a hug, and told me she *did* want something better for me than what she had—that's what all parents want. It was the perfect apology acceptance, in that it actually made me feel even more guilty.

"Oh my God, I mean really, are you okay, Lydia?" MacKenzie asks. "That was some no-joke, straight-up fire in your yard last night."

"Yeah, six of them," I tell her, tossing my phone aside.

"It was all over social media," she tells me. "Liz Dayforth did not waste a second getting her pics up."

"I know," I say. "She had her phone out and was taking video before she even checked to see if we were okay. The firefighters had to ask her to move twice."

"Nice neighbor," MacKenzie says, rubbing her arms as goose bumps pop up. It got down to twenty by the middle of the night last night, and Dad says there's no point running the heater with the living room standing wide open and facing north. The tarp Dad taped over the gaping hole sucks and pulls with the draft every time anybody opens a door.

"So, really, you're okay? Like, everything's fine? You sure you don't want to come stay with us for a little while? Mom said you could," MacKenzie says.

"I know, Dad said you guys offered—and thank you, but no. I'm not going to be chased out of my own house."

"I figured you'd say that." MacKenzie sighs and gets off the bed, pulling aside the curtain on the balcony door. I know what she sees without joining her: crime scene tape draped from tree to tree circling the front yard, six burned stop signs, dark circles of singed grass surrounding them.

"Why aren't they gone yet?" MacKenzie asks, letting the curtain fall closed. "I mean, sorry, but they're kinda creepy."

"They're doing an investigation," I say. "The cops don't want anybody touching the signs or whatever. I guess they're bringing in an arson guy from upstate."

"Can fingerprints survive fire?" MacKenzie asks.

"I seriously doubt it," I tell her. "But they can probably identify the accelerant, and that could help lead to whoever did this."

MacKenzie takes a deep breath and gives me a hard stare.

"What?" I ask.

"I'm going to say something you're not going to like," she says.

"Is this about *Hamilton* again? Because you've never even listened—"

"No," MacKenzie says sharply. "It's about . . . Jesus, seriously? You don't see it? You're Lydia Chass and you can't figure this out?"

"Can't figure what out?" I ask.

"Who did this!" MacKenzie says, waving out the balcony. "I mean, Mom made one phone call and—"

"To who?" I demand, getting to my feet. "What did she find out?"

"That six stop signs were taken out of the ODOT garage last week. Know anybody that has connections there?"

"You're not serious," I say, ignoring the gaping hole that has just opened in my midsection and swallowed my heart. "Bristal would never—"

"Oh, of course!" MacKenzie yells, throwing her arms into the air. "Your best friend Bristal, who you've known for about a month and has a rap sheet, by the way."

"Your mom shouldn't tell you her parolees—"

"Screw that!" she says, kicking my bed. "Oh God." Her face contorts, and MacKenzie goes down. "I think I just broke my toe."

I watch her cradle her foot, then rock back and forth over it,

217

mewling like a kitten. In third grade, she had insisted on being driven to the emergency room for a thorn in her foot, so I'm not too concerned. MacKenzie's pain tolerance is about as high as an unconscious ant.

"You're fine," I say, but I join her on the floor and stick a sequined pillow under her foot.

"Sorry about kicking your bed," MacKenzie, says palming tears off her red face.

"It's okay. Karma caught up fast," I tell her. "Better?"

"Yes." She nods, dead serious. "The sequins helped."

"Look," I say, leaning back against my bed. "What you're saying about Bristal makes sense, okay? I see it. She's a career criminal, and she had access to the signs. But there's no motive."

"What do you mean?"

"No reason for her to have done it," I explain.

"I know what motive is, jackhole," MacKenzie says. "I mean more, like, how do you not see the motive? Your parents are singing her praises all over town. Badass Bristal jumped out the window and chased down the person who threatened your family. She's a hero—"

"Heroine," I correct.

"And she's got one of the best families around eating out of her hand."

"But you said it yourself," I counter. "She chased down whoever did it—and got her ass handed to her. Bristal's eye was swollen shut, and that gash on her cheek was no joke."

But MacKenzie shakes her head. "Bristal doles out and takes

beatings all the time. She had to make it look legit, and she knew exactly how."

"I don't buy it," I say, getting up from the floor and looking out the window myself, taking in the six dark sentinels now standing in our yard, the yellow crime tape twisting in the breeze.

"Why not?" MacKenzie asks, wincing as she puts weight on her foot and joins me.

"Because I . . ." My voice fades out, catching in my throat. "Because I just don't think Bristal would do that to me, okay?"

"Wow," MacKenzie says. "I never thought I'd say this in my life."

"Say what?"

"Lydia Chass, you're being stupid."

TWENTY-SIX

Bristal's escape plan works perfectly. I land in a crouch on our front porch, the tarp covering what used to be our bay window billowing in the breeze. It's chilly, and past midnight, Mom and Dad turned in a long time ago, and the Dayforths' motion-sensor light points in the other direction—toward the neighbors they trust less, I assume. I pick my way over the gravel to my car and ease the door open, covering the overhead light with my hand, like Bristal had said. I ease the transmission into reverse, and my car begins a slow roll to the end of the driveway.

I turn on the engine and my headlights illuminate South Lincoln Street, empty except for an orange tabby cat that slinks across the road, giving me a hard glare as I slide past it. As much as I don't like MacKenzie's theory about Bristal being involved with what happened last night, she has some good points. The ODOT connection is glaring, but what I had said to MacKenzie still holds true; Bristal doesn't stand to gain anything from it. Sure, Mom and Dad are saying nice things about her, but it's not like they bought her a car, or tried to adopt her.

Still, she had made that comment about the extra bedroom with the silver tea set, and building a connection with a family she perceives to have money certainly wouldn't hurt her cause in any way. I shake my head, turning on my signal at the intersection, even though there's no one to witness me going left. I could ignore all the signage outside of town and drive as fast as I want. There's no one out here. No one for me to hit, and no one to see me speeding, the farther I head out of town and the closer I get to Far Cry Road.

My mind continues to cycle, gnawing on the problem that MacKenzie had dropped in my lap. If Bristal hadn't set the fires, then who had? Dad had been on the phone all day today, working from home and refusing to go into the office until we knew who was responsible for it. The sheriff had come by, and a guy who is going to replace the window had come and taken measurements. There had been a lot of murmured conversations, as Dad tried to keep gossip from rising through the radiators of our old house and reaching my bedroom.

But I still heard things.

Josephine Walters wasn't the only person who connected the dots and figured out where the signs had come from. All the county employees at ODOT had been questioned, but they don't have security on their buildings, and nobody was particularly surprised to learn that they don't lock their doors, either. It's Henley, and quite frankly, no one had ever seen a reason to. They knew that Helen Gurtz occasionally snuck in and scooped some of the road salt for her front walk, but when a report came out that regular road salt was abrasive to cat's paws, she'd gone the noble route and started buying kitty-safe salt.

The truth was that everybody had an idea about who might have done it, but nobody had any proof. While I'd shut down commenting for *On the Ground in Flyover Country*, there was nothing I could do about the Block Watch page on Facebook, other than choose to not expose myself to it.

I turn right onto Far Cry Road, dimming my lights as I slip past the few houses that are out here. There's an old homestead with a crumbling barn in the back. The moon is bright enough that I can see the construction year, fashioned in slate tiles across the roof—1889. The other houses I pass are trailers, one surrounded by a dog fence that hangs heavy with signs warning off intruders, trespassers, and liberals. I spot Bristal's Neon tucked into an overgrown turnaround, and I pull in beside her.

"Dear God, she actually did it," Bristal says when I open her passenger door, releasing a cloud of vapor. "Lydia Chass, breaking the law."

"I'm not breaking any law," I inform her. "I'm eighteen and have all the rights and freedoms of an adult."

I wish I could say that Bristal wasn't breaking any laws, either, but the open container by her gearshift says otherwise.

"Aren't you on probation?" I ask her. "What are you thinking?"

"I *am* thinking," she contradicts me. "It's a Friday night, I'm

222

gonna catch bigfoot, and not to hurt your feelings or anything, but my leg hurts like a fucker on fire. So instead of lighting up, or popping an Oxy, I'm doing the intelligent thing and indulging in some underage drinking. Won't show up on a piss test."

"You were smoking weed the other day before we interviewed Bailey Foxglove," I point out.

"Yeah, but"—she exhales, and I roll down my window—"my piss tests are at the end of the month, and Jo-Jo has never hit me with a surprise one."

"Jo-Jo? Oh, never mind," I say.

Of course Bristal would have an affectionate nickname for her probation officer. She turns her head, and for the first time I get a good look at her black eye. But *black* isn't the word—it's a deep purple, the swelling pushing the soft skin under her eye into a glistening bulge. It's hard to look at, and I turn away, knowing she caught that punch on my account.

"How's your leg?" I ask.

"Decent," Bristal says, stiffly pulling her left leg up and propping it on the dashboard, then rolling the cuffs of her jeans so that I can see the gash, neatly stitched with purple thread—as promised.

"Your mom did a good job," I tell her. "Those are nice and even."

"She's got enough practice," Bristal says, pointing to another scar on her leg, then shoving her sweatshirt sleeve up and showing me a third on the inside of her upper arm. "I kind of attract trouble."

"Yeah," I say, not wanting to follow that particular line of conversation any further. The question of whether Bristal attracts trouble—or wholeheartedly throws herself into its path—isn't one I want to consider, given MacKenzie's suspicions.

"Hey, so, seriously, about that—"

"I don't want to talk about it," I say stiffly.

There's a moment of quiet as Bristal lifts her beer and takes a swig. Staring down into the can, she says, "You still pissed at me?"

"Pissed at you?"

"About the podcast?"

"What—oh . . ."

"'Cause I am sorry, okay? I was trying to help, in my own way—which I know probably isn't always the best way. You said your mom and dad were all upset about the first episode catching so much flack, and all the aggressive weirdos in the comments. I just thought, *Hey, I'll do something stupid and have fun at the same time, and maybe they'll get off your back.*"

"No, it's . . . look, I actually think I'm the one who should be apologizing."

"Oh?" Bristal's voice for once isn't thick with sarcasm, or feigned innocence. She's truly surprised.

"You did something creative, and funny, and you did it your way. I shouldn't have yelled at you."

"That was yelling?" she asks.

"In the Chass household, it qualifies," I tell her.

"Lightweights," she says under her breath. Then, "So we're cool?"

"Yeah, we're cool," I tell her, meaning it. Unless, of course, it turns out she was involved in torching my yard.

"Fuck," I say, and impulsively grab her beer, taking a deep swig.

"Whoa, hey, slow down, Drinky Drinkerton, that's spiked with Jack."

"With what?" I cough, holding the beer can out to take a look at it. It's off-brand and super cheap, and while it had tasted like water, it burned going down.

"Mr. Jack Daniel's," Bristal explains. "Friend to you and me, and extra-close confidant of our guidance counselor, who we have to thank for being out here in the first place."

"Amen," I say, raising the can and finishing it off. "Do you have more?" I ask, turning in my seat to check out the back of Bristal's car, my head pleasantly humming.

"Yes, but I'm cutting you off," Bristal says firmly. "I'm not assisting in your first-ever home escape only to have you crash into pots and pans and puke all over the place as soon as you try to get back inside."

"Thanks," I say, clapping a hand onto her shoulder. "See? You're a good person. I knew it."

Bristal snorts. "I'm the best fucking person."

"Maybe," I say, lifting a finger in the air. It wobbles more than I'd like it to, so I hold on to my wrist with the other hand to keep it steady. "But you were totally making fun of me reading off the Civil War dead when you identified roadkill."

"Heh, yeah," she says, smiling. "That was a direct hit. But it was damn funny, and people liked it."

"People like *me*!" I insist. "Are you sure you don't have more beer?"

"One more for you," she says, reaching into the back seat. "There's no Jack in this one, and if you puke in my car, I'm leaving you in a ditch, bigfoot or no bigfoot."

"Why would I pee in your car?" I ask, snapping the can open.

"*Puke* in my car," Bristal corrects, grabbing a can for herself. "And if you pee in my car, you can forget the ditch. I'll just leave you in the road."

"No, you wouldn't. You like me," I argue, which brings me back to my thought from a second ago. "People like me."

"Adults like you," she says, downing half her beer in a gulp. "With the under-thirty crowd you're highly suspect."

"Pfffffttt . . . ," I say, which has never struck me as a good counterargument before, but seems to be all-inclusive and damning in the moment.

"Did you see our stats?" Bristal asks, pulling out her phone. "Our downloads for the last episode were high."

Bristal turns her phone so I can see. We've got over two thousand downloads for that ep alone, and the numbers for episode one are ticking upward as well, the newer airing pulling in listens for the backlist.

"I want to turn the comments back on," Bristal says. "Yeah, it can get nasty, but people are talking, and if they aren't talking on our platform, they'll do it on someone else's. Things could get missed."

I consider it for a moment, letting her words process through the growing haze in my mind. "You're not wrong," I tell her. "Even just alluding to Denise in the first episode drew comments. People remember her, even if they don't want to admit it."

"Right," Bristal agrees. "And the more people get chatty, the more clues we can catch."

"I know, but Mom and Dad would flip if I turn commenting back on."

"What's the whole thing you just said about being eighteen and having the rights and privileges of—"

"I still need them to pay for my college," I shoot back, the words seeping out even though they might no longer be capable of such a thing.

"Wow, talk about privilege."

"Besides, I'd rather get information from a source that actually knew Denise, like when we talk to your uncle. Picking through online arguments and trying to infer who is blowing steam and who actually knows something valuable feels a little pointless if we can just straight-up ask Dover."

I don't mention that the interview is going to go a lot deeper—and get a lot darker—than that.

"Okay, I'll let it slide for now," Bristal says, resting her phone on her leg as she takes another drag from her vape pen. "But if Dover's a dud, I'm revisiting the subject. So tomorrow is a go?"

"Yeah," I tell her, trying to take another drink of beer, but misjudging the distance to my mouth and dumping some on my chin instead. "I talked MacKenzie into picking me up and claiming we're going shopping. We'll meet up with you and go on to the prison."

"That's a good friend." Bristal nods.

"Mostly she's convinced you're going to kill me," I admit.

"Even better friend, then, if she's willing to take the risk on your behalf," Bristal says. "How's the tornado episode coming along?"

"Okay." I sigh, rolling down my window all the way and hanging one wrist limply out of it. "There's just a ton of material, and I've got to sift through it all. Talking to Dover is the last thing on my list. We've got that video of him from the day after the tornado, and I think it's a good way to start the conversation with him, move on to Denise from there."

"Yeah, the 'at least I didn't get hurt' video," she says, still clearly impressed by her uncle's nonchalance about his own injuries. Given the line of purple x's marching down her calf right now, I can see that the apple doesn't fall far from that particular family tree.

"Which reminds me . . ." She reaches into the back again, pulling her backpack up to the front. "Despite the steel-bear-trap, crystal clear clarity of my memory, I did actually take notes when I talked to everyone out here on Far Cry about Randall Boggs. When I told them we were working on a podcast about the long stretch, they all wanted to share their tornado story."

"Of course they did," I say, leaning my head back against the head rest, which promptly falls off and lands in the back seat. "I think I broke your car."

"My car's fine," Bristal says, waving it off as she digs in her backpack, producing a yellow legal pad. The first four pages are filled with her writing, precise and neat, running margin to margin. She hands it over to me, and I flip through. The dates, times, and locations of the people she'd spoken to are all recorded, along with some direct quotes.

"Nice work," I tell her, impressed.

"I know everybody's got a tornado story," Bristal goes on. "But the people out here on Far Cry have a different perspective. They weren't actually in it, but they watched it go through town, had people's stuff falling out of the sky and landing in their yards. Every single person out here wanted to tell me about their dogs, too."

"Their dogs?" I ask, looking up from the paper.

"Yeah, you know how they say animals know when a storm is coming? They act funny, or whatever?"

"I've heard stories like that," I say. "Something like they can feel the barometer pressure more keenly than humans can."

"It's definitely a thing," Bristal says. "But people in town had a more immediate experience of the tornado. What they remember is buildings coming down, cars flying through the air, toppled poles and lost people. Out here, they didn't get that, so the smaller details stand out."

She reaches out and taps the yellow pages of the legal pad. "Every single one of these people out here on Far Cry wanted to tell me about their dogs losing their damn minds right before the tornado came through."

"Huh," I say, lifting the pages to scan them. "That could be interesting."

"I thought so, maybe," Bristal says, pulling off her vape pen again. "Different angle."

"Hey, can I try that?" I ask, eyeing her pen.

"Nope," she says, shaking her head. "Shit's expensive. And all the gas stations got it locked up tight, so I can't lift it. Just bum some cigs off your mom."

"For the last time," I say, letting the pages fan back into place. "My mom doesn't smoke."

"Uh-huh," Bristal says, picking up her phone.

Mine vibrates, and I reach for it only to see a text from Bristal—the picture of my mom smoking.

"Whatever," I say, about to rattle off a nasty reply when I stop, my unfocused eyes seeing something for the first time.

"Bristal," I say, my voice tremulous and wavy, the cool air of the night slipping into the car and raising goose bumps on my skin, "my mom doesn't smoke," I say.

"You do stick to your guns, I'll give you—"

"No, look." I pick up my phone and zoom in on the picture: the girl with dark hair, the black hole of her mouth, the stream of smoke exiting it . . . and the barely discernable blue flowers on her shirt.

"My mom doesn't smoke," I repeat, holding the phone out to Bristal.

"But Denise Halverson did."

TWENTY-SEVEN

"Holy. Fuckin'. Hell."

Bristal stares at the picture, vapor escaping her mouth as she moves the phone first one way, then another, trying to change the clarity of a thirty-year-old photo when she can only see out of one eye. "Hold on," she says, grabbing her phone and flipping through her pics to find the original.

I take my phone back, staring at the smoking girl, who is staring back at me.

"Okay," Bristal says, widening the screen on the original photo she took of David Swinton's pictures. "Here's the whole thing, not cropped."

The girl is tall and slim, with loose black hair. Her right arm is bent at the elbow, holding the cigarette away from her body in the relaxed posture of a seasoned smoker. The trio is too far away to make out much more, but I can identify my dad, even in profile. I'd simply made the assumption—as had David Swinton—that the girl standing with him was my mom. They'd been a couple all through high school, and Denise Halverson was built like my mom, with the same hair color.

"Did your dad say anything about knowing Denise Halverson?" Bristal asks, cutting straight to the point.

"No," I say, the single word coming out reluctantly. "He never mentioned her."

"But he knew you were looking into her disappearance?"

"Yes, I mean . . . we never talked about her specifically. Mom and Dad were both upset about the podcast in general, and how explosive the comments got."

"Which was because of Denise," Bristal says, but for the first time, I poke back.

"Not necessarily," I tell her, still gazing at the picture, zooming in and out and taking in all three of the teens standing in a group next to the railroad tracks. "People were upset about me describing the Lytles as a military family, and of course just having a feminist view overall."

"Right, but . . ."

I trail my finger over the screen, lingering for a moment on the third party of the trio. I'd never taken a closer look after identifying my dad and who I thought was my mom, tucking the picture away as an interesting piece of nostalgia, squarely placing my parents—teenagers themselves at the time—in the path of destruction.

Now, though, this picture has taken on an all-new meaning. And a very sinister one.

"Bristal," I say, zooming in on the third person in the picture and handing it over to her. He's tall and lean, tanned arms hanging loosely from a white tank top and low-slung blue jeans.

"Shit," she says. "That's Dover."

"It is," I admit. "But we already knew that Denise and Dover hung out, so it's not that big of a deal that he's there."

"Right," she agrees. "It's your dad that's the weirdo third wheel. I mean, we could play one of these things does not belong, but I can't carry a tune real well and I'm guessing you already know the answer."

I don't say anything but start frantically scrolling through my phone. "Swinton wrote something on the back of that photo, the date it was taken and the location. Did you happen to—?"

Bristal hands over her phone, David's neat, heavy hand fills the screen.

June 11, 1994, Henley, Ohio N/S Railroad Tracks, Sweet Corn Festival

"Two days before the tornado went through," I say aloud.

"And the day Denise went out the window," Bristal adds. "She's technically a missing person in this photo."

We're quiet for a second, each of us staring at our phones, and the blurry face of a girl with black hair, wearing blue roses.

"You realize this is probably the last time anyone saw her, right?" Bristal says.

"Yeah," I say, my hand tightening on my phone. "I get that."

"And one of the last people to see her was your dad," she adds.

"And your uncle," I tack on, a little too quickly. "If we're going to start pointing fingers—"

"No," Bristal says, waving her hand and shooing the last ribbons of smoke from the car. "I'm not pointing at anybody—yet. All I'm saying is that your dad knew that even the mention of her name was getting people's hair up all over town, and here we have a picture of him talking to her, after she'd supposedly ran away. It's just—sorry—but it's weird that he wouldn't have said anything."

"Maybe," I say. "But then again maybe not. This picture was taken during the Sweet Corn Festival. It's a big event, everyone is there. And it's Henley, everyone knows everyone. I don't think it's that weird that some teens from the same class would stop and say hi to each other."

"Would you stop and talk to me, before we were doing this podcast together?" Bristal asks, flipping her phone around so I can see the picture again.

I sigh, the happy, fuzzy edges of the buzz that I'd been working on filtering out into the cool night air. "I don't know why my dad is talking to Denise, and I don't know why he wouldn't mention it to me, okay? But you have to admit that it's totally possible that this is just three teenagers who happened to bump into each other."

"And then one of them fell off the face of the planet," Bristal adds.

"He might not even remember this conversation," I say, raising my phone but not able to drop my point.

"Only way to find out is to ask him," she says quietly.

"I'll find a way to do that, good idea," I snap. "Should I wedge it in there before I tell him that I snuck out to try to catch bigfoot after someone targeted our home, or make sure I ask him about his connection to a missing girl after—"

A scream rips through the night, rising and falling, overriding my words.

"Oh God!! Oh my Gooooooooood!"

Everything I have contracts. My hand tightens on my phone, my arms and legs pull into the fetal position, and I swear it feels like every cell inside of me grabs the one next to it, holding on in fear. Bristal, on the other hand, leaps out of her car.

"What are you doing?" I whisper-scream after her, just as the scream comes again.

"Oh God!! Oh my Gooooooooood!"

My hair is standing on end, goose bumps like an army of sentinels marching across my skin. My numb fingers fumble with my phone. "I'm calling nine-one-one," I announce.

"Don't be a fucking idiot," Bristal says, then opens my door and jerks me out into the night. I yelp, dropping my phone, then scrambling after it.

"You don't need to call nine-one-one," Bristal says, hauling me up by the shoulder.

"Oh God!! Oh my Gooooooooood!"

"What the hell are you talking about?" I ask, arms wrapped protectively around myself as she sits on the hood of her car. "Someone is screaming for help!"

"They're not," Bristal says calmly, nodding her head toward the strip of woods that follows the line of the stream through the fields. "Listen."

"Oh God!! Oh my Goooooooooood!"

"Screaming for help from God still counts," I say, but Bristal only shakes her head.

"C'mere, and calm down," she says, patting the hood of the car next to her. I reluctantly do as I'm told, the heat from the cooling motor seeping through my jeans.

"Listen," she says calmly.

"I've heard it enough—"

"No, listen to everything else. What do you hear?"

I go quiet, aware that I'm not going to get anything out of Bristal until I play along. "Crickets," I say. "Some insects."

A high trill joins the insect hum, and Bristal lifts a finger. "That's a screech owl."

"Cool, thanks. It's good to have identified the last thing I'll hear before I'm murdered."

"You're not getting murdered—well, at least not tonight," Bristal says. "My point is this; you can hear insects, and an owl, because they're all just chilling out and doing their night business."

"Oh God!! Oh my Goooooooooood!"

"Shit!" I yelp, and grab Bristal's arm, the cry all the more terrifying now that I'm not inside the car. "I don't care about nocturnal animal business, I want to go—"

"They're still doing it," Bristal says calmly. "Listen. The insects, the frogs, the owl . . . they're still doing their thing. They're not scared of that noise, because it's something they're accustomed to."

"If you bring up bigfoot, I swear, I am knocking you over and taking your keys."

"Good luck," she says. "Besides, keys are in the ignition. And no, it's not bigfoot. That's a fox. A female fox."

"It's not," I say firmly. "They don't speak English."

"It's not *saying* anything," she tells me. "You know how if you close your eyes you start to see shapes in the dark?"

"Yes," I say. "MacKenzie had this whole thing in sixth grade where she was certain her dead grandma was trying to material-ize in her bedroom every night, and I had to explain to her how our brains are constantly working, looking for familiar patterns to identify, even if there's nothing actually there."

"Exactly," Bristal says. "That fox isn't calling out to God . . . unless she landed a really awesome mate this time around."

"Gross," I say, letting go of her arm and wrapping myself in my jacket as the breeze kicks up.

"Not gross—nature," Bristal says. "And that's precisely what I'm pointing to. There's not someone out there yelling for help. Animals get real quiet around humans. Sadly, I have to admit that it's probably not a bigfoot, either, because I think they'd shut that shit down for him, too."

"I'm sorry all your hopes of bigfoot have been dashed," I tell her, a chill tripping down my spine as the call comes again.

But Bristal is right; without my brain attempting to force the sound into human words, it doesn't sound like a person screaming for help. It comes again, and with the layer of fear removed, I can make more observations.

"It's the same every time, too," I tell her. "If it was someone who actually needed help they wouldn't yell the same thing, over and over, at the same volume."

"'Specially if they're bleeding out," she says helpfully. "You'd get quieter, real fast."

"Beautiful," I tell her. "So what was the whole point of this?"

"I just wanted to bring you out here," Bristal says. "This lot that we're sitting in is where Randall Boggs's trailer used to be. The neighbors"—she points to the three houses I had passed—"are all the same people that lived here back in the nineties. Things don't change out here."

"Yeah," I say, my eyes wandering to the dark outline of the barn built in 1889, in the distance—but far away. "Somebody could've taken their time with Boggs and nobody would've known."

It's a depressing thought, that an old man had died out here—slowly. Even if neighbors had heard his cries they might have dismissed it for the lonely calls that sound like a plea for help, coming all too perfectly from a place called Far Cry Road.

"So what's the plan for tomorrow?" Bristal asks as I slip Bristal's neatly lined notepad into my pack.

"Our meeting time with Dover is at eleven, right?" I ask, and she nods. "Nearly an hour to drive to the prison . . . so, we'll pick up you up at nine thirty?"

"So MacKenzie is really driving us?" Bristal asks, flopping into the driver's seat. "I can't vape in front of Jo-Jo's Mac-Mac; she'll rat me out."

"Probably," I tell her, slamming the passenger door shut. "So maybe just don't do it."

Bristal considers this for a second. "Do you think if I told her I'd kill her for squealing she'd believe me?"

"Yes," I say, getting into my own car. "And then she'd report it to her mom, and you'd be in even more trouble."

"Ugh!" Bristal punches the roof of her car, making the plastic protector of the dome light fall off. "I get grumpy when I can't vape."

"I consider myself warned," I tell her, turning on my car and cranking the heat. I roll down the window for my parting blow.

"But you still have to be nice to MacKenzie!"

TWENTY-EIGHT

Asking Bristal to be nice to MacKenzie is one thing, but asking MacKenzie to be nice to Bristal is another.

"I just need you to keep it civil," I tell her as I strap on my seat belt. "I'm not asking you to be her best friend."

"Well, I think that position is taken already," Kenzie snorts as she backs out of my driveway.

I ignore the jab and chalk it up to jealousy. Between the podcast, avoiding flying bricks in my living room, and trying to keep my GPA above a 4.0, I haven't had a lot of time to do things with MacKenzie. I've known her my whole life, so I'm prepared for the passive-aggressive fog that's going to settle over this entire day.

I just don't know how Bristal is going to take it.

"You know what he's in for, right?" MacKenzie asks, eyes fixed on the road, a small muscle at the edge of her jaw jumping in anger. I glance up from my phone and a text from Bristal letting us know to pick her up at the library.

"Who's in for what?" I ask. "And you'll need to turn around. Bristal said to meet her at the library."

MacKenzie heaves a huge sigh and does an illegal U-turn at the end of Lincoln. "Probably she doesn't want me to see which trailer she actually lives in, so I can't tell Mom next time she has to issue a summons. And you know damn well what I meant—Dover Jamison is in prison for beating the shit out of his ex-girlfriend."

"Ah . . . ," I say, letting my phone slide back into my lap. It's another weight on Dover Jamison's scale of judgment in my mind—and it's not currently tilted in a positive direction.

Bristal is leaning against her car, vape pen in hand, casually blowing smoke into a gathering cloud above her head when we pull in next to her.

I roll down my window. "Hey."

"Hey," she says, giving me an up-nod and leaning over to glance at MacKenzie, who stares pointedly forward. Bristal gives me a small smirk and then climbs into the back seat.

"You can't smoke in here," Kenzie says automatically, glancing up into her rearview mirror. "My mom would kill me."

"Incorrect," Bristal says. "I don't think your mom would kill anybody. But I bet you are high on the list, if she has one."

"Do you have any questions for Dover?" I ask loudly, hoping to change the subject as we leave Henley behind. It's a forty-five-minute drive to the prison, but it's going to feel a heck of a lot longer than that if these two are going at each other the whole time.

"Not really," Bristal says. "Hey, can we swing by the gas station? I need to steal a few things."

MacKenzie doesn't bother replying, just turns on her signal and pulls onto the highway, grinding her teeth.

I turn in my seat and give Bristal a glare. "Be nice," I hiss.

"Yeah, Jo-Jo said I'm supposed to be working on that," she says. "Hey, Mac-Mac, do you have child locks on?"

"Yes," MacKenzie says. "And how did you figure that out? Did you—did you seriously try to open your door on the highway?"

"I wouldn't call it *opening the door*. More like *performing an experiment*."

"With physics? And your body? As we go down the highway at eighty miles per hour?"

"If you're going eighty, then we're speeding," Bristal says calmly.

"OH MY GOD," I scream, and turn up the music very loud. I can't stop this war; but I'm done participating in it. As we fly past another semi I glance at the speedometer to see that MacKenzie isn't going eighty; she's going eighty-five. But I'm not about to point it out.

The sooner this car ride is over, the better.

When we pull into the prison parking lot, MacKenzie takes one look at the armed guard patrolling the door marked VISITORS and says she's decided to stay in the car.

"It's too cold," I tell her. "And besides, you don't have to come all the way back with us. We have to go through security and everything. You can just wait outside of that. It's not that different from the airport."

"Except for the high percentage of murderers in the population," Bristal adds.

"I'll keep the car on and run the heat," MacKenzie says. "I'd rather stay out here."

"Whatever makes you comfortable," I tell her. "And seriously, thanks for driving us."

MacKenzie narrows her eyes at me and says, "You're just making sure I'm still here when you come back out."

"Maybe," I admit. "But also I'm confident Uber is pretty familiar with this place as a pickup location. So we'll manage if you ditch us."

"Whatever," she says, and rolls her eyes. But there's a smile curving at the edge of her lips as I get out of the car. It disappears fast when Bristal starts banging on her back seat window.

"You need to let me out!" she screams—way more loudly than necessary. "Child locks!"

I open the door for her, and she gets out, giving Kenzie a wave as she pulls away to find a spot. We show our IDs to the guard at the door, who checks them against a visitors' list for the day. We're led into a small room lined with lockers and told to put all our stuff in them.

"I can't take anything?" I ask the guard. "Paper? Pencil? Pen? Phone?"

All I get is a headshake for every noun I produce, so I toss everything in a locker, and Bristal's stuff follows suit.

"You could've warned me," I say as I take a seat next to her on a wooden bench. Other families wander in, everyone signing off on the clipboard and choosing a locker for their things.

"You'll just have to take notes the way I do," she says, pointing to her temple. "Between the two of us, I'm sure we can catch everything."

I'm not worried about catching everything as much as I am about misinterpreting it—or misremembering. I haven't cleared all my questions with Bristal; she's mostly here to get me access to Dover. Once I start drilling down on some of my points, I might have two Jamisons pissed at me.

"How much talking are you doing, and how much am I doing?" Bristal asks.

It's a good question. I need her to warm him up, but I also need her to back down once it's my turn to take over.

"What all does he know about why we're here?" I ask.

"I told him that I was doing a podcast for a history credit and that we wanted to ask him some questions about the tornado, but that's really it. I figured you'd want me to talk first, get him comfortable."

"Yes," I say, relieved. "Exactly."

"But," she goes on, "I will tell you that he can get squirrely sometimes. Don't expect a lot out of him about Denise Halverson."

"What do you mean?"

"Sometimes my dad will talk to him on the phone, and he'll ask him, like, where this old shotgun of his grandpa's is, or something like that, and Dover will tell him he can't really answer that without talking to his lawyer first."

"Why would that—"

"Unregistered gun," Bristal says. "Dover might be in jail, but he's not stupid. He keeps his mouth shut about just about everything, and if he catches even a whiff of something that could lengthen his sentence, he says he has to talk to his lawyer first."

"What's he in for?" I ask, popping the question that I already know the answer to.

"Various things, some drug charges," Bristal says nonchalantly.

"Various like what?" I ask, pushing.

"Uh, menacing, I think. Aggravated assault for sure," Bristal says, walking along beside me as we come into a room that looks like it doubles as a cafeteria, complete with vending machines.

My blood pressure spikes, and black spots swim in my vision, my hand clutching convulsively as it looks for the comfort of a pen, or a notebook to squeeze. I was expecting booths and bulletproof glass lined with chicken wire, old corded phones hanging in each one. I didn't think I'd come to prison and have snack time with a felon sitting right across from me. I'm so frozen Bristal has to propel me to the table with the plastic number seven on it when the last name of Jamison is called.

"Aggravated assault?" I ask, my tongue thick on my dry lips. "How is that different from regular assault?"

"It's the level of intent of harm meant for the victim," Bristal says. "But it totally needs to be renamed because I've never committed an assault where I wasn't aggravated first. There he is!"

Bristal stands and waves as Dover comes into the room, and my heart rate picks up yet another notch. He's not handcuffed.

He's not even wearing prison orange. Dover Jamison walks over and gives his niece a hug wearing a navy-blue T-shirt and a pair of gray sweatpants. He looks like a dad on a lazy Saturday. Actually, he looks like a hot uncle on an off weekend and I need to get my crap together. Thirty years ago he made a grown woman blush on camera, and he was the first person to separate my mom's ass from her underwear. I'm eighteen and not immune, but I promise myself that smile isn't going to have an effect on me.

"Bristal," he says, stepping back from his niece and giving her a once-over. He spots the black eye right away, touching the same spot on his face. "What's the other guy look like?"

"We all wish we knew," Bristal says, shooting a glance at me as they take a seat at the table. "He didn't give me his name before he ran off after throwing a brick through my friend's front window. Dover, this is Lydia Chass. She's the one I'm doing the podcast with."

"Nice to meet you," I say, offering my hand across the table. Dover takes it, shakes it once, and pulls away. His skin is warm and dry, his eyes hard on mine.

"Lydia Chass," he says, like he's tasting the name. "Your dad Brent?"

"Yes," I say. "Do you know him? Wait, you graduated together, right?"

It's the dumbest thing in the world to say. Of course they know each other; it's Henley. But also, I know Dover never graduated, because Bristal is doing this podcast with me specifically so that she can be the first person in her family to do so.

"Sure, I know him," Dover says. "Class of '94."

It's a kindness to me, and a smart move for him. He's not claiming he graduated, and he's not making me feel stupid. It almost makes me feel bad for the bomb I'm about to drop on him. Almost. That smile might be smooth, and his skin might be warm, but there are teeth behind those lips, and that hand has made a fist more than once.

"We saw you were interviewed about the tornado," Bristal jumps in. "So we thought it might be good to talk to you about that day."

"Sure," he says, nodding. "Not something you forget."

"Great," I say, regaining my composure and leaning forward. "You said in your interview then that you were staying with some relatives in town, right?"

"Yep," he says. "It was so hot you'd see fire hydrants chasing dogs, trying to get them to piss on 'em."

Bristal laughs, but I just offer the polite smile that I've tested out over years of Mrs. Nathans's jokes during blood drive meetings.

"So yeah, I went into town. Had an aunt with air-conditioning. She suddenly had a lot of family members that liked her."

"It looked like you were hurt, in the video," I continue. "Can I ask what happened?"

"Sure." Dover nods. "I was helping clear some of the rubble where the old hotel came down, the Fairlawn. The one wall had gone over, and they'd cleared us to start cleaning up that area. Pretty much everybody brought in their own wheelbarrows, chain saws, that kind of stuff. I thought I'd be smart and work over in the shade of the wall that was still standing, but it wasn't super stable. One of them bricks came down, hit me *bam*, right on the head."

He slaps his hands together, bringing attention from everyone in the room. A female guard gives him a small headshake, but the lesson is delivered with a smile and a wink. I want to tell her to take them back. I want to remind her that the reason he's here is because he hits women.

"Anyway," Dover says. "That set me back a bit."

"Not much, though," Bristal says, her pride in him showing. "In the video you're all like—well, at least I didn't get hurt."

"Not by the tornado, nope," he agrees, smiling.

"You lived out on Far Cry Road at the time, is that right?" I ask, starting to slip the wedge in, knowing that it might turn around to be jammed between my teeth.

"Yeah, Far Cry. Hell of a place to grow up. Me and your dad had some fun out there."

I'm still for a second, wondering if he's talking about Bristal's dad—whoever that might be. But he's looking right at me, and I'm blank. I clear my throat.

"My dad?"

"Yeah, your dad," he says, pointing his finger at me to add clarification. "His grandpa used to bring him out there to fish. The Chasses own most of the land out by Far Cry, you know that, right?"

I didn't know that, but I don't want to look like I didn't know that. Also, judging by Mom's comment the other night, I'm pretty sure we don't own most of anything anymore.

"So you two went fishing together when you were little?" I ask.

"Fishing when we were little, bit of hunting when we got bigger, lot of drinking when we were older," Dover says, eyes holding mine. There's a challenge in them, one that I see staring back out of Bristal's eyes all the time; one that I have to answer or never be respected.

"Did you ever find your dog?" I ask, and he pulls back like I kicked him.

"What?" Bristal asks, turning toward me. "What are you talking about?"

"In Bailey Foxglove's notes," I tell her, keeping my eyes on Dover. "He called her about his missing dog. Twice, actually."

"Dodger," Dover says. "He was a good old boy, that dog. Taught him how to open the fridge. He could bring you a beer and everything."

Dover feeds me his award-winning smile, and I smile back, but we're both just showing our teeth to each other now, and we know it.

"Never did close the door behind him, though," he adds, turning the smile to Bristal, who lights up.

"Mom told me about that," she says. "Said the dog would let himself in the house, too. But couldn't manage shutting it."

"He had that screen door all figured out," Dover agrees, nodding. "And you feed him something, you can guarantee it would come out the other end in one piece. Seriously, you would not believe the things that dog could pass. We used to put bets on it. Stuff came out clean, too, let me tell you. Stomach acid put a nice polish on something, once you get the shit off it. Dodger shined up an old .50 caliber bullet from World War Two that Grandpa Sandy had. Looked straight out of the box."

"Amazing," I mutter. "He sounds like a pretty smart dog, but he couldn't find his way back home?"

"Lots couldn't," Dover says, the canine smile still holding. "Pound was full when the flood came through."

"Was Dodger there?" I ask, and Bristal kicks me under the table.

"Seriously?" she asks. "You come to prison and ask a man about his dead dog?"

"*Did* he die?" I ask, turning to Dover.

"He didn't drown, no," Dover says.

"Why are you—" Bristal begins, but I cut her off with a brisk question.

"Did you know Denise Halverson?"

"Denise!" he says her name like she just walked into the room and he's overjoyed to see her. "Everybody knew that girl," he goes on, his smile widening. "If you catch my drift."

"Did *you* know her?" I ask again, my own smile gone.

"You don't have to answer that," Bristal says, pushing against my arm as she turns her attention from her uncle to me, suddenly remembering that I'm a dog myself; a terrier, specifically, and I've got a bone I'm not going to let go of.

"You're his niece, not his lawyer," I tell her.

"It's okay," Dover says to Bristal. "Yeah, I knew Denise. Haven't heard that name in thirty years."

"A lot of people haven't," I tell him. "We wouldn't have, either, if we hadn't spotted some discrepancies in the reporting of the tornado. Do you know what happened to her?"

"Happened to her? Last I heard she'd run off."

"When was the last time you saw her?"

The smile slips, and I think I spot true confusion in his pale blue eyes. "She was still around after the tornado, I think," he says. "Can't say for sure."

I would love for this to be my moment. I would love to whip out the picture dated June 11, 1994, which shows him standing next to Denise at the railroad tracks. But my phone is in that locker, and I already made an argument in defense of my dad not mentioning seeing Denise, either. And Dover isn't denying seeing her. Even if he did, he could claim a fuzzy memory due to a concussion from the brick hitting him.

Bristal was right about her uncle; he's smart. He's giving me half answers and shallow nods. Nothing I can get my teeth into. But he's not only smart—he's also mean. Bristal can't see it, or maybe she just has a different definition of the word. She hasn't put together the puzzle pieces to form the picture that I already see, one that I have all the corner pieces for. I'm just filling in the middle now.

"What are you in here for, Dover?" I ask.

"I already told you—" Bristal says, but her uncle motions for her to be quiet, and she does. His eyes are on mine, unblinking.

"A few things," he admits, one shoulder rising in a half shrug. "But what you're digging for is aggravated assault, I believe."

"Against?"

"My girlfriend," he says. "Broke her jaw, her arm, and two ribs."

He ticks them off on his fingers like a grocery list. Beside me, Bristal goes silent, perhaps seeing this side of him for the first time.

"Takes a lot to hurt someone like that," I say, keeping my voice even. "It takes practice."

"Mmmm," Dover says, a nonanswer that gets me nowhere. But I don't need an answer to my next question; in fact, I don't even need to listen to his words. All I need is his reaction.

"Did you start young? Did you practice on Denise?"

"What the fuck, Lydia?" Bristal full-on shoves me this time, but I keep my eyes on Dover's.

The smile is back, slow and feral, spreading ear to ear.

"Sorry, ladies," he says, crossing his hands behind his head. "I'm afraid I can't say anything more without speaking to my lawyer first."

"I'll make a note of that," I say, just as steely. "Who's your lawyer?"

The smile spreads, the well-laid trap sprung. "Your dad."

TWENTY-NINE

"What the fuck?" Bristal is on me the moment we're through the door, the guard giving us a wary glance as she trails me to the curb.

"Hey!" she yells, grabbing my shoulder and spinning me around. "Seriously, what the fuck, Chass?"

"Oh, come on," I shout, my own temper flaring. "It never occurred to you? Not once? Dover is the only person Denise was known to associate with—a guy that goes on to become a felon and is incarcerated for domestic abuse?"

"He is *not* the only person she hung out with," Bristal shoots back, madly thumbing through her phone and raising it to show me the picture of Denise, Dover, and my dad.

"One picture," I tell her, raising a single finger. "One picture, one time. My dad's name *never* came up when we talked to David

Swinton or when I talked to Erin. She hung out with a Jamison—that's what they said, and that's *all* they said."

Bristal is seething, her hair a dark storm around her head as the cold wind whips it, her black eye bulging as a tear leaks from under the lid.

"Right," she says, her voice cracking a little. "Of course, and who is the more obvious choice here? The Jamison or the Chass? You don't know shit about shit."

"Go ahead!" I yell, crossing my arms. "Go ahead and make your case. Do it. Right now. You can make it about public perception and socioeconomic levels, predisposed notions about family names and the plight of the poor. Stitch it all together and make it look pretty, but in the end—do you think it was the lawyer or the felon?"

"Fuck you, Lydia."

Bristal isn't crying anymore. Her face is cold and stony, the heat of anger replaced by the chill of resentment. Brandon Childress told me to fuck off at the blood drive, and I didn't feel it, partly because he didn't mean it, not all the way. Bristal means it. Right here, right now. I can see it in her eyes.

"Fuck you," she says again. "I asked you from the beginning—at what point am I sacrificed at the altar of your success? Honestly, I'm surprised it took this long, little miss class president."

My blood goes cold, even though my pulse has picked up a beat. "What do you mean?"

Bristal smirks, aware that she just dealt a blow. "I saw you throw the votes in the dumpster," she says, her voice low. "I was out at the track, picking up trash for my community service, when the service doors came crashing open and out comes Lydia Chass. I didn't even know your face could look like that, twisted and pissed like a bear that just got poked. And you did, didn't you, Chass? The senior class wanted to oust you as president in favor of Brian Phillabrant, but you weren't about to let democracy stand in the way of the real winner, were you?"

"Don't," I say, my own voice low as Kenzie pulls up to the curb. "You can't—"

"Can't what?" Bristal asks. "Let your perky little friend know who you really are, underneath the GPA and the volunteer spreadsheet?"

I move closer to Bristal, panic squeezing my throat. "Brian plays baseball, and the senior class president is in charge of prom. He can't even remember to get his parking pass—he would have done a horrible job handling his season and planning prom at the same time. It would have been a disaster."

"Maybe." Bristal shrugs. "But I don't give two shits about prom. I'm pointing at you, making decisions about what you think is right—and that's you, winning. Every time. Even if the rest of the world disagrees."

I look over to Kenzie's car, where she waits, window up, silently observing our standoff.

"Why didn't you say something?" I ask, a gust of wind tearing at my words.

"I already tried that once, remember? I ratted you out in kindergarten and nobody believed me, because you're a Chass and I'm a Jamison. I might not have a long line of college degrees in my family, but I learn fast. And I think the lesson is over here. I'm done."

"Wait, what?" I ask, any fear I had of Bristal outing me as an enemy of democracy overwhelmed by something larger.

Bristal throws her hands in the air, disgusted. "What did you think I was going to do? Be like: *You totally used me to get to my uncle and accuse him of murder. But that's okay, it'll make good material for the podcast. I understand.* No!" she says fiercely, shaking her head, her teeth chattering as the wind tears at her slim jacket. "It's not fucking okay, and I'm not playing. Fuck you. Fuck the podcast. Fuck graduating. Fuck Henley. I'm done."

She turns away to head back to the building, and I grab her elbow. "Bristal, wait—"

Bristal spins, one hand curled into a fist. It hovers as her lips pull back, rage contorting her face, rippling the purple skin of the bruise she got defending me and my parents. There are fresh cuts on her knuckles where she went after whoever attacked us, but now that fist is aimed at me, and I'm certain it's about to fall.

"Stop!" MacKenzie screams, jumping out of the car and throwing herself between us. "I swear to God, you hit Lydia and your ass is in jail!"

Bristal's lip flickers, a wild animal delivering a warning. I put my hands on Kenzie's shoulders, feel the tension pulsing through them.

"She's not going to hit me," I say.

And she's not. There was a moment when she would have, right when she spun on her heel and located a target. But it wasn't me she saw; there was a lifetime of hurt in her eyes, for every person who had ever taunted her or hurt her first. Bristal's punch was primed to land—and she stopped when she realized it was me—her supposed friend. A person she's protected in the past, and still is.

"She's not going to hit me," I say again, more loudly, fully realizing it. And she's not going to tell Kenzie that I stole the class election, either . . . because she knows no one will believe her.

"Get in the car, Lydia," Kenzie says, the voice she uses for her little siblings. "And you . . ." Kenzie's finger comes out, shaking in Bristal's face. "You ever raise your fist to Lydia again, you're done. You hear me? I don't give a shit."

"MacKenzie, stop," I warn her, watching as Bristal's arm comes down, her face falling into the cold, cement pattern I've seen her wearing when she comes out of the office, suspension slip in hand. This is a Bristal who doesn't care, or, at least, wants people to believe she doesn't.

"Find your own ride home," MacKenzie sneers, finally backing away as she moves to get into her car. "This isn't a dump truck, and I don't drive trash around."

"Fuck you," Bristal says.

"Great comeback, write it down for future use," MacKenzie says blithely, sliding into the driver's seat and pushing open the passenger door for me. I stand still, rooted to the sidewalk.

"Lydia," she says sternly. "Get in the car."

"We can't just leave her here," I argue.

But Bristal shakes her head and pulls out her phone. "I'm fine. Get the fuck out of my face, Lydia Chass."

"Let's go," MacKenzie says, and Bristal turns her back on me, walking toward the prison, phone up to her ear. I turn to Kenzie, torn.

"We can't just—"

"We can," my friend insists. "She's fine."

Bristal isn't fine, and I know it. But the cold ice at the bottom of her eyes when she said my name—hitting hard on *Chass*—had matched her uncle's when he blithely enumerated the bones he'd broken on a woman's body. And I've played with fire enough for one day.

I climb into Kenzie's car, crank the heat, and curl into a ball, my chin buried in the down fleece of my winter coat. I try not to look back as we pull away, try not to wonder how Bristal will get home, try not to think about her thin jacket as the first heavy patters of ice hit MacKenzie's windshield when we pull onto the highway.

But mostly, I try not to think about the single tear I'd seen streaming out from under her black eye, and the absolute betrayal that had shown in the other one. Open, blue, hurt.

Hurt like a dog that's been kicked by someone it trusted.

THIRTY

Excerpt from podcast episode "What Was Lost in a Hometown Tornado" of On the Ground in Flyover Country

Welcome to Henley, Ohio, a place you can always come back to.... I'm Lydia Chass, inviting you to join me as I explore the past and traverse the present of our hometown. This week, I'm covering the first in the series of events locally known as the long stretch of bad days.

Everyone has a tornado story....

Ask anyone in Henley where they were on June thirteenth of 1994, and they'll know, right down to the hour. Janice Pascale was pulling hornworms off her tomato plants when she says everything went very still.

"The light was just wrong. It was like everything turned

pink, and it got real quiet. I straightened up and looked toward town, and there it was, just like the movies. A black snake coming down out of the sky. It touched down, and I could see things flying. I just ran for the house fast as I could. Ran right out of my flip-flops. They were still sitting there, by the garden, when I came back out."

Next to Janice's flip-flops was a cast-iron stove, later identified as being part of the front lobby of the Fairlawn Hotel. Those in town had a more direct experience of the tornado, like Bill Milhaus.

"I heard that sound, not something you forget. Like a train, but a train if God was driving it. The siren started going, but it wasn't much of an early-warning system. I saw the damn thing bearing down on Main Street before the siren went off. Then it just chewed up the courthouse and spit it out, siren and all."

Bailey Foxglove was sixteen at the time and pressed into service to answer all the emergency calls for the sheriff, which were rerouted to her home. As the daughter of Sheriff Foxglove, she held the fort, helping those she could. Everyone who called was panicked, at a loss, searching for a loved one. Some couldn't even find their own homes.

"Trees were down, buildings were gone. We navigate by certain things, you know? When you use the church steeple to tell you where you are on Main Street, and then the steeple's gone, suddenly Main Street looks real different."

Without points of reference, citizens wandered the streets.

The Fairlawn Hotel had collapsed, as well as the fire station, resulting in the deaths of three of the four citizens of Henley who were lost that day. James and Jessica Beckley were a young couple with a newborn whose names are etched onto the memorial near the water tower, along with Laura Richardson, the tornado's fourth victim.

Helen Gurtz cleans and maintains the memorial, and the Whitesides' Family Flower shop donates geraniums to be planted each year. The village council recently announced plans to put up a park bench nearby, to invite people to sit and think awhile about what was lost that day. As Mrs. Gurtz says, there is more than one tragedy here.

"We lost people, yes, and that young couple and their baby—there's nothing sadder than that. But this town isn't what it used to be. Those bricks were baked in a kiln built down by the river right when Henley was founded. The trees that built that steeple were some of the first downed in Markham County. You drive through Henley now it looks like any other place: block buildings, square windows, concrete steps. All the beauty is gone—the carved cornices, the old stone foundations, the hitching post for horses was still outside the Fairlawn when the tornado came through. That's all gone now. We lost a lot in 1994. A lot of history."

History was lost, but the future is still bright for the citizens of Henley. As the thirtieth anniversary of the tornado approaches, citizens are working hard to decide the best way to commemorate the day. Anita Levering, who has taught fifth grade for more than two decades, plans to take her class on a walking tour of town, showing the children what buildings used to stand in each place. David Swinton, former owner/operator/reporter/photographer for the *Hometown Henley Headlines*, is planning to reprint the newspaper editions that cover the tornado and its aftermath, selling them at 1994 prices—a little under a dollar.

"I haven't settled it all yet, in my head. If I have to lose money, I will. Paper's more expensive today, but this is important, and I want everyone who wants a reprint to have one."

Commemorative postcards and placards are also in the works. Follow the Markham County Historical Society Facebook page to find out more!

Tune in next week as coverage of the long stretch of bad days continues.

THIRTY-ONE

I pull off my headphones, dully scrolling through the transcription of the tornado episode. It's crap, and I know it. After accumulating a pile of paper, tons of notes, and talking to anybody who wanted to chat, I'd just grabbed pull quotes from a handful of people and reiterated the old stories that everyone knows. My heart wasn't in it, and I skipped out, phoned it in.

And, of course, people love it.

I'd turned comments back on, knowing full well that there's nothing here to flare tempers or ignite passions. I didn't say anything inflammatory, didn't point fingers, didn't chide anyone, or tell them how to feel. I played the straight and narrow and am being rewarded for it. I'm pretending to be just what everyone thinks I am—Ivy League–bound, buttoned-up Lydia Chass, who would never kick a kindergartener in the balls, rig an election, or leave someone stranded at a jail.

> **Mrs. Levering:** More great coverage, Lydia! Thank you for honoring our past and keeping your language clean in this episode!
>
> **BigMacKenzie:** Hard work pays off! Harvard bound!
>
> **Jo-Jo-Mac:** Always a pleasure to hear your voice, Lydia. Much preferred.
>
> **Swinton_D:** So glad to see young people caring about their roots! Thank you for mentioning the reprints!
>
> **HenleyHistSoc:** Looking forward to the thirtieth anniversary! We have lots more planned so stay tuned!

"Hooray," I mutter to myself. "The pearl anniversary of death and destruction. Come celebrate with us as we polish a stone and put up a bench so you can sit and look at the stone."

"Lydia?" There's a timid knock at my door, and Mom pushes it open an inch. Steven wiggles through, his wheels forcing it to swing open.

"Hey, buddy," I say, leaning down and unhooking his wheels to pull him into my lap. He cuddles in, purring, a tight coil of fur and warmth, comfort radiating from him. I click my laptop shut, and Mom's eyes follow my movement.

"What's up?" she asks, sitting on my bed cross-legged and pulling a pillow across her knees. "Still working on that episode?"

"No," I admit, burying my face in Steven's fur. I'd been avoiding Mom and Dad ever since coming back from the prison, not wanting to admit to them that I'd pulled the rug out from under

Bristal and left her out in the cold—literally. After Mom and I had our version of a knockdown drag-out, we've all been playing it careful and polite around the house.

"I already posted the episode," I tell Mom. "It's the least interesting thing since the minutes from the septic system edition of the village council meeting. And everyone loves it."

"Well . . ." She smiles, trying hard. "That's a good thing, right?"

"You mean—at least no one is setting our yard on fire this time?"

"I mean"—she puts her hands in the air, as if weighing one thing against another—"it is nice that the house doesn't smell like a tractor pull anymore."

I snort, puffing out Steven's hair. He turns to touch noses with me, his whiskers tickling my cheeks. Then he looks over at Mom and begins to wiggle, suddenly aware that the grass is much greener, and the cuddles more dependable, on the other side of the fence. I carry him over to the bed, and he slides into her arms like water, the purr kicking up a notch.

"Sit down," Mom says, patting the bed next to her. "I need to tell you something."

"Oh God," I say. "You need to work on your lead-in."

"It's a good thing," she insists.

"Then don't tell me to sit down first," I tell her, bopping her gently in the face with a pillow.

"Okay, let's start over," she says gamely. "Lydia, I have something great to tell you. Now lie down on the floor and receive your news properly."

"That sounds like the beginning of a porno."

"You are really stealing my thunder here," Mom says. "I can't compete with porn."

"We're definitely done talking about porn now," I tell her. "Seriously—what is it?"

"Two things," Mom says, holding Steven's front paws to illustrate. "First of all, we know who torched our yard."

"What?!" I yell. "How? Who was it? What happened?"

"Keep your knickers on, Nellie Bly," Mom says. "Just let me tell the story."

"Don't do it like Dad, though, okay?" I plead.

Mom holds her hand up in a solemn vow. "Chronological, I swear."

"'Kay, but I'm holding you to it."

"All right." She settles back into the pillows, Steven nestled against her chest. "Yesterday I got a call from Michelle Denney— Bob's mom?"

"Right," I say slowly, wondering where this could be going.

"She's good friends with Jess Childress—"

"Brandon's mom," I say, filling in all the cracks on my own, in case she's tempted to draw this out any longer. "Whose little sister was on the bus that Lytle hijacked."

"And it turns out that . . ." Mom looks down into Steven's adoring eyes, her hair falling in a dark sweep over both of them. "It's hard. People can be so horrible."

I don't know if she's talking to me or Steven, but there's true distress in her voice.

"What, Mom? What happened?"

"You can't be repeating this," she says sternly, looking back up at me and sweeping her hair out of the way. "I wouldn't even tell you if it wasn't pertinent—"

I raise an eyebrow and she sighs.

"Dale Childress has been sleeping with Randi Bean—"

"The Sweet Corn princess?" I ask.

"How would you even know that?" Mom asks, perplexed, and I wave toward my laptop, letting that stand for an answer.

"Anyway, Jess found out that Dale was cheating. So she hit back. Called Michelle Denney and told her that it was Dale who stole those signs and put them in our yard. Michelle called me, and I called your dad, and the sheriff went out to talk to Dale about it. Turns out he had all these scratches on his face, and a busted lip, with no real good explanation of where they came from."

"I don't know," I tell her. "He could've said *Bristal Jamison* and I'm pretty sure that would cover it."

"Well"—Mom shakes her head—"I don't know that Bristal really strikes me as the scratching type. I bet Jess got a few licks in, herself, once she heard he'd been cheating. Regardless, Dale wasn't a hard nut to crack. He folded right off, told the sheriff things haven't been too great lately and he's been making a lot of bad decisions."

"Aww . . . ," I say, clutching my chest with one hand while holding up my middle finger with the other.

"Now, seriously, Lydia. It's not funny. He got laid off, you know? And I guess Dale got all down on himself. His marriage was falling apart—"

"His fault," I interject.

"Well, I don't know if he cheated first and then they had trouble, or things were going south and then he went shopping. We can argue chicken and egg if you want, but the point is that Dale Childress is who put those signs in our yard," Mom says.

"And set them on fire," I add.

"Yes, that too." She nods.

"And threw a brick through the living room window."

"Right."

"While we were *in the living room*," I say, my voice rising.

"Yes," Mom agrees, her tone matching mine. "Your dad and I talked about it, and we both agreed that we're not going to press charges."

"You—are you fucking serious, Mom?" I screech. Steven lays his ears back, eyebrows going into a flat line.

"Lydia! Don't talk like—"

"Like an outraged person?" I ask. "Because that's what I am right now. Out-fucking-raged."

"You're starting to sound like Bristal," Mom chides.

"There wouldn't be words if I was Bristal," I tell her. "It would just be fists."

"Don't ever talk like that, Lydia—do you hear me?" Mom says, her parenting tone coming in and hitting down hard. "That's a threat, and if you make those noises outside this home, who knows what it could bring down on this household!"

"Bricks?" I ask. "Fiery signs?"

"Your father has gone through hell for backing Abe Lytle," Mom says. "We all have. This is an opportunity for this family to turn the other cheek. It could gain us some support, and Lord knows we need it."

"That, and a security system," I tell her. "You just open-invited anyone who has a beef with us to walk on by and toss a brick. We'll just put in a new window and say we understand."

"That's the other thing," Mom says, shifting uncomfortably and adjusting Steven on her chest. "You Dad called ADT, and they're coming tomorrow."

"Seriously?" I ask, stunned.

"Yes," she says. "But we're not putting the signs out. We don't want people to—"

"Have their feelings hurt?"

Mom sighs and avoids my eyes, making a show of inspecting Steven's ears for cleanliness. I fall forward, face-first into a sequined pillow.

"This town . . . ," I mutter. "I don't even know."

"Well, I do," Mom says. "I know a lot, more than you might guess. So do you want my other piece of good news or not?"

"Sure," I say in a monotone, my disinterest flipping over a few sequins.

"Denise Halverson is alive."

THIRTY-TWO

"What?" I spring up like a jack-in-the-box, and Mom gives me a coy smile.

"Yep. Your podcast did more than ruffle feathers, and it reached further than you thought. Michelle got curious and started looking through Facebook—"

"Denise isn't on—"

"*And* she couldn't find her there," Mom says, raising her voice to talk over me. "So she went to Classmates.com."

"What the hell is Classmates.com?" I ask.

"A site for old people," Mom says. "She didn't see her there, either, but she posted in the message boards, looking to reconnect, or see if anyone knew anything. Couple of hours later she gets a friend request from a Denise Chivington, in Missouri."

"Chivington?" I repeat, and Mom hands me her phone.

Denise Chivington's Facebook profile shows a good-looking woman with dark hair smiling directly into the camera, a golden retriever at her side. She's sitting on the front step of what looks like a suburban dream, with a brass door knocker and glass insets on either side of the front door. I flick through the photos to find an equally attractive husband, a smiling set of twins, and a well-attended backyard barbecue complete with tiki torches.

"Damn, Denise," I say under my breath. "You did okay."

"Well," Mom says somewhat dubiously. "It's Facebook, so everything looks perfect. But—she's definitely not dead."

"And that makes me definitely a bitch," I say, handing Mom's phone back.

"You get one more swear word today, Lydia," Mom says sternly. "One more. Use it wisely. Now—what did you do?"

"I may have insinuated that Dover Jamison killed Denise Halverson and then interrogated him in front of his niece and really, really pissed both of them off."

Mom's head is shaking back and forth, her mouth falling open a little farther with every swing. "You—you talked to *Dover Jamison*? When? HOW?!"

"I uh . . . went to the prison with Bristal and MacKenzie this weekend instead of shopping."

Her head stops moving. "Mother. Fucker."

"Whoa, Mom!" I say. "That's your one for the day. And it's a solid!"

"Don't make jokes with me, Lydia Helen Chass," she says, whipping out the middle name. "You lied to us, and you went to a prison? To talk to Dover Jamison, of all people?"

"Yes." I nod. "And I'm sorry, but I thought . . . I really thought he might have killed Denise."

"And you were *really* wrong," Mom says, holding up her phone and flashing the smiling woman with the golden retriever at me. "So you sat down with a felon for no reason. And specifically—" She takes a deep breath, and I can tell she doesn't want to say his name again. *"Him?"*

I contemplate shooting back at her that I did learn something. Mainly that Dad is his lawyer, and I've got a few questions about *that*, but given the complicated history she has with Dover, I figure any more questions I have about him should probably be addressed to Dad . . . but minus the fact that I've met him and snuck out of the house in order to do so.

"It was stupid, Mom. I know, okay?"

"Stupid is one thing; reckless is another," she says. "I've got my full-mom face on right now. Lydia—please don't go into maximum-security prisons without asking me first."

"I can make this promise," I say, after considering it. "But what's the staying power on this? Do I still have to check in when I'm, like, forty?"

"Forty-three," she insists as Steven reaches up to pat her face. She dodges his paw, then kisses the pads in apology.

"Please don't tell Dad?" I whisper.

"Oh, your father will never know this happened," she says, crossing herself even though we're Protestant. "He'd shit a brick."

"That's two, Mom," I say.

"It's been a long day," she shoots back. "I just found out my daughter taunted an abusive man."

"And slandered him, technically," I add.

"Yeah, that's another reason to not tell your Dad," Mom says, now fanning herself. "And I can't imagine how Bristal reacted. I'm surprised she didn't take a swing at you."

"She definitely thought about it. MacKenzie stepped in between us."

"She's a good friend," Mom says.

"So is Bristal," I say, meaning it. "And I threw her under the bus."

Mom winces. "Maybe don't use that phrase around your dad, okay?"

"Right," I say, nodding, even though my mind is chasing something else. Mom brought me two pieces of news, and both of them exonerate a Jamison. Not only was I way off base by accusing Dover of murdering someone who isn't dead, but I realize now that I also still carried a shadow of a doubt that Bristal might have been involved with setting our yard on fire.

"Hey, you're good at apologizing, right?" I ask Mom, who quirks her head to the side.

"Are you inferring that I do a lot of things wrong?"

"No, just that you always know the right thing to say. Does that sound better?"

"Yes, but maybe say the words in your head first before trying them out loud," Mom says. "Just a tip, for the future. Maybe on dates."

"Yeah, those," I say, tapping out a text to Bristal. I haven't tried reaching out since our blow-up at the prison. It comes back as undeliverable.

"Fuck," I say, slamming my phone down. "She blocked me."

"Strike three," Mom says. "You're out. And by that I mean drive your ass over to her house and make amends. This family owes that girl."

"Yes," I say, reaching for my shoes. "I know we do."

"Tell her Steven says hi!" Mom calls after me as I step out into the hall. I don't have to look back to know that she's waving his paw.

THIRTY-THREE

I rehearse on my way over to Ash Park. Bristal has already given me a hard time for being rusty on apologies, and she's right. I'm not good at admitting I'm wrong, and even worse at vocalizing it, so this is going to be like eating humble pie with crow for dessert. I pull into Ash Park and scan the long lines of trailers. They're all set at angles, like Matchbox cars pulled into a parking lot in a diorama. Luckily, Bristal's Neon is easy to spot, the four mismatched doors standing out like a beacon.

I pull in behind her and scan the trailer for signs of life. There's a punching bag hanging from a tree, utterly still in the lack of any wind or breeze. If I needed any more confirmation that Bristal lives here, the punching bag is it.

I know she has a younger sister, Mariana, a freshman. There could be more siblings, and if the lore of the fecundity of Jamison girls holds true, there probably are. A shadow passes in front of a window, the outline of a cigarette held in one hand. Bristal has mentioned her mom before, and I think her dad lives with them, too, but I couldn't swear on it.

"Lydia, you're kind of a dick," I whisper to myself, alone in my car.

Bristal had texted me to make sure everyone in our house was okay after Dale Childress vented his rage on our front lawn. She even asked how Steven was—and I don't know how many siblings she has, or if both of her parents live in the trailer I'm about to go into . . . if she'll let me in. There's a good chance I get a door shut in my face and might have to dodge a fist immediately before that. But if I really do want to launch a career as an investigative journalist, I need to be okay with slamming doors and awkward moments on front steps.

Might as well start now.

I hear a child's cartoon music through the thin walls of the trailer as I knock, but there's no movement. Aware that the music might be louder than I am, I knock harder. This time a bellow comes from inside, "Bristal! Somebody's at the door!"

"Cause and effect, Mom," I hear her say. "Cause and effect."

The door opens, and I'm face-to-face with Bristal, her dark hair jet-black from a shower, the angry bruise on her eye now a weltering red. The swelling has receded, and the pupil is now visible—as is the anger that flashes there.

"Wait!" I say, shooting an arm out to stop her from shutting the door. "Denise is alive! Michelle Denney found her online."

I'm here to apologize, but first I've got to gain entrance, and I know that piece of news will stop Bristal in her tracks.

"What?" she asks. "Are you serious? How?"

She's wearing an oversized sweatshirt, the scabs on her knuckles barely visible as she clenches the door handle, still considering slamming it closed.

"And *that* was Dale Childress," I say, pointing to her fist, and then her eye.

"Heh," she says, cracking a smile and rubbing her knuckles. "Felt like a Childress's cheekbone."

There's an awkward moment where we look at each other and finally she shrugs and says, "Don't just stand there, asshole. You're letting all the heat out."

I breathe a sigh of relief and follow her into the trailer. There's a couch and love seat jammed tightly together to form a right angle, facing a TV. Mariana is cuddled with two smaller girls under a flannel blanket; she tosses me a wave, and the girls look at me curiously, but Bristal doesn't bother introducing us. Instead, she pulls me to the right, where there's a kitchenette and a small round table. I'd interrupted a card game; the table is covered with poker chips, peanut shells, and ash from her mom's cigarette.

"We're seeing who has to do the laundry tonight," Bristal says, waving me into a chair as she slides into her own.

"Mostly we just both try to make the game last until the next day so that neither one of us has to do it," the woman says, eyeing me up and down. "Damn, you look like your dad."

"This is my mom," Bristal says, by way of introduction.

"Hi," I say, not sure what else to tack on.

"Madison Jamison," she says, holding her hand out. "And I'll just spare you the whole part where you wonder why I never married the girls' dad. It's mostly 'cause I don't need the government or any church's blessing to legitimatize my personal relationships."

"Oh," I say, nodding and trying to hide my surprise.

"Yeah, we're not all dumb out here," Bristal says, seeing right through me.

"Also, my name is badass," Madison adds. "And it kinda sounds like a porn star. Madison Jamison."

"So Dover is your brother?" I ask Madison, and she nods.

"I need to apologize to both of you then," I say, drawing in a deep breath.

"Nah," Madison says, waving me off. "Dover's a dickhole. Anything you said about him, he probably deserved."

"Ummm . . . well, I actually accused him of murdering someone who is still alive, so yeah, I think I need to apologize."

"Bristal told me all about it. But—beers first," Madison demands, smacking a hand on the table. "Take it from me, honey, apologizing is a lot easier if you're drunk."

Bristal hops up and grabs three beers from the small fridge. I look at mine dubiously as Madison cracks hers open.

"What? You watching your calories? Bristal, grab Lydia a light beer."

"No, it's—"

"Illegal," Bristal finishes for me. "Lydia doesn't do illegal things."

"Huh." Madison regards me carefully, as if I were in a zoo.

"No, it's not that," I say, turning to Bristal. "I need to apologize to you, and I should be sober when I do it—you deserve that much."

"'Kay," Bristal says, eyeing me over her own beer. "Let's see if you've gotten any better at it."

"I'm sorry," I say simply, then take a deep breath and dive in. "I'm sorry that I thought the worst of Dover and your family. I'm sorry that I left you behind at the prison. I'm ashamed that you physically defended my house, my family, my parents, and I still let others cloud my thinking about what kind of person you actually are."

Bristal and Madison both consider me, Madison nodding a little.

"That was pretty good," she says to her daughter. "I'd let her off the hook."

"Fair," Bristal says, tipping her beer toward me. "But I still think there's a stick up your ass."

"I was born with that," I tell her, and Madison chokes out a lungful of smoke.

"So," Bristal says. "What's the story on Denise?"

I explain about Michelle Denney finding Denise online, and how Mom connected with her as well. By the shared friends count on her Facebook page, I'm guessing there was a pile-on of requests from Henley people that left Denise feeling more well-liked than she'd ever been when she actually lived here. Bristal takes my phone from me, scrolling through the pictures.

"I'm glad she's not dead, but damn . . ."

"What?" I ask. "You seem disappointed."

"She's all—" Bristal waves her hands in the air, trying to find the right words. "Suburban, and shit."

"Did you want her to be in prison?" I snap back, then regret my words. "Sorry."

"Honey." Madison shakes her head. "Dover *is* in prison. That's his fault, not yours."

"No," Bristal says, handing my phone back to me. "But maybe like a bounty hunter, or a game warden. Something. Not a mom and a golden retriever owner."

"There's nothing wrong with golden retrievers," I argue.

"They're the MacKenzie Walters of the dog world," Bristal shoots back. "Hey—she earned that," Bristal warns me, a finger coming up as I'm about to mount a defense of my friend.

"Dogs," I say instead. "Let's talk about the next episode— assuming you're still in?"

Bristal shares a glance with her mom over the table and taps her finger against her beer can, making hollow music. "Yeah," she finally says. "I'm still in."

"Great!" I say. "How is the Boggs episode coming? You're up next."

"It's done," she says. "Just need to upload it. I was told I was supposed to wait until Monday to publish stuff, and I'm a good golden retriever, so I listened."

"You're a horrible golden retriever," I tell her. "And you can publish whenever you want."

"Score," she says, and belches. "Your tornado episode was shit."

"Randall Boggs," Madison says, leaning her head back and staring at the ceiling. "He was a piece of work. Dirty old man, that one."

"Did you know him?" I ask.

"Same way anybody knows anybody else in Henley, on sight but not real well." She taps the ash of her cigarette into an empty beer bottle. "He tried to get me to give him a blow job for a penny."

"What?!" I say, and Bristal shouts, "Only a penny?!"

"He was a slick fart, that guy," Madison says. "I used to work at the Fairlawn, in high school. You know that used to be a whorehouse back in the seventies, right?"

"*What?*" I say again, adding volume this time.

"Yep." She laughs. "That's not something you'll find documented at the historical society, but those beds were rented by the hour, not nightly. Did a pretty brisk business, too. The Horvaths owned it at the time."

"Horvath." Bristal kicks me under the table, while she thumbs through her phone, finally pointing at the commenter from our first shared episode of *On the Ground in Flyover Country* who had identified themselves as whorevath1977.

"Oh yeah," Madison goes on. "There's all kind of great jokes there. The Horvaths owned it. It's called Fairlawn. The girls that worked the front desk had a whole bit about it."

"What were you saying about Randall Boggs?" I ask.

"He got skunked one night and came in, must have thought it was still 1972, or whatever. Tried to get me to go upstairs with him, but all he had on him was a penny. I wouldn't've touched him if he had a five-hundred-dollar bill; he smelled like a distillery and looked like an outhouse.

"He got all irate, said used to be a man could buy a Jamison girl for a dollar, and I told him a penny ain't a dollar and he said it wasn't a penny, it was a nickel. So I told him he wasn't getting near my nips for a nickel, either, and besides that I wasn't stupid, the damn thing was clearly copper.

"And that's when he *really* got mad and told me I was a dumb slut and he wasn't wasting his treasure on me, and my pussy wasn't worth a penny anyway. Then he threw the bell at me and went out the front door hollering—"

"Wait, wait, wait, wait," Bristal interrupts her mom, the hand holding her beer wavering side to side. "He said it was his treasure? You hearing this?" She turns to me.

"What did it look like?" I ask, whipping my phone out. "Do you remember? Are you sure it was a penny?"

"Yeah." Madison nods. "It said *one cent*, right on it. Had a—"

"Indian princess on the other side," Bristal interrupts, sliding her phone to me across the table. "Check it out."

It's an auction listing for an 1864 Indian Princess copper nickel, the crack on Bristal's screen sending an eerie crevice across Lady Liberty's face.

"Holy crap," I say, looking up at Bristal. "He had an Indian Princess in the family after all. But . . ." I scroll down, looking at the asking price. "It's hardly a treasure. This isn't even pulling in two hundred dollars."

Bristal waves for me to give her phone back, and I hand it

over, picking up my own and tapping away. Madison looks between us.

"What's going on?"

"I think this is what Randall Boggs was murdered for," I tell her. "He always ran his mouth about having a family treasure, and an Indian princess in the family. Turns out he might not have been lying, but he definitely overvalued the coin."

"Says here a mint condition could net a grand," Bristal says, tapping her screen.

"But even that is hardly a treasure," I counter, but Madison laughs.

"Your life must be nice," she says, tipping back the rest of her beer. "There's been days I'd kill for a grand, easy."

"Okay," I say, feeling a blush rise. "But why would whoever killed him leave drugs sitting on the table? Those had to be worth money."

"What kind of drugs and how much?" Madison asks automatically.

"A bag of heroin and a bag of coke," Bristal says.

"Nah." Her mom shakes her head. "That shit was cheap, and easy to get. If somebody came after Boggs looking to score some cash, they might have passed that up. Plus, that way if they get stopped for any reason, they don't have drugs on them. No reason for a search. No links to a murder."

"You're a really useful person," I tell her.

"It's not like I'm a lawyer or anything," she says, and I jump at the opening.

"Dover said my dad is his lawyer. Is that true?"

Madison goes quiet, then looks at her daughter across the table. Over in the living room, the little girls sing along to a cartoon, their dark little heads bobbing up and down in unison.

"Should I tell her?" Madison asks Bristal, who shrugs.

"She asked."

"All right, girl," Madison says, reaching across the table to crack open my beer. "But drink this first."

THIRTY-FOUR

The beer goes down like acid, and I almost lose half of it out my nose before Bristal pulls my arm down. "Dude, she said drink it. Not slam it."

"Sorry," I say. "Am I drinking wrong?"

"Kind of," Madison says, scrunching her nose at me from across the table. "But how's the head feel after that?"

"A little fuzzy," I admit, tapping myself on the chest to encourage the rest to stay down.

"Okay." Madison nods, then turns to Bristal. "Take the rest of that away from her. You weren't kidding."

"Light. Weight," Bristal says, pulling my beer can over to join hers.

"I'm going to start off by saying your dad is a good guy, all right?" Madison says, lighting up a fresh cigarette. "I've been around and I've known some men, and Brent Chass is a solid dude."

"Okay," I say, anxiety building in my chest. I already knew these things, had believed them my whole life. If Madison is about to tell me something that contradicts that—and it's certainly looking that way—I'm going to need the rest of that beer.

"Dover said they were drinking buddies. Is that true?" I ask. My dad has never turned down a drink, but I've only ever seen him sipping with Mom after dinner or having something around the fire on a cold night. I've never seen him drunk, and I got the impression that Dover is the person who doesn't drink leisurely—he drinks to get drunk.

"They were, but that's the end of the story. I'm going to start at the beginning. My brother and your dad hit it off back when we used to live out on Far Cry Road. I wasn't very old at all, but I remember Dover walking in the door with your dad behind him, both of them with fishing poles over their shoulders, thinking they were just two boys enjoying the summer. But they weren't, and even I knew it.

"Dover always had a high opinion of himself, so I don't think he ever considered the fact that he was barefoot while your dad had shoes, or that his hair was long and your dad's was short, because the price of a haircut could make all the difference in a house like the one we grew up in. Dover didn't see it, and to his credit, I don't think your dad did, either. They thought they were two kids catching frogs, not realizing that one of them was doing it for fun, while the other one was counting on it for his dinner."

"Was he at your place a lot?" I ask.

"Quite a bit, yeah." Madison nods her head. "But things were different then, this was the eighties. Kids left home in the morning on their bikes and didn't come back until the evening. Now that's called *free-range parenting*, but back then it was just how we lived. Your dad would ride his bike out here, or Dover would walk into town. I've got to say, I think your grandma tried her best to like my brother. Added him to the family pool pass, and everything. But Dover got kicked out of the pool one day for snapping a lifeguard's bikini straps, and he was struck from the official record."

Madison makes air quotes around the last phrase. "Meaning, your grandma took him off their pool pass and started asking your dad where he'd been all day once he got home."

"But they stayed friends?" I ask.

"More or less," Madison says. "They both got older. Found other boys that fit their socioeconomic status a bit better. Your grandma made sure they were never in the same classes together through grade school. When high school came around, Dover had figured out that he liked to hit things, and the bass drum looked like a good outlet for that."

"Uncle Dover was in marching band?" Bristal spits out. But she's blown through her beers and finished off mine, so it comes out more like *marshing band*.

Madison rolls her eyes. "Not for love of music. Randi Bean was the marionette, and she did *not* wear a lot of clothes for that gig."

"So my grandma kept them apart throughout middle school,

but high school comes around and they're thrown back together," I say.

"Pretty much," Madison says. "They didn't have the same classes together or anything, but fall of freshman year they got real tight again, and once your dad got his license his mom didn't have a lot of say in where he went, what he did, or who he was with."

"My dad *partied*?" I ask, not quite able to see it.

"Kiddo, it was the nineties. There wasn't anything else to do," Madison says. "Drink down at the riverbed or out at the old barn on 96. I mean no, not everybody drank, but back then most of us did. There was some pot at a few parties, and the really rough customers could get a hold of heroin, but your dad never had anything to do with any of that—pot neither. He just drank and hauled Dover's ass out of places when he tried to start fights."

"Sounds about right," Bristal says, trying—and failing—to blow a note over the open mouth of her aluminum can.

"You need a bottleneck for that," her mother tells her. "And no, you can't have one. I'm cutting you off."

"'Kay," Bristal says agreeably, and I look at her in shock.

"I don't fuck with my mom," she says in reply.

"Smart girl," Madison says. "Anyway, one night Dover got into it with Mark Donnelly—Randi Bean's boyfriend. Brent hauled his ass out of there and put him in his car, which usually was enough to calm Dover down. But Dover had got it into his head that he was beating the shit out of Donnelly, and your dad had to leave the party altogether—and he shouldn't have been driving.

"They don't even get five miles before they hit somebody—it

was the Milhaus family, if I remember right, coming back from the movies. Your dad and Dover went careening into a pole. Your dad was out cold, but Dover didn't miss a beat. He knew it was his fault they'd had to leave, and that Brent was just trying to save his ass and ended up with his own on the line. Dover dragged your dad over into the passenger seat and made out like he'd been the one driving."

"Shit," I say, glancing over at Bristal, who nods, her mouth a thin line. "He did that for my dad?"

"He did," Madison says with a heavy sigh. "And they both paid for it."

"How do you mean?"

"Dover got a DUI and a gross negligence charge. Lucky they didn't kill anybody in that wreck or it would've been manslaughter. Worst part was, he didn't even have a license—we didn't have the money to go through the courses, so he'd always just been driving without one. It all piled up, and he ended up going to juvie. Came out of there with bad tattoos and a worse attitude. Turned eighteen and didn't go back to school. Things just kinda went downhill from there."

Madison goes quiet, taps some ash from her cigarette into an empty beer can.

"Shit," I say. "Meanwhile my dad goes on to become a defense lawyer."

"Explains a lot, doesn't it?" Madison asks, with a sad smile.

"Yeah," I say, the clouds in my vision clearing a little as I think of my dad, his own beer, and the firepit behind the house, talking about how good people can do bad things. And then there was Dover, covering my dad's ass and paying for it with his own future. I know the man sitting across from me in that maximum-security prison didn't have a soft spot left in him, but it wasn't always that way, and maybe bad people can do good things, too.

"I'm sorry," I say again, staring at a scratch in the Jamisons' kitchen table.

"You don't need to be," Madison says. "Your dad's paid for it, in spades."

"How do you mean?" I ask.

"Listen, my brother . . ." Madison shakes her head, stubs out the cigarette. "He belongs in prison, okay? Maybe he did this one thing right, one time. Or maybe it was a dumb move, but either way, Dover would've found himself behind bars, eventually. He was mean, deep down. It was a streak that your dad could overlook when they were kids, but it got bigger, became a smear, then a crevice. The only things Dover has ever been good at was getting girls' pants off and landing a punch. He got better at both, but never smart enough to avoid the law. He's got your dad dangling. Anytime he needs a lawyer, he can get one for free—or else tell a story the whole county would eat up like it was a fish fry at the legion hall."

"Shit," I say again. "That's . . ."

"Really fucking shitty," Madison finishes for me. "Dover's my brother, but I feel for your dad. Nobody wants a Jamison as an enemy—but if it's Dover, it's even more dangerous to be his friend."

"What do you think of all this?" I ask Bristal, who rouses herself from staring at the table.

"I think your dad's a decent guy that made a dumb mistake, and my uncle's an asshole that maybe made a dumber one."

"That about sums it up," Madison agrees.

"I just don't want it to be a thing. With you and me, I mean," Bristal says, pointing between the two of us, her finger tracing an irregular path between us. "It's just dumb. I hate all of it. It's dumb."

"What my daughter is saying, is that she's sorry, too," Madison explains. "It's just she's drunk and when she's been drinking she stops swearing and it becomes hard to understand her communications without it."

"You don't have to apologize for anything," I tell Bristal.

"I told you to—" Her voice peters out, her face coming together into the squish of an ugly cry.

"Oh my God, stop!" I yell, coming to my feet. "If you start crying—"

"Told you to f-f-f-f-fuck off," Bristal says, her face totally collapsing as the tears come in a rush.

"It's fine! It's . . . I forgive you!" I grab Bristal as she falls forward, a deep sob coming from her chest.

"Crap," I say, crying now as well, my hot tears falling into her still-damp hair.

"Oh, dammit, you two," Madison says, wiping her own eyes.

I pull back from Bristal, giving her a serious look. "You need to unblock me."

"Huh?" she says, face suddenly blank. "Oh, yeah. Of course."

"Wait, let me do it," Madison says, diving for her daughter's phone. "All I have is work friends. We don't have any high drama. I've never had to block anybody. Or unblock them." She stares at the phone for a second, perplexed. "How do I do it?"

"Here," I say, reaching for Bristal's phone and unblocking myself.

"Never get old, kids," Madison says, her eyes following my fingers as they flash over Bristal's phone.

"Never get married, and never get old."

THIRTY-FIVE

I walk with Bristal out to her car, deflated and a little tipsy. Even though she's had more to drink than me, Bristal heads over to her punching bag and delivers a few solid kicks to it before sitting down—hard.

"You okay to drive?" she asks me as I fumble with my car keys.

"I had, like, half a beer," I tell her.

"Yeah, and you're Lydia Chass, so I'm still asking. Also, it was more like a quarter of a beer because I think some of it came out your nose."

I give up on my keys and sit on the hood of my car, looking down at Bristal, who is hugging her knees as the wind kicks up a notch. I can hear a TV from the trailer next to theirs, a loud snore coming from another one across the gravel pathway.

"Your mom kind of broke me," I admit. "How long have you known about Dover and my dad?"

"It's always been like a family joke. Free lawyer. Who needs that more than the Jamisons? But I got curious in high school, asked Mom about it, and she told me the story about Dover taking the fall for your dad."

"How do you not hate me?" I ask, my voice small and lost in the dark, tree branches creaking around us as someone screams from the television nearby.

"I kinda did, for a little bit," she admits with a shrug. "But I saw how much having a lawyer for a dad blew back at you. Like the Pascale chick dumping her lunch over your head, and dicks like Childress. I just kind of figured you'd crawl through your shit. I'd crawl through mine."

"Not everyone would see it that way," I tell her.

Bristal belches and reaches up to take a half-hearted swing at the punching bag. "Mom kinda broke me, too—a whorehouse, in Henley?!"

"Tell me about it!" I say, happy to let her change the subject.

"Can I put that in the Boggs episode?"

"Yes, do it," I say automatically. "I'm actually jealous. You're breaking a real story."

She pushes on the punching bag again, and the chain squeaks. "Nah, I bet everyone in Henley already knew about the whorehouse, they just didn't talk about it. You know, being nice and all."

"True, but I mean the 1864 copper nickel," I tell her. "That's a scoop. There's always been a rumor that Boggs had a family treasure hidden away. Now we know what it was—thanks to your mom."

I kick my foot against the bumper of my car, my mind running. "You could probably even look at the case file, see if the copper nickel came up in an inventory of the house. The coin literally had *one cent* printed on it. Any burglar would overlook that. Or . . . wait—didn't you say there were loose coins in Boggs's couch? The cops aren't exactly numismatists."

"I don't know," Bristal says. "I wouldn't put anything past them."

"What?" I ask blankly. "No, Bristal. A numismatist is a coin collector."

"Oh," she says, her unfocused eyes staring down at the grill of my car. "I thought it sounded illegal."

"Anyway, I bet you could ask for an inventory of those coins, if they still have them, which I bet they do. It *is* an unsolved crime, and—"

"Do you want the ep?" Bristal looks at me, her gaze still slightly unfocused.

"What? No!" I insist, my voice rising. "You called this episode all the way back at the beginning. You literally chanted *Murder, murder, murder* in the historical society after hours."

"Yeah, but . . ." She kicks at the gravel, and I see that the rubber sole is separating from the cloth of her shoe. "It's a real story now, and you're the journalist. I pushed you toward Denise because I thought we were going to be avenging this great wrong, but you were right. It turned out to be nothing, and you put a lot of work into running down the lead. You need a real story out of this podcast so that you can go on to a great college and do good things. I just need to graduate from high school. You need this more than I do. You should take the Boggs story."

I consider it for a moment, fixated on Bristal's shoe, and the widening space where I can see the beginnings of a hole, and the flash of her sock.

"No," I say. "Your mom was the source, you ran the risk of procuring the case file, you did the research. This is your episode. I'm not letting another Jamison stick their neck out for a Chass. The Boggs's episode is yours, murder pennies and all."

"Murder pennies," Bristal growls under her breath, then brightens up. "Can I talk about the price of a blow job in 1994?"

I hop off the car and stick a hand out to help Bristal to her feet. "Why do you ask permission? You're just going to do what you want anyway."

"Awww," she says, grabbing on to my hand and pulling herself up. "It's like you know me."

"You still want to come with me to the dog pound to interview Linda Chance after school?" I ask.

"Planning on it," Bristal says, tapping away at her phone. "First I've got to make a note here to add to the Boggs's episode that the older generations in Henley all need to get tested for STDs."

"If they had any STDs from the Fairlawn, they'd certainly know by now," I tell her, pulling open my car door.

She shakes her head. "Not if it was blue waffle. That can take some time to become symptomatic."

"I don't really know much about STDs," I admit, starting my car and flicking on the heated seat.

"Definitely Google it," Bristal tells me. "I mean you are going to college, right?"

"Fingers crossed," I tell her, my stomach taking an unexpected plummet. I draw in a deep breath. I was right to give Bristal the episode, but that doesn't mean that it won't hurt me in the end. There's still time, I know. I could change my mind, tell Bristal I want the episode. She'd give it to me, and maybe it would be the tipping point that makes Harvard or Columbia recognize that I'm doing real work, here in Henley.

The leather underneath me heats up, radiating warmth through my body, easing out the chill from the wind that had settled into my bones. I look at the hole in Bristal's shoe.

"I'll see you tomorrow," I tell her.

THIRTY-SIX

Excerpt from podcast episode "Your Grandma Mighta Been a Ho" of
On the Ground in Flyover Country

Welcome back to *On the Ground in Flyover Country*. I'm your host, Bristal Jamison, and this week we'll be talking about the fact that your grandpa was probably a cheater and your grandma might've been a ho. Mrs. Levering, don't turn this off. I swear there's historical significance. This episode picks up where last week's left off—with the long stretch of bad days—and I'll be focusing on the one and only murder that Henley has on the books.

Randall Boggs lived a solitary life out on Far Cry Road—which, by the way, has two origin stories for its name. Yes, it's a far cry from town, but any resident that lives near the creek bed can tell you there's a more sinister tale as well. One that will raise the hair on the back of your neck and make you dive for safety, if you hear it. Well, it will if you're Lydia Chass. If you're me, you can recognize a fox call when you hear it. And yes, it's a fox. All you bigfoot weirdos can get aggressive with me in the comments. Let's go.

Boggs preferred the isolation of Far Cry Road, and everyone was pretty happy with the fact that he didn't come into town all that often. He wasn't easy to talk to and even harder to look at. There's no record of how he smelled because people are too polite around here, but judging by the crime scene photos—not too good. And I mean even before he floated in rainwater for a few days sporting a JFK haircut circa November 11, 1963.

Randall Boggs was a rough customer, and he met a hard end. Though his body would not be discovered until June 15 by Dale Childress and Larry Jamison—one of whom is real good at walking onto other people's property—the autopsy showed that he likely died on June 12. How he died was something of a matter of contention. He definitely didn't have his brain anymore—that was partially stuck on the wall, partially floating around with empty chip bags and old raccoon shit—but Boggs had been severely beaten before his death. Although the killing bullet was delivered execution-style, Boggs likely would have died anyway from internal injuries delivered by his tormentor.

But why was he beaten? What did this old man out in the middle of nowhere have that someone would kill for?

Although Boggs's murder remains unsolved, it's been long assumed that his use of recreational drugs is what led him facedown to a bad end. But both heroin and cocaine were left behind, sitting innocuously on the coffee table as the water rose around it. Which means that whatever the intruders were after, it wasn't drugs.

So again—what did the old man have?

One thing Boggs definitely had was diarrhea of the mouth. It was always running, and anyone that saw him coming crossed to the other side of the street to avoid yet another alcohol-fueled tale of a family treasure, one that he kept hidden and secret, biding his time while it doubled and tripled in worth.

Randall Boggs was good for three things—reminding you that personal hygiene is important, long stories about hidden wealth, and periodic reminders that he's not white trash. He couldn't be, because there was an Indian princess in his family.

Here's the part where I call your grandma a ho.

Another thing Boggs definitely had was an itch in his pants. Our AARP listeners already know this, but the beautiful Fairlawn Hotel provided services far beyond a pillow for your head in the 1970s. It ran more along the lines of a sheath for your sword, and did a brisk business. And no, I'm not claiming that your grandma specifically worked there, but somebody had to, that's all I'm saying.

Regardless, my mom *did* work at the Fairlawn—and before anybody says, *Well, of course she did*, let me clarify—Madison Jamison worked at the Fairlawn Hotel in the 1990s at the front desk. But that didn't stop Randall Boggs from trying to give her a taste of history one evening, when he asked if she'd come upstairs with him and offer up the turn-down service along with a blow job—for a penny.

Mom wasn't into it for a few reasons, but she did get a good look at that penny, and recently described it to myself and my cohost, Lydia Chass. A quick search revealed that the coin in question was likely an 1864 Indian Princess copper nickel, and by Boggs's standards, definitely worth its weight in gold. He walked out of the Fairlawn Hotel with it after throwing the front desk bell at my mom in a fit of rage, and that coin was never seen again.

Neither was Randall Boggs.

Not with his brain inside his skull, anyway.

Whoever murdered Randall Boggs worked him over for a prolonged period of time, presumably to get him to give up the storied family treasure. Furniture was slashed, and though the Boggs's residence was always in disarray, photos of the crime scene suggest that someone was looking for something—and was determined to find it.

If the police are still interested in finding out who

murdered Randall Boggs on June 12, 1994, I suggest they go looking for someone in possession of an 1864 Indian Princess copper nickel. Or . . . it could be just somebody he managed to get a blow job out of for a penny.

Either way, I'd keep my mouth shut, if I were you.

THIRTY-SEVEN

"Blue waffle?" I ask as Bristal climbs into my car after school. "Thanks a lot."

"Hey, man, you're the one after a higher education," she says. "I'm just filling in those lower cracks, too. You're going to be a well-rounded individual. A real Renaissance woman."

"Speaking of that higher education . . ." I take a deep breath and open my app, flashing my phone at Bristal to show her that both Columbia and Harvard have accepted me.

"Well, slap my ass and call me toned," Bristal says. "You're bound for the Ivy Leagues." Her smile is broad and honest, true happiness for me radiating.

"Oh no, wait," she suddenly says, putting her hands up in the air. "Don't start on how choosing between first-rate colleges is going to be such a difficult task. Talk about first world problems."

"I won't," I tell her, and it's true enough—she doesn't need to know that the real problem is going to be paying for it.

"Amazing job on that ep, by the way," I tell her. "And I don't just mean that it might have played in a role in my acceptance. My phone has been blowing up with tips."

My in-box is full as well. Just this morning I've received thirty-five emails from people claiming they know something about Randall Boggs. Five of them say they know someone who has an 1864 copper nickel and want to meet with me to divulge names.

"Mine, too," Bristal says, raising her screen to show me 146 unread text messages. "So far I've got three death threats and one job offer as a topless Uber driver."

"Topless Uber driver?" I ask, turning out of the school parking lot. "The podcast is all audio. They don't even know what you look like."

"Yeah, I don't think it had anything to do with the podcast. It was like literally just a random guy texting me asking if I'd pick him up and not wear a shirt while I did it."

"How is this your life?" I ask.

"An ex," she says blithely, pulling out her vape pen. "I broke up with him and he posted my number on some site. So now I've got plenty of job opportunities, if becoming famous for calling people's grandmas hookers doesn't work out."

"But seriously," I say. "We could really have something here. I've got some solid leads in my in-box."

"Oohhhh . . . and I've got a voice mail from the sheriff," Bristal says, holding up her phone to show me. "Do you think they want to deputize me, or arrest me?"

"Maybe both," I tell her, my heartbeat rising. "Dude, this could be the real thing. We might have cracked a cold case."

"Cool," she says nonchalantly. "Too bad there's no reward money."

"No," I agree. "But the real reward is in—"

"Justice, blah-blah," Bristal says, rolling up her window. "And admittance to Ivy Leagues."

"Or in listens," I tell her. "If we actually manage to see this through . . ."

I'm so excited I have to break off, visions of exploding download numbers and guest appearances on big-time true-crime podcasts. *On the Ground in Flyover Country* could become *the* podcast overnight, which we might be able to monetize to help pay the hefty Harvard tuition fee—if, of course, that's where I decide to go. If the podcast goes big, everyone is going to want me—and if I play my cards right, losing my college savings won't be a roadblock.

I flip on my blinker, turning left to head out of town to the county dog pound. "The only thing I want to do right now is tear through my phone and start taking notes, but we've got to finish out this series about the long stretch, and it would be a disservice to Linda Chance if we didn't give the flash flood decent coverage."

"Yep," Bristal agrees, cracking the window and exhaling vape out into the cold air. "Have you seen our download numbers lately? I think news got out that the Denney lady found Denise Halverson, and everyone knows the podcast is to thank for it. Have you talked to her at all?"

"Denise? No," I admit. "She sent me a friend request, and I accepted it, but we haven't talked yet. I mean, I'm not trying to be crass, but—"

"If she's not dead, she's not all that interesting and there's no story," Bristal finishes for me. "Plus, you've already got what you wanted out of this deal. I get it."

"That makes me sound pretty horrible," I say, pulling into a slot near the pound's front door. Dogs run loose in the outdoor play area, noses poked through the fence, hind ends wagging away as Bristal and I get out of the car.

"You are pretty horrible," Bristal says. "Only you do it on the lowdown, real sly. That's what I like about you."

"Thanks, I think?" I say, following her as she heads for the fence and the eager dogs, not the front door.

"Hey, boys and girls," she says, squatting down and scratching their noses. "Who's the good girls? Who's the bad ones? There you go—that one," she says, pointing at a terrier of some type that is wagging its tail but also showing its teeth to Bristal. "That's the interesting dog."

"Hey, ladies," Linda Chance says, propping the front door. "Glad we could work something out. Your show is all anybody is talking about, and I've got a thing or two to say about what went down during the long stretch."

Linda's been saying a thing or two—possibly three or four—long before *On the Ground in Flyover Country* went on the air, but I know she'll make for a good interview. I've seen her opinion pieces in the *Hometown Henley Headlines*. They are always concise, to the point—and worded to wound.

The three of us settle into her small office, even though there are only two chairs; Bristal climbs onto a stack of dog food bags that are Saran-Wrapped together, her heels dangling inches from the floor.

"So," Linda says, getting comfortable behind her desk. "Which one of you is in charge of the flash flood episode?"

"I am," I say. "Is it okay to record you?"

"Of course," Linda says, moving a framed monogram that reads, "You're Not Drinking Alone If Your Dog Is Home," so that I can set my phone in the middle of her desk.

"You were the dog warden in 1994, correct?"

"Yes," Linda says, nodding her head. "I'd taken on the job a couple of years earlier. People used to joke that I was still wet behind the ears, even after the flood. But I tell them I do have a choke chain and I've been known to use it. Just never on a dog."

"Cool," Bristal says.

"Tell us about the flash flood, in your own words," I continue.

"After the tornado went through, everything was just a mess. I know that isn't news to anybody, but I don't just mean people's underwear was lying in the road. Roads were blocked, electricity was out, cars had been tossed around. You couldn't get anywhere, even if you had somewhere to go. Pretty much everybody just picked a spot as close to where they thought their home had been and started gathering their stuff, and piling it there—anything that was still useful, that is.

"We were told dumpsters were coming in, but we had to wait because two hundred of the three hundred and forty-eight bridges in the county were out of commission, and half the roads had big trees lying across them. A lot of people just started burning what would burn, so we had a couple of little fires break out, too. It was just this godawful, end-of-the-world mess, and add to it about three hundred animals running around loose, lost, scared to death."

My pen is flying, my journal page filling up. "Is that just dogs? An estimate on cats?"

"I don't deal in cats," Linda says. "That's the Humane Society, but they were filled up to the rafters, too. And I mean that. There were literally cats in their rafters. And people won't collar a cat like they will a dog. I think only twenty or so of those cats ever got claimed. Of course, they never made the news because they didn't get flooded out."

"So the physical state of the county contributed to the disaster that took place on June fourteenth?" I ask.

"Definitely," Linda says. "I'm the only employee, and I had a handful of volunteers, but they were all busy taking care of their own—which, I totally get. The pound used to be down by the creek, you know the place?"

"Yes," I say. I'd already gone out to the location, seen the old cinder-block building, no bigger than our gardening shed. It's empty now, though you can still see the waterline above empty cages if you peek through the windows. I'd estimated it to be about eight feet high.

"I drive the dog truck home every night and to work in the

mornings, which turned out to be a blessing because you couldn't even get down to the pound. Trees and limbs were everywhere, plus the roof to the old granary had landed in our parking lot. I still had my truck, though, so I just drove the roads, calling in loose dogs when I saw them, hauling them back a few at a time and walking them down to the pound. I had three dogs to a cage by then, which wasn't good for anybody, but half those dogs had tags, so I figured we'd be emptying out sooner rather than later."

A door slams in the hallway, and a high female voice calls out, bringing a chorus of greetings from the dogs that are still indoors. It's loud and overwhelming, and absolutely lovely to hear, knowing what comes next in Linda's story.

"That's one of my volunteers," Linda says. "Never had any trouble bringing them in before. But after the flood, I've had to turn people away. Guilt weighs heavier than taxes, you know."

"Would you like to explain that?" I ask.

"Sure, but it doesn't need to be," Linda says. "We'd been running campaigns for ten years to get a levy passed to build a new pound. Always voted down . . . until 1995. Thank you, taxpayers of Markham County," Linda says, her smile holding more shades of gray than a M. C. Escher drawing.

"So you were underfunded until 1995?"

"And overworked," Linda adds. "But never like that week. Never. Like I said, I had three dogs to a cage, and a few had more than that. We lost thirty-seven dogs, when the waters rose."

"Can you talk about that night?" I ask.

"Sure . . . ," she says, though her voice has lost its vibrancy.

"The day after the tornado it was hot, real hot. Everything that got soaked then got baked, and everybody was working around the clock, trying to get the roads cleared so that the telephone and electric crews could get their work done. About midafternoon the clouds were piling up and everybody had their radios on, expecting to hear an emergency broadcast system warning any minute. It was like none of us had ever seen a tornado in our lives, and here we were looking for another one, right on top of the first."

"But it wasn't a tornado," I say.

"No, it was rain. Crazy rain. Rain like a blanket. I was out on 96 chasing down a shepherd mix—he had a collar because I could hear his tags jingling, but he wouldn't let me get close enough to grab him. I knew he had to be somebody's dog, so I just kept trying, and he kept luring me out farther from my truck. Pretty soon those first big fat drops of rain start falling, and I look up and there's a wall of water coming at me from the west. I got a good visual on my truck and ran straight for it, hoping I could get there in time. I didn't, and when that rain hit me, it was like somebody dropped a veil over my eyes. Couldn't see my truck. Couldn't see the road. I kept going what I thought was straight and ran into the bed of my truck so hard I dented it."

"Ouch," Bristal says, her voice coming from a few feet above my head.

"Knocked me over, tell you what," Linda says. "I went down hard but pulled myself up by the rear wheel. I knew I had to get down to the pound, and right now. That creek has always been prone to flooding, and there's more than once I waded in there and found the doggos standing on their crates, whining. But this was something else entirely. This was worse, and I knew it.

"I drove like a crazy person. Couldn't see shit. Couldn't hear shit. Just water and the sound of it bouncing off my windshield. I missed my turns two or three times, and I can't tell you how often I've counted up the seconds it took me to back up, cover my tracks, trying to figure out if it would've made a difference."

I remember the waterline inside the old building, above my head, and way higher than any dog's. "I don't think it would've," I tell her.

"Probably not, but you still think about it," she says. "Anyway, I got down to the crossroads right before the pound, and Foxglove was out there. There'd been an electric crew working, and they were all huddled in their trucks. Foxglove hit his lights as soon as he saw me, pulled up, and blocked the way. He knew well enough that I'd try to get down there, try to save those dogs. Even though . . ."

She stops, swallows. There's a click in her throat, and the edges of her mouth turn down as her eyes drop to her desk. She takes a second, raises her chin, keeps going.

"Even though the water was up to the windows by then. I could see it, from where I was. I tried to push past him, but Foxglove stopped me, grabbed my arm and told he'd put me in cuffs if he had to, but I wasn't going down there."

"Was he right?" Bristal asks.

"He was," Linda says, sighing. "It took me years to see it, though. I was just this side of twenty and ready to dive in, fight the current, save those animals that I'd condemned to death when I shut them in their cages. But the water was already at our toes a mile out and that stream was running with a sound like a freight train. I knew those dogs were dead already, but I couldn't help it. I wanted to try."

The three of us fall silent, and a high *yip* from the play yard reaches the office. In the hallway, I can hear the volunteer talking to a dog whose name seems to be Buster, and who is going for his bath time.

"That is the most horrible thing I've ever heard," Bristal says. "Seriously. I'm glad you've got this episode, Lydia. I couldn't do it."

I turn in my chair, looking up at her over my shoulder. "But you can cover a murder?"

"I'll swerve to miss a dog," Bristal says. "Humans get a fifty-fifty."

"Amen," Linda says.

"I won't air that, for both your sakes," I say, then turn back to Linda. "The sheriff's daughter was taking phone calls during the long stretch, and she took quite a few about missing dogs as well. Do you know how many of the dogs who passed away had families looking for them?"

"Twenty-eight," Linda says automatically, the number seared into her mind. "There were twenty-eight of those dogs who had tags on, or their families came in and identified them after the fact. The other nine might have been true strays, or just nobody cared enough to come look."

"What'd you do with them?" Bristal asks. "Sorry . . . I'm not trying to be gross, but just—that's a lot of dead dogs."

"And in the heat of the summer," Linda agrees. "We had to move quickly, you're right. You did the episode about the roadkill, right?"

"Yeah, that was me," Bristal says.

"So you know ODOT just has a mass site they toss them in. That's what we did with the dogs, most of them, anyway. A few families came by and gathered the remains, but the majority just went into that grave outside of town."

"Thank you so much, Linda," I say. "I know this isn't easy to talk about."

I'm about to flip my notebook shut and turn off my phone, when Bristal pops one last question.

"Might be weird, but . . . do you know if my uncle Dover's dog was out here? Bailey Foxglove wrote in her notes that he called asking after Dodger."

"Twice, actually," I confirm.

"Yeah, Dodger was one of them," Linda says. "He didn't have tags on him or anything like that, but I knew Dodger by sight. I'd picked him up four or five times wandering out on Far Cry. He was a smart dog, sweet boy. I'd call him and he'd jump right up in my cab. I'd drive him home, didn't bother taking him in. I knew your . . . Sorry, but I knew your family wouldn't be able to pay the release fee, and the pound couldn't afford to feed any dogs we didn't have to.

"Looking back on it, I wish I would've just taken him home that day, but I had a full truck and he was way out at the edge of Far Cry, right where it hits the county road, and Dover lived out the other side, where a bunch of trees were down. I didn't even recognize Dodger, poor bastard. He was covered head to toe in mud. Thought he was just some stray when I loaded him in the back, realized he was Dover's dog once I got to the pound and started walking them down the hill one at a time."

There's a quick knock on the door, and a young woman pokes her head in. "Sorry," she says, spotting us.

"Just checking to see if Barley needs his bandage changed or not?" she asks Linda.

"We'll let you get back to work. We really do appreciate your time," I say, grabbing my phone as Bristal slides down from the stack of dog food. Her knee knocks a box over, and it topples to the floor, a slew of pamphlets splashing across the linoleum.

"Sorry!" Bristal says, bending to pick them up.

"Nah, don't worry about it," Linda says. "Those are a shitload of misprints I got back from the printer for the neuter and spay clinic."

I'm down on hands and knees, helping Bristal scoop pamphlets back into the box when the bright red lettering across the top grabs my attention.

"Neuter and *slay*?" I ask. "That's a heck of a misprint."

"Yeah, I wasn't too happy, seeing as we're a no-kill shelter. Don't really know what to do with two thousand pamphlets saying otherwise."

"I can drop them off at recycling," I tell her as Bristal hefts the box from the ground. "I don't mind at all."

"That'd be great, Lydia, thanks. One less thing for me."

We head toward the door, and Linda goes in front, holding it open for Bristal as she edges her way out, balancing the heavy box.

"Give me a call sometime, if you want to coordinate another adoption drive," Linda says.

"Sure thing," I say, buckling my seat belt as Bristal climbs into the passenger seat. "And thanks again for your time!"

Linda waves as we back out, and Bristal immediately goes for her vape pen. "Well, that was fucking horrible," she says. "I need to adopt a dog, like right now."

"Do it," I say.

"Can't," she says, pulling in a lungful. "No pets at Ash Park."

"You can volunteer," I say. "I'll swing by and pick you up next time I go in. I try to hit it at least once a month. Walk the dogs. Brush them, stuff like that."

"I could dig it," Bristal says.

I drop her at Ash Park and head for the recycling drop-off, glancing down when my phone vibrates in the cup holder. I'm expecting an unknown number, yet another voice mail from someone claiming to have information on Randall Boggs.

Erin Hendrix is calling me.

THIRTY-EIGHT

"Erin, hey," I say, putting her on speaker as I turn left at the only stoplight in town.

"Lydia! Thank you! Thank you! Thank you!" Her voice cracks as it wavers between laughing and crying, her emotions blasting across the spectrum with just those seven words. I pull up next to the huge green recycling container and put the car in park, flicking my wipers on as a light mist starts to fall.

"Thirty years, I've thought about her," Erin goes on. "And you come in like an angel and put all those pieces together. Your mom is over here and showed me how to sign up for Facebook, and I asked Denise to be my friend right away! I just can't . . . I don't even know how to thank you!"

"You don't have to thank me," I tell her, but there's a swell of pride in my chest. "It's just such a relief to know she's okay. I really . . ." I fade out, unsure how much to share. "I think I was assuming the worst."

"That's easy to do in Henley," Erin says. "Good news can be in short supply sometimes, and it makes the bad hit you all the harder."

"Like a brick from the old Fairlawn Hotel," I say, thinking of Dover and his bloody bandage. "Or maybe I should say Fairlawn cathouse."

Erin goes silent on the other end, and I realize that my youth minister might not be ready to talk about sex trafficking just yet.

"Sorry," I say, reaching for my door handle. "I didn't mean to—"

"No, it's not that," Erin says. "Gosh, everyone knows about that. It just set me back because the Fairlawn wasn't brick. It was old timbers."

"You sure?" I ask.

"Yes," Erin says. "The firehouse was brick, and the old police station. I think maybe the library, too. But the Fairlawn was made out of timber. Helen Gurtz might like to talk about everything that the tornado destroyed, the truth is that the Fairlawn wouldn't have been standing much longer, regardless. The society was looking into having it declared a historical site, and applying for some grants for restoration money, but then the tornado took out most of Henley and, well . . . that was that."

The rain kicks in harder, the mist developing into a spray.

"Oh, I've left my upstairs windows open. We had to fumigate on account of some carpenter ants," Erin says, indulging in the long Midwestern tradition of explaining her actions before she performs them. "I suppose I should— Rebecca! You don't have to . . . Well, now your mother has gone up the stairs and—"

"I'll let you go," I say. I crack my door, the cold pellets of rain smacking against my face as I raise the hatch and pull the box of neuter-and-slay pamphlets out of the car. A gust flaps the box open, grabbing the first seven or eight papers and scattering them across the parking lot.

"Shit!" I cry, tossing the box back into the car and taking off after them. Most are long gone, but a straggler is snagged at the bottom of the sign reminding people that K-cups aren't recyclable. I stomp on it right before a shift in the breeze can free it, my sneaker coming down hard on the face of a well-groomed, nearly smiling golden retriever. The end of his left ear peeks out from under my shoe, the front door of his suburban home now sprayed with mud and rainwater.

Wait.

I snatch the flyer and wipe it as clean as I can, the corners flipping madly as the wind tries to tear it from my hands. My hair whips in my face, and I claw at it, trying to clear my vision, hoping to see something else.

The dog on the flyer is Denise Chivington's dog.

Linda Chance didn't put a lot of effort in designing the pamphlets. The picture is badly cropped; half of the smiling face of a brunette woman hovers next to her pet.

"Fuck," I say as I turn, running back toward my car. I dive into the driver's seat and slam the door behind me just as a stiff wind rocks my car. I pull up Facebook on my phone and find Denise Chivington, comparing her profile photo to the flyer.

"Fuck," I say again, my heart racing, my throat closing. "Fuck. Fuck. Fuck."

I copy the photo, and—as a last grasp at hope—drop it into a Google Image search. An exact match comes back at the top of the returns, from a stock photo site.

My phone vibrates with a call from Bristal.

"Hey," she says as soon as I accept the call. "My mom said if I really like the snappy little terrier down at the pound that Ash Park can eat her uterus, and I should see if Linda will let me volunteer and waive the fee—"

"Bristal," I cut her off, my hand tight around my phone. "You need to get over to my house, right now."

"Um, okay. Why? Did you just figure that *The Great Gatsby* isn't actually that great and you need emotional support?"

"No," I tell her. "But Denise Halverson is dead, and I'm pretty sure she was murdered."

THIRTY-NINE

Bristal bounds into my room, her hair plastered to her skull by the rain. She takes one glance at the papers and notes I have fanned around myself on the floor and sits down facing me, crossing her legs.

"Hit me with it."

I hand her the mud-stained and water-wrinkled neuter-and-slay pamphlet with the golden retriever front and center.

"Look familiar?" I ask. "Not the dog, the half-cropped-out owner."

"Oh, shit," Bristal says, smoothing the flyer out. "That's Denise."

"Except it's not," I tell her. "It's a model. That picture is from a stock-photo company, and if you search for other photos with the same model, every single one of them is used on Denise's Facebook page."

Bristal goes quiet, her finger tapping against her knee. "Okay, that's super fucking suspicious, I'll give you that. But could Denise actually *be* a model? Like, what if that is her and she uses her professional photos for—"

"No, sorry," I tell her, shaking my head. "There's more. Remember when we talked to Dover at the prison?"

"Yes," Bristal says, her mouth going into a grim line.

"Listen," I say cautiously. "I'm going to ask you some things, and I just want you to answer me as you remember them."

"Okay," she says, but her eyebrows are coming together, and I sense a storm brewing inside my bedroom to match the gale outside.

"According to Dover, how did he get hurt when he was cleaning up after the tornado?"

"He got hit in the head by a brick," Bristal says.

"A brick from where?"

"From the Fairlawn, the old hotel," she answers, and I nod.

"That's what I remembered, too," I tell her. "We couldn't take any notes because we weren't allowed to have our phones, or anything to write with. I wanted to double-check with you to see if I was remembering right," I explain as I click through some keys on my laptop before turning it to Bristal.

"The Fairlawn wasn't made out of bricks," I say, showing her an old photo. It's sepia-toned, the double-decked porches of the Fairlawn holding that evening's guests, their wagons and horses lining the street outside.

"Okay," Bristal says stiffly, pushing the laptop away. "But he was telling us a story from thirty years ago, Lydia. He could've just gotten a detail wrong, or maybe he didn't even know what building he was working on. Bailey Foxglove said herself some people couldn't find their own houses, with all the landmarks gone. And he could have had a concussion, too. You saw that video. Something definitely hit him in the head."

"Yeah," I agree. "Something did. And I think it was Randall Boggs's fist."

"What the fuck?" Bristal says, coming to her feet, no longer able to contain her anger. "Let's just be clear—my uncle suddenly went from killing exactly nobody to murdering two people?"

"Yes," I say, my tone even. "I'm sorry, but I truly think so."

She stands over me, motionless, hands curled into fists. I see the feeling in her eyes, see her lips forming the words. Bristal Jamison is going to tell me to fuck off again, and this time, we won't come back from it. Her mouth quivers, and she takes a deep breath, then closes her eyes.

"Prove it," she says, her words coming out shakily.

I say nothing, tapping keys until I find the video from June 14. I look up at Bristal, who is buzzing with energy, every line of her body infused with rage and the attempt to rein it in.

"Hear me out," I say, then click play on the video.

Dover Jamison, eighteen, was staying with family in town when the tornado hit . . .

Bristal comes to my side, sinks to the floor next to me as the reel plays.

"They got air-conditioning, and I don't," Dover says. "Thought I'd be able to get some rest, but . . ."

"Was it worth it?" the reporter asks.

"Well . . ." Dover scratches at the bandage above his ear, the grin still spreading. "That AC unit is sitting in the nonfiction section of the library now, and the couch I was on at the time got moved down to Third Street, but hey—at least I didn't get hurt."

I hit pause, the screen frozen as Dover's lopsided smile can't quite reach the eye that's swollen shut, the skin a deep, dark purple.

"Look at his bruises," I say, pointing to the screen. "Those aren't fresh. They're two days old, at least. Which would mean they happened right around the time Randall Boggs was getting the shit beaten out of him. But he didn't go down easy. Remember in the police report? It said the knuckles were busted on both of his hands, and there was skin under Boggs's fingernails."

I reach for the copy of the police report, but Bristal doesn't say anything, only turns the laptop toward her, zooming in on the screen. "The blood on that bandage isn't fresh, either," she says, reluctantly. "Damn it, Lydia. How—"

"Wait," I say sternly. "I'm going to ask you something else, and just give me the answer you think is right. How did your uncle say his dog died?"

Bristal closes her eyes, thinking. "He didn't."

"Right," I agree. "So you remember him saying Dodger *didn't* die at the pound?"

"Yes," Bristal says. "For sure."

"That's how I remembered it, too," I say, then push play on the audio file I have paused and ready on my phone. Bristal's voice from earlier in the day soars out, loud and confident.

"Might be weird, but . . . do you know if my uncle Dover's dog was out here? Bailey Foxglove wrote in her notes that he called asking after Dodger."

"Twice, actually," I say.

"Yeah, Dodger was one of them," Linda says. *"He didn't have tags on him or anything like that, but I knew Dodger by sight. I'd picked him up four or five times wandering out on Far Cry. He was a smart dog—"*

Bristal's hand snaps out, stopping the audio. "But why would he lie about that? Why would he lie about how his dog died?"

"Because Dodger was carrying around the only proof that Dover killed Randall Boggs," I say.

"Jesus Christ." Bristal pinches the bridge of her nose, closing her eyes in disbelief. "He fed it to his dog. He fed that fucking 1864 copper nickel to his dog, didn't he?"

"Great place to hide the proof of your crime." I shrug.

"Or polish up a trade-in," she says, her face lighting up as the first excited feelings of discovery take hold, no matter what it points to. "Remember what he said, about Grandpa Sandy feeding a World War Two bullet to Dodger to clean it up?"

"'Stomach acid put a nice polish on something, once you get the shit off it,'" I say, quoting Dover directly.

"I mean, he might suck, but that was a good line," Bristal says, her hands now going to the papers that are strewn on the floor around us, searching for her own clues. "But if Dover killed Boggs—and I'm willing to admit it does not look good for him on that point—what does this fake Denise Chivington person have to do with anything? And—" Her hands freeze, her eyes coming to mine. "Who the hell is friending everyone on Facebook?"

"I looked harder at that profile once I got suspicious," I tell her, going back to my laptop. "It falls apart pretty quickly. Denise Chivington doesn't have a lot of friends outside of Henley people who responded to her requests, and a few bots. I'm sorry I have to ask this, but does your uncle have access to the internet in prison?"

"Yeah," she says, not fighting the pile-on. "He does. Let me guess. That profile was created the day we visited him."

"The day after, actually," I admit.

"Fuck," she says quietly. "Fucking dead dogs and—" She breaks off suddenly, her hand coming down hard on my wrist, squeezing tight. "Far Cry," she says.

"Ouch!" I say, twisting out of her grip. "What?"

"Far Cry," she says again, with no explanation other than to push play on Linda Chance's interview from earlier. It picks up where it had left off.

"—*sweet boy. I'd call him and he'd jump right up in my cab. I'd drive him home, didn't bother taking him in. I knew your . . . Sorry, but I knew your family wouldn't be able to pay the release fee, and the pound couldn't afford to feed any dogs we didn't have to. Looking back on it, I wish I would've just taken him home that day, but I had a full truck and he was way out at the edge of Far Cry, right where it hits the county road, and Dover lived out the other side, where a bunch of trees were down. I didn't even recognize Dodger, poor bastard. He was covered head to toe in mud—*"

I tap off the audio, looking at Bristal. "I still don't—"

"My notes," Bristal says, crawling over me and sifting through loose pages. "From interviewing people out on Far Cry?"

"Here," I say, grabbing her journal pages and handing them over, still mystified.

Bristal snatches them and scans them, reading aloud, her thoughts melting into a stream that overflows as much as the creek had in 1994. "Dale Childress . . . so that would've been heading west, around ten a.m. . . . Sammy Aldridge, same direction, his dogs started barking about ten fifteen. . . . Then it's ten thirty by the time Lucy Hemming—*fuck!*"

She yanks my laptop toward her and pulls up a map, her finger stabbing at different points along Far Cry Road, the houses and yards standing out starkly from the fields in the aerial view.

"Here's where Boggs's place used to be, you head out to the west and you hit the Childress place, then Aldridge's, and that abandoned farmstead—that was a Hemming place. I talked to the old lady, Lucy. She's in the old folks' home now, but they all said the same thing, about their dogs going nuts before the tornado came through—but none of them at the same time."

"Okay . . . ," I say, still not following.

"What did that fox sound like to you, out on Far Cry? What words did you think you heard?"

"*Oh my God,*" I say, my mouth almost too dry to speak. "But panicked and drawn out. Like someone—"

"Screaming for help," Bristal finishes for me. "Screaming for help and sounding so much like the sound people out there were used to hearing that nobody noticed."

"Except the dogs," I say, following the path of Bristal's finger along the map. "Like you said that night we were out on Far Cry, nothing reacted to that scream because the animals were so used to hearing it. No dogs barked that night we were out there, and the dogs back in 1994 weren't barking because of the barometer pressure, either."

"Nope," Bristal says. "Somebody was out there screaming. Somebody who was making their way west and stopped making noise right here." She taps the screen, the image pixelating where her finger presses down. "Right here in this copse of trees where Far Cry intersects with 96."

"Where Linda Chance found Dodger," I say.

"Covered in mud," Bristal adds. "Because he was digging something up."

We're both silent, the lessening patter of the rain on my windows fading with the last of the sun, the evening clouds eating what's left of twilight.

"We gotta go out there," I say, staring at the map.

"And we should probably take a shovel," Bristal says.

FORTY

I pull into the abandoned Hemming place and yank my jacket hood over my head before getting out of the car. Bristal does the same, hitting the hatch and retrieving the shovel I'd grabbed out of Mom's gardening shed. She still wasn't back from Erin Hendrix's when we left the house, and Dad hadn't returned from work, either. I'd shot them a text on our family chat that I was going over to Bristal's, while Bristal texted her mom to let her know that she was going to go dig up a dead body, to which Madison had responded, **Cool**.

I whip out a flashlight, and we push our way through the overgrown yard, out past an empty granary, hugging the side of a half-collapsed shed at the back corner of the property before we break out into the open field. I can see the thin, white bodies of the birch trees at the edge of the culvert, a few hundred feet from the intersection of Far Cry Road and County Road 96.

"If we see any cars, you need to turn your light off," Bristal says as we step out into the field. "Technically we're trespassing, and I don't feel like explaining why."

But she doesn't need to worry; nobody is out on a chilly, rainy night, and we reach the copse of trees without hearing the sound of an engine or seeing the flash of headlights.

"Okay," I say, pulling my hood closer around my face as the rain picks up again. "How do we know where to dig?"

Bristal rests the shovel against a tree, and blows on her hands, rubbing them together for warmth. "It's not a huge area," she says. "When he buried her, he would've wanted to stay under cover, and you've got to imagine these trees have grown quite a bit in thirty years, and the canopy has spread. So we don't look around the edges, first of all.

"Second, not to be awful, but I doubt he bothered digging the required six feet. He was burying a body, and probably fast. A shallow grave would settle, so we need to look for—"

"A depression, about the size of a human body," I say, sweeping my flashlight around the copse of trees. "And not too close to the culvert because he'd know that running water would uncover her, sooner or later."

"Look for a puddle," Bristal advises, curling her arms around herself. "This rain is cold, but it might do us some favors."

We search the south side of the culvert without finding anything that looks promising, ducking down low once when we hear a car. I flip the light off, hovering next to Bristal as our breath makes clouds in the air, the warmth of our bodies evaporating in front of our eyes. The car passes by, and I turn the light back on as she hops the culvert and the thin steam of water running there, then turns to me.

"Toss me the flashlight," she says.

"Why?" I ask.

"Because you're going to fall when you jump," Bristal explains. "And I don't want to lose the light."

"I'm not going to fall!" I insist.

"Just toss me the light," she says. "Save me the trouble of saying—"

I flex my knees and jump, expelling what feels like Herculean effort as I fly through the air—and collapse into a heap, the light rolling away from me.

"I told you so," Bristal finishes, with a sigh. "Just once, you're going to listen to me. And when it happens, that will be a beautiful moment."

"Sorry," I say, pulling myself to my knees and brushing mud off my ruined jeans. I head for the light, which had flown from my fingers to land just outside the copse of trees, its beam spreading across the open, empty field. I trip on something and fall again, catching myself just in time. Cold water spreads up past my wrists and I gasp as it hits my face.

"Lydia?" Bristal says cautiously, her voice eerie in the dark. "You okay?"

"Yeah . . . I just landed—" I fall silent, realizing. "Could you maybe get the light?"

Bristal moves without talking and I see the light swing back around toward me a moment later, as I'm coming to my knees. I grab a branch and haul myself upright, the light blinding me for a moment.

"Sorry," Bristal says, moving the beam away from my face and toward my feet, where water has gathered. It whirls in dirty pools where my hands had been, dead leaves spinning on the surface.

"Do you think?" I ask, and Bristal hands me the light.

"Only one way to find out," she says. Bristal digs, and I hold the light.

She moves the water first, letting it pool inside the shallow basin of the shovel, then tossing it aside, occasionally splattering my legs. But even though I've fallen twice, she's soon way filthier than me, sinking deeper into the muck as she digs. The rain has let up, but it still flows through the ground, backfilling almost as fast as she can empty the ever-widening hole. Bristal is working methodically, the pile of mud beside the hole growing. She eventually strips off her jacket, sweating despite the chill, and steam rises off her skin visibly as I hold the light on her as she works. The shovel makes a sucking noise every time she pulls mud from the ground, and her breathing becomes labored before long.

"Want me to take a turn?" I ask.

"Nah," she says, driving her foot onto the top of the shovel and tossing out a hefty wad of wet soil. "Shoveling isn't as easy as it looks. You actually have to know what—"

There's a splitting noise, and Bristal's hands go still, her eyes wide in the brightness of the flashlight.

"Bring that over here," she says, her voice flat. I come closer to the hole she's standing in, the beam trailing down the muddy handle of her shovel to the rusted head—and a curl of dark, human hair erupting from the ground at the end of it.

"Oh fuck," Bristal says, collapsing at the knees, and sitting down hard at the edge of the grave. "I think . . . I think I split her skull."

"It's okay," I say grimly, leaning over the edge. I wiggle the shovel and delicately pull it free, then step gingerly down on either side of the patch of dark hair.

"Hold this." I hand the light over to Bristal, who takes it with shaking hands.

"I felt it," she says, her voice tremulous. "I felt the bone. When it hit the shovel it just . . . it cracked."

"It's okay," I say again, pulling a pen out of my pocket. "Just hold the light still."

I lift the curl of hair by the end of my pen and follow it down to the ground, pushing mud out of the way with my other hand.

"Lydia, I don't know if you should—"

But I'm not listening. I drop the pen and push both hands into the muck, clearing a path down past the driven trough of Bristal's shovel blade, moving handfuls of dirt aside until I see a bright flash of bone. I pull back, and Bristal leans forward, shining the light over my shoulder.

Under the spray of hair is a bright white spinal cord, the cervical vertebrae running like a ladder down into what's left of a pinstriped shirt, with little blue roses.

"It's okay," Bristal says, echoing my words. But they're not for me, and they're not for her.

"It's okay," she says. "We found you."

"Oh my God," I say, my hand covering my mouth as the sobs start to come, panic hitching my lungs upward, then down, a vibration taking over my whole body as shock settles in.

"Shit," Bristal says, digging in her pockets. "My phone must've fallen out when I was digging. Lydia, you need to call nine-one-one. Tell them—Lydia!"

But her impatience is cut off as her eyes follow mine to the road, where the single beam of a flashlight shines down on us.

"Girls?" a man's voice calls. "What are you doing?"

FORTY-ONE

I shade my eyes against the light, and he moves it, the beam bouncing off the grave at my feet.

"What are you doing?" he asks again, and without the rush of fear in my ears I recognize his voice.

"Dad?" I ask, relief bubbling over as I climb from the grave. "Dad!" I stumble upward.

"Lydia," Bristal's voice is cold and even, holding a warning.

"We found her, Dad," I say, moving toward him, arms outstretched. "We found Denise Halverson. She's been out here ever since the long stretch, all along she was—"

"LYDIA!" Bristal yells, her voice deep, the beam of her own flashlight illuminating Dad—and his other hand.

"Dad?" I ask, incredulously. "Why do you have a gun?"

It's a picture that makes no sense, my father, grim-faced, holding a weapon—and it's pointing at us.

"Lydia," he says, very slowly. "Go up to the road and get in the car."

"What?" I ask, stepping backward instinctively, toward Bristal—and Denise. "No! Dad! You don't—"

"Just go up to the car," he says, still advancing. "And tell the Jamison girl to get that light out of my face."

"Don't think I will," Bristal says, her voice just over my shoulder, her hand reaching out to stop me right before I tumble backward into the grave. "You got out here fast," she says, her voice low as she steps out of the grave, light still trained on him. "How'd you find us?"

"Called your mother to check up on you girls when Lydia didn't answer her phone. Your cover story of going to dig up a dead body wasn't a very smart move."

"But you knew right where to find it, didn't you?" Bristal growls.

"Dad?" I ask, jerking my eyes to his. "How? How did you know?"

The pages spread out on my bedroom floor splash through my head, the picture of Dad, Dover, and Denise Halverson standing together by the railroad tracks during the Sweet Corn Festival, the round, black O of Denise's mouth as she exhaled smoke.

"Shit, Dad!" My voice cracks, panic spiking my veins. "Did you kill her?"

"No, Jesus!" His gun hand drops, the light wavering as well. "I didn't . . ."

Rain sprinkles us all, picking up again, a breeze kicking in from the west as each drop falls, lit by our dual beams.

"She was as good as dead when I got here," he says, his voice heavy.

"How?" Bristal says, her voice gaining energy and a tone that I know well, one that says she's about to drill down and not back up. "How could she have been as good as dead when she was screaming all the way from Boggs's trailer to here?"

"She made it to the road," Dad says. "She . . . she ran out in front of my car. I think maybe she . . . she thought I was going to help her. But it was too late." Dad raises his head, eyes meeting mine. "It was too late by then."

"Why?" I ask. "What did he do to her?"

"It was in her joint," Dad says. "Dover had been beating Boggs, and Denise was going along with it until the gun came out. She lost it when he shot the old man, tried to run. Dover stopped her, got her calmed down. But she was such a mess, he didn't trust she could keep her mouth shut. Dover said her hands were shaking so hard she couldn't even get her cigarettes out of her pocket, which gave him the idea.

"He told her she needed something stronger and offered her a joint. She went out and sat on the front step, said she wanted fresh air. He kept an eye on her while he rolled it, and while she had her back turned her grabbed some d-CON off the floor of the trailer and rolled that in, too."

"Jesus," I say. "She smoked rat poison."

"Yeah." Dad nods, his face twisting. "It ate her lungs up. She was bleeding from the nose and the mouth by the time I found her up on the county road."

"He called you?" I say, putting it all together. "She figured out something wasn't right, and she ran from him, didn't she?"

"Knew by the first drag, I bet," Bristal says.

"I didn't know, Lydia," Dad says, his eyes searching my face. "I swear. Boggs. Denise. Any of it. I didn't know. All that Dover said when he called was that he needed me out at Far Cry right now, or else everyone in Henley would know who was driving the car that night we hit the Milhaus family."

"So you did it," I say, numb. "You came out here and you found her?"

"She was bleeding so much," Dad says. "There wasn't anything I could do for her, Lydia. I swear it. Dover was right behind her, drug her back down to these trees."

"But she wasn't dead," Bristal says. "Not yet. And a car accident might scare a teenager into keeping their mouth shut, but not a grown-ass man. Dover has a hell of a lot more on you than just a fender bender. He made you do it, didn't he? He made you kill her," Bristal pushes, the edge of her voice growing harder.

"He's a mean son of a bitch and a hell of a nasty bastard when his blood is up, and it was already up, wasn't it? He'd killed Boggs, and you could place him out on Far Cry that night, and he damn well knew you owed him for that crash but not enough to cover for a murder. Not enough for a good kid like you, am I right, Chass?"

Dad's shaking his head, the rain splattering off the barrel of the gun, each drop breaking into hundreds more, all of them spinning in the light. "You don't understand—"

"I *do* understand, goddammit," Bristal shrieks. "Jesus Christ, I grew up with Jamisons, and I know some of us go bad, and a few worse than that. He had you, didn't he? He had you running scared from the minute you woke up in that passenger seat, and you were terrified every day that he'd rat you out. So when you show up to find a dying girl, he digs his claws in just a bit deeper, upped the ante and made sure none of it would ever see the light of day.

"He made you kill her," Bristal says, her voice dropping low again. "He made you kill her, and you dug the grave together."

A low rumble of thunder rolls across the west; a flicker of lightning branches in the sky. Rain pelts my cheeks, pooling around the bones of the dead girl at my feet.

"Is that true, Dad?" I ask.

"He said . . ." Dad pulls in a deep sigh, words that have been stale for thirty years finally crawling out. "Dover said it didn't matter. Said she was good as dead, and it was true. She couldn't have lived. Lydia . . . her breath . . . she was foaming—"

"How'd you do it?" Bristal pushes, her voice cold iron. "How'd you kill her?"

"He held her hands," Dad says. "I covered up her nose and her mouth. It only took a minute."

"Oh, Jesus . . . Dad," I breathe, my heart breaking. I can feel it, his pain, in this place, thirty years ago. The pressure of his father's gaze and the demands of being a Chass, the knowledge that he had already fucked up once, and that Dover would throw him to the wolves—always anxious for a taste of Chass blood.

"She's been down here thirty years," Bristal says. "Each day damning you a little bit more. You couldn't come clean, could you?"

"No," Dad says, his gun arm straightening. "And I'm certainly not going to now. Lydia," he says sternly. "Move."

"What?" I ask.

"He wants you to move so he can shoot me," Bristal says, her voice flat.

"What? Dad, no! You can't shoot *Bristal*!"

He takes a step closer, the gun not wavering. "You need to move," he says again. "It's just a Jamison girl. There are probably five more back at home."

"Three!" I shout, rage taking over incredulity. "There are three other Jamison girls back at her home, and Bristal is my friend. I'm not going to let—"

I'm shoved from behind, and I go down hard, clipping my teeth on the flashlight. The shovel flies through the air, hitting Dad square in the chest. His shot goes wild, and I hear the bullet zip through the overgrowth near my head. Dad falls over backward, his light spinning away, as Bristal lunges forward, stepping on my hand. Bone crunches and I scream, but she doesn't pause, her bare feet flashing in the beam of my dropped light, as I realize she must have slipped out of her muddy shoes so that she could move faster.

And she is flying, diving for the shovel before Dad can get to his hands and knees. She swings and he ducks, the metal zinging as it clips the top of his head, and a chunk of scalp flies. Dad yells and goes for her legs, but she dodges him, raising the shovel above her head, ready to bring it down in a crunching blow.

"Bristal! No!" I yell, finally moving, crawling on my hands and knees through the muck, my injured fingers curled around my light, hot needles of pain shooting through them. My good hand hits something cold and hard in the mud and I grab it, coming to my feet with the gun. I swing around, my light illuminating the two of them, Dad bleeding from the temple, eyeing Bristal, who stands above him, lips in a snarl, shovel raised, Denise Halverson's grave between them.

"I already busted one skull tonight, Chass," Bristal says, rocking on her heels. "I don't have to be done."

"No, Bristal—wait," I say, stepping forward, keeping my light on both of them, the gun pointed somewhere between them. Dad takes advantage of the distraction, knocking Bristal down. She falls into Denise's grave, and the shovel flies, Dad crawling after it, blood running freely down the side of his face. Bristal screams and erupts from the grave, grabbing his ankle and dragging him backward. He kicks her in the face, and she falls to the side, boot tracks embedded in her cheek and blood streaming from her nose. Her head swivels, searching for a target, but the light in her eyes is dim, her gaze unfocused. Dad raises the shovel, ready to bring it down.

"STOP!" I scream. "Dad—no!"

My voice breaks on the word *Dad*, and he pauses, the shovel held high in midair. His eyes go to my gun, and I adjust my grip, fingers cold and clammy against the wet metal.

"Lydia," Dad says calmly. "Think about this—think hard. Nobody has to know. It's been quiet for thirty years, and it can stay that way."

"Fuck that," Bristal says, her voice groggy as she spits a mouthful of mud to the side. "You're not putting a girl in the ground and walking around like your shit don't stink. Henley forgot about her, but I won't let it stay that way."

"They'll forget about you, too," Dad says. "I made a deal with the devil a long time ago so that I could have a future. Everything I ever did was for family—the one I had then, and the one I have now."

His eyes shift to the gun in my hand, my shaking fingers. "Think about everything you've done, Lydia. Everything you've worked for. You molded your life to fill a very specific résumé— and nowhere does it say that your dad is a murderer. You got what you wanted—Harvard, Columbia. You're in, kid. Take what you've worked for and let everything else go."

"Dad . . . ," I say, my voice shaky, the gun heavy in my hands.

"If you let this happen, I'm done," Dad says, eyes locked on mine. "*You're* done. If you let this happen, I can't help you get through college. I can't provide for your mother."

"I can't . . . ," I say, a line of warm blood slips out of my mouth, my front tooth swinging loosely against my upper lip. I think of Mom, crying and lost on the couch, more tears falling when I told her I never want to be like her—a Henley housewife. I still could be. There's a future where the Chass name equals murder and we no longer live on South Lincoln Street. There's a future where I visit Dad on the weekends in prison because I'm still here, in Henley.

"I can't . . . ," I say again, my own tears falling, warm alongside the cold rain. But the thing is, I can—and I know it. I've cheated and lied, hurt people and climbed over others in order to get what I wanted.

"You can," Dad says, his voice gaining strength. "You can and you have to, or else everything I've built and all your hard work collapses. Denise watched Boggs get the shit beat out of him and never said a word. She wasn't some lost angel, and this Jamison girl is a delinquent. You're *Lydia Chass*, and you're going to be something. But you've got to make a decision, right now. You've got to take control of your own future, or else you won't have one."

It's true and I know it. An entire life of following the rules, nodding and smiling, doing the right thing and going along to get along, biting my tongue and choking back the bile have culminated in this—my ticket out of Henley. I've burned the midnight oil, stayed up late, felt my tendons tight in my wrists, the ache of filling out every form, checking every box, and always, always being the best—and winning. There's only one small movement left: the curl of my finger on the trigger. The only thing standing in my way is Bristal Jamison.

Bristal Jamison and the truth.

"Bristal?" I ask, my voice shaking, the muzzle of the gun dancing between the two of them.

"You do what you're gonna do, Chass," she says, her eyes never leaving the mud-slicked handle of the shovel, and Dad's knuckles white against it. "I'm not begging for a damn thing."

I take a deep breath, and steady the gun.

"Sometimes good people do bad things, right, Dad?" I ask.

Then I close my eyes.

"I'm sorry," I say.

And I pull the trigger.

FORTY-TWO

Excerpt from podcast episode "Clearing the Air" of On the Ground in Flyover Country

Welcome to Henley, Ohio, a place you can always come back to. . . . I'm Lydia Chass, inviting you to join me as we explore the past and traverse the present of our hometown.

Bristal: Which, honestly, has been kind of a shit show lately.

Lydia: As you have probably guessed, my cohost, Bristal Jamison, is joining me today as we untangle the Gordian knot of gossip from the past couple of weeks.

Bristal: I just want to say right off—Lydia shot her dad, and it was badass. Badass Chass.

Lydia: Could you maybe treat it with a little more gravity, though?

Bristal: Why? He's not dead. You shot him in the shoulder. He's fine. By the way, listeners, if you're interested in commemorating the historic moment—and I know Henley is big on commemorating shit—I'm selling "Lydia Shot Her Dad" patches on my Etsy site.

Lydia: That is definitely not okay. We did not talk about this.

Bristal: No, but I've been telling you we should monetize since my ODOT episode. Have you seen our numbers lately?

Lydia: Speaking of that, I'm going to assume that quite a few of our listeners aren't local—

Bristal: Considering that the population of the entire county is about thirty thousand and our last download count was ten times—

Lydia: I think we can contribute that to you dropping the f-bomb live on CNN.

Bristal: It was a hot-mic situation.

Lydia: You spoke directly into it and made eye contact with the camera.

Bristal: CNN was awesome.

Lydia: I'm not sure they felt the same way about you. You may have garnered them a few FCC fines, and you were only on air for thirty seconds.

Bristal: Speaking of censorship, we have to use the word *allegedly* quite a bit in this episode, because we can't necessarily prove some of the things we'll be talking about.

Lydia: Correct. While Bristal and I can both speak about

what we ourselves witnessed, we can only surmise about what went down in Henley thirty years ago.

Bristal: But our surmises are totally right.

Lydia: We'll start with Denise Halverson, a name that everyone in Henley—and now, most of the nation—knows. Denise was a foster child with a tough background, who came here with her fists drawn and her back up, ready to face what her past had taught her to prepare for. But Paul and Erin Hendrix offered her a real home—something she'd never known and didn't know how to respond to.

Bristal: Sometime on June 11, 1994, Denise ran away from home, climbing out of her bedroom window and meeting up with my uncle Dover Jamison.

Lydia: And my dad, Brent Chass, at the Sweet Corn Festival.

Bristal: We don't have to say allegedly about that part because we have photographic evidence.

Lydia: Dover and Denise went to Randall Boggs's house, and Dover beat Boggs until he gave up the location of his often-bragged-about family treasure—which, as Bristal revealed in her earlier episode, he believed to be an 1864 Indian Princess penny. Once the pair had it, Dover shot Boggs in the back of the head.

Bristal: Allegedly. And I'm not just saying that because he's my uncle. We don't want to get sued.

Lydia: At this point, Denise panicked, and—frightened that his partner in crime might give him away—Dover offered the girl a joint that he had laced with rat poison. Aware that something was wrong, but too late to save herself, Denise ran out of the trailer and into the cornfields surrounding Randall Boggs's trailer. It was Dover's turn to panic.

Bristal: He called Lydia's dad, who he believed owed him for taking his place behind the driver's wheel after a car crash. Brent Chass complied and drove out to Far Cry Road, unaware of what he was looking for—until a bloodied girl ran into the road, choking on her own breath, and foaming blood from her mouth and nose.

Lydia: We don't need to linger on the gory details—

Bristal: Brent Chass smothered her while Dover Jamison held her wrists, and the two buried her in a shallow grave in a copse of birches. Allegedly.

Lydia: Where she would remain for thirty years, a forgotten footnote to the infamous long stretch of bad days in Henley, Ohio.

Bristal: Until Lydia spotted a discrepancy in the number of missing people in the reporting from the *Hometown Henley Headlines*, and ran that shit down.

Lydia: We'll be covering the breakdown of our research and how we put together the pieces in future episodes.

Bristal: But all you people who friended Denise Chivington on Facebook might want to unfriend her, real fast. It's actually Lydia's dad. Do I have to say *allegedly* after that one?

Lydia: I'm not sure.

Bristal: My uncle called her dad from prison after we went to visit him for an interview about the tornado and let Brent know that we were onto them.

Lydia: And the fake Facebook profile worked. I stopped looking for Denise and started working on the flash flood episode for this podcast—which will be airing at a later date.

Bristal: We've kind of had a lot going on.

Lydia: It was through a conversation with Linda Chance, the Markham County dog warden, and a misprinted neuter-and-spay flyer that cracked everything wide open.

Bristal: Lydia's big on details—and she promises there will be more later—but mostly what it boils down to is her dad might be smart, but he doesn't really know how to use Facebook and she caught his ass in the cookie jar.

Lydia: It's "caught him with his hand in the cookie jar." Or you could use "caught him red-handed."

Bristal: She caught his red ass in the cookie jar.

Lydia: Oh, boy. Okay—regardless, Bristal and I were able to deduce where Denise was buried and went to discover for ourselves if we were right.

Bristal: But her dad was onto us, and we ended up in a real knockdown drag-out.

Lydia: Well, Bristal and my dad did. I mostly just laid in the mud after you broke my fingers.

Bristal: That was an accident. Also—toughen up.

Lydia: A struggle ensued. I ended up holding the gun and ultimately had to choose between the two.

Bristal: And Lydia shot her dad. Patches available on Etsy.

Lydia: In the shoulder!

Bristal: Allegedly.

Lydia: We know that part is true. You don't have to say *allegedly*.

Bristal: Yeah, but maybe if you want to change your story later. I got you.

Lydia: First of all, I wouldn't do that. Secondly, we're airing this live.

Bristal: We're live? I don't think you told me that.

Lydia: I totally did.

Bristal: I'm checking my Etsy sales right now.

Lydia: Anyway, it has been a hectic couple of weeks. But we wanted to provide a follow-up to what you've likely been seeing, hearing, and reading in the national and state headlines.

Bristal: Consider this your local news blast. Also, I'm not pregnant.

Lydia: When Bristal and I chose to share the information that Dover's dog had likely been fed the 1864 penny, we did not expect everyone to run with their metal detectors to the ODOT roadkill dumpsite.

Bristal: But seriously—props to you guys. It smells out there.

Lydia: After a couple of weeks of the not-so-exciting rediscovery of dog tags and collars, we would like to share that yesterday, little Cody Lytle did in fact uncover the lost Boggs family treasure.

Bristal: But before you go getting excited, listen to the next part.

Lydia: It turns out that Boggs's understanding of coin values was a bit hazy. Many factors go into determining the worth of an old coin, including the alloy used, and who struck them.

Bristal: Long story short, the one Boggs had is going on eBay for about a buck right now.

Lydia: And Denise Halverson died for it.

Bristal: So there you have it, folks. What's a girl's life worth? About a buck.

Lydia: But it's going to cost all of us so much more.

Bristal: Dude, can you take me to Hobby Lobby after this?

Lydia: Uh, sure. Why?

Bristal: Because I need to buy stuff to make, like, five thousand patches.

FORTY-THREE

The prison didn't issue Dad the same gray sweatpants and navy-blue T-shirt that Dover had when Bristal and I met with him. Dad is wearing orange, his bad shoulder bandaged and in a sling. He looks like a criminal. Which . . . I guess he is.

"Hi, Dad," I say. My voice gets stuck halfway, the familiar words not tripping off my tongue the way they're supposed to. This is a phrase for at home, for being shouted up the staircase or from the front porch as his headlights sweep the front yard when he gets back from work. It's something I should be yelling from the firepit, welcoming him to join Mom and me. These aren't words for a prison.

But that's where we are, and it's because of me—and I have things to say.

"Hey, Lydia," Dad says, and somehow he says it just right, as if he's not wearing orange, as if we aren't in jail, as if we are just a father and daughter having a chat.

"How's your mom?" he asks.

It's kind of him to ask, and not just for her sake. I can answer this, can put together the words, even if they aren't easy to say, or for him to hear.

"She's hurting," I tell him.

"Yeah," Dad says, his gaze breaking from mine. "I can't even imagine."

Maybe he can't, but I've watched Mom plow through bottle after bottle of wine, Steven's fur is matted with her tears, and she's not eating.

"She said she has to question everything now," I tell him, not mincing my words. "The man she married has been a liar from the beginning. She's wondering if she ever really knew you and how else you betrayed her."

Dad nods, his eyes filling with tears. "I deserve it, but if you could tell her . . ." It's his turn for his voice to break, and my turn to look away. "If you could tell her, that was the worst thing I've ever done in my life, and if anything could wash me clean of that, it was her."

"I'll tell her," I promise him. He won't have the chance to tell her himself. She's refusing to come see him and won't take his calls.

"But, Dad . . ." I go on. "The worst thing you've ever done

in your life is murder. You killed someone. You killed Denise Halverson."

"I did, yeah," he says. "And I've been waiting since I was seventeen to say so."

"Dad," I begin, but he interrupts me.

"No, listen, Lydia," he says, leaning forward. "Thank you."

"What?" I don't know what I'd been expecting. Anger, maybe. Disappointment. A story about being a Chass, and what that means, the weight of our name and all the responsibility that comes with it.

"Not a day went by," Dad says. "There wasn't a day that passed I didn't think about Denise Halverson. Every morning as soon as I woke up. My wedding day. The day you were born . . . Lydia, it colored everything. No matter how beautiful a moment, no matter how right everything else was going in my life, I always knew it could be taken away in a breath.

"I don't have to do that now," he says, his good shoulder lifting in a shrug. "I wake up and there's nothing hanging over my head. I've had clients try to tell me before, there's relief in doing your time and paying your dues. I never believed them, until now."

"Dad," I try again, but *I'm sorry* sticks in my throat. Dad doesn't want me to be sorry. I came here to apologize to him, and he's thanking me.

"You don't have to do that, Lydia," he goes on. "You don't have to live like that. You will never have to wake up and wonder if everything is going to be taken from you today, because you did the right thing, in the right moment. Even when I was telling you not to."

"I *shot* you," I finally gasp, the word spitting from my lips.

"I deserved it," he says. "It was my penance, and a lesson."

"A lesson?" I ask, finally raising my eyes to his.

"Sure," Dad says, a smile playing across his lips. "You can be wrong . . . or you can be Lydia Chass."

FORTY-FOUR

Eight Months Later

Bristal is working over her punching bag when I pull into the driveway behind her Neon. She gives me a little wave and yanks her gloves off with her teeth as I get out of the car, scooping the skirt of my graduation party dress out of the way so it doesn't get shut in the door. I join Bristal on the picnic table as she starts to unroll her wrist wraps, leaving the tails hanging loose as she reaches for her vape pen.

"Good party?" she asks, wiping sweat from her brow as she sits beside me.

"Okay," I say, shrugging. "Kind of hard to know how many people would show, with everything going on."

"You're leaving it all behind, though," she says. "Saw in the paper you committed to Columbia. Was it hard to pick?"

"Kind of," I admit. "All the best schools were offering me a free ride, on account of my *journalistic integrity*."

"Right, but what they mean is you shot your dad."

"Could you stop putting it that way?" I ask, turning to her. "You make it sound so—"

"Violent?" she asks, both hands up in the air. "It was, Lydia. Shit got intense out there."

"I know," I say. "I can't forget it."

We're quiet for a moment as a gust of wind picks up, sending some empty off-brand beer cans scuttling into her driveway from under the trailer next door.

"How's your mom doing?" Bristal eventually asks.

"Not so good," I tell her. "Everything knocked her flat on her back, and now with me leaving for school in the fall . . . I just don't know."

"Think she'd want me to come around? I'd be happy to go over and see her every now and then, unless . . . I mean, if she doesn't want to see me, I'd get that."

"No, I think it would be good," I tell her. "And I'd appreciate it. Thanks."

"Yep. Thanks for shooting your dad instead of me."

"Oh my God, could you—"

I turn to look at her, but Bristal's smile is infectious, and I end up laughing. How, after everything, I don't know. But Bristal Jamison can still make me laugh. I sigh, and lift my hair off the back of my neck, where sweat is trailing.

"What about you?" I ask. "I heard some broadcasting schools reached out?"

"They did, but . . ." Bristal shrugs, avoiding my eyes.

"But what?"

"But a lot of things. Couple of them offered free tuition, but I still gotta cover room and board, plus get my ass out there and back." She looks off into the distance, eyes squinting against the sun.

"We could've paid for that," I tell her, and she snorts.

"Hate to break it to you, Chass. But that's not true anymore."

Bristal's right. With Dad stripped of his license to practice law, there's no money coming in. And even though he can choose to represent himself in his own criminal case, we need to hire someone to defend us in the civil case that the Milhaus family brought against us once they learned that my dad had been driving the car that night thirty years ago. They knew there was blood in the water and thought it smelled like money. Chass money . . . even if that money no longer exists. Turns out we're not the only family in Henley with a completely legendary fortune.

"We still could have helped come up with something," I tell her. "I don't want to see you let an opportunity—"

"See, that's where you've got it all wrong," Bristal interrupts me. "I actually *like* it here. Henley's my home, and being a Jamison means something now. Well, something different, anyway."

"I thought you might say that," I say, reaching into my pocket for an envelope. "I brought you something."

"Awwww . . . is it a graduation present?" she asks, taking it. "Because you didn't need to spot me a card and twenty bucks. You shot your dad for me."

I roll my eyes at the continued jabbing. "Just open it."

She does, unfolding the pages of neatly typed, notarized documents. "What's this?" she asks, looking up.

"I had Judge Whiteside draw up a formal agreement. *On the Ground in Flyover Country* belongs entirely to you now."

"Seriously?" her eyes light up, scanning the pages.

"Yes. I mean"—I sigh, hating to admit it—"your episodes are the ones bringing in the most downloads. People love you, and yes, you're right. We should've monetized a long time ago. So, it's yours now. Do with it what you will."

"Dude," Bristal says, her wrist wraps blowing in the wind. "I kind of want to hug you right now."

"Go for it," I say, arms out. She walks into me, her skin hot from the sun, sweat dripping from her hair onto my neck.

"You stink," I tell her.

"Yeah, I've been experimenting with organic deodorant," she says, stepping away and raising her arm to sniff her armpit. "It can't keep up with me."

"Organic deodorant, seriously?"

"Yeah, I don't want boob cancer."

"But you *vape*?"

"I can get a lung donated," she says blithely. "I don't think they do boob donors. But I'd love to see how they indicate that on your driver's license."

"It's not organ specific," I tell her. "If you sign up to donate organs, you're offering up anything you've got that anyone needs. And it's a heart they put on your license, by the way."

"I know, dipshit," Bristal says. "And by the way, I kind of heart you."

"I kind of heart you, too," I say, tears pricking at my eyes.

"But we already hugged and I've got a strict one per year, per person on that expression of affection," she says, wiping her nose on her wrist bands and looking over at me. "Go home, Chass. You're emotional."

"At least I'm not drunk," I say, getting to my feet and heading to my car.

"Give me two seconds and half a beer," Bristal calls.

"Oh, shut up." I toss over my shoulder, climbing into my car and rolling down the window. "Hey," I yell, and she turns, still sitting on the picnic table. "Want to come visit me at Columbia sometime? I'll pay to get your ass out there, no excuses."

"Sure, I can dig that," she says, nodding. "Can I swear in front of all your smart friends?"

"You can swear *at* my smart friends," I tell her.

"Deal," she says. "See you, Chass."

"See you," I call as I back out of her driveway and leave Ash Park for Lincoln Street, and the other side of town. I cruise slowly down our drive, eyeing the branches of the old oak that never sprouted buds this year and remains leafless, the fire from the stop signs reaching high enough to kill sections of it. Mom never got around to seeding the sections of front yard that had burned, either, and weeds are starting to fill in the dead areas, life forcing a way in—even if it's not the right kind of life.

I sigh, and sit in my car for a minute, not quite ready to go inside. I don't know how much longer I'll live here, but I know it will always be called the Chass house, as long as history clings to the bricks and our name is still in people's mouths. It might be said in different ways, sometimes with affection, maybe tinged with anger, or rich with the deep tones of repeated gossip.

But I won't be here to listen to it.

And Bristal Jamison will probably beat them up for me.

ACKNOWLEDGMENTS

I made a joke on social media that I'm running out of people to dedicate books to, as I've written more books than I have friends. That being said, my acknowledgments are easy to write, because I truly have a great team of supportive people behind me.

As always, thanks goes to my agent, Adriann Ranta Zurhellen, who pulled me out of the slush pile back in 2010 and told me that it's perfectly fine to kill off the love interest. Included under that umbrella is my editor Ben Rosenthal, who continues to support the myriad of ways that I come up with for killing whatever character I think is best, and is okay with swearing, too.

My team at Katherine Tegen Books continues to be amazing. I've been working with many of the same people for over ten years now, which is rare in this industry. Thanks to my cover and interior designer, Erin Fitzsimmons, and the genius behind the art, Corey Brickley. In another medium, I've been lucky enough to have Brittany Pressley perform, or be included in, the majority of my audiobooks. I can't tell you how many compliments I get on both the cover art and the quality of my audiobooks, which I can take no credit for.

Lastly, anyone familiar with my tiny hometown will find recognizable historical events included in the plot of this book. I'll clarify that I know there was never a whorehouse on the square and that we have no unsolved murders. Don't come up to me at the county fair to correct me on this point . . . unless of course there totally was a secret house of ill repute or you know about some questionable deaths.

In that case, I'm all ears.

Mindy